the*Lost*
SAPPHIRE

BOOKS BY BELINDA MURRELL

The Locket of Dreams
The Ruby Talisman
The Ivory Rose
The Forgotten Pearl
The River Charm
The Sequin Star

The Sun Sword Trilogy

Book 1: The Quest for the Sun Gem
Book 2: The Voyage of the Owl
Book 3: The Snowy Tower

For Younger Readers

Lulu Bell and the Birthday Unicorn
Lulu Bell and the Fairy Penguin
Lulu Bell and the Cubby Fort
Lulu Bell and the Moon Dragon
Lulu Bell and the Circus Pup
Lulu Bell and the Sea Turtle
Lulu Bell and the Tiger Cub
Lulu Bell and the Pyjama Party
Lulu Bell and the Christmas Elf
Lulu Bell and the Koala Joey
Lulu Bell and the Arabian Nights
Lulu Bell and the Magical Garden
Lulu Bell and the Pirate Fun

the *Lost* SAPPHIRE

BELINDA MURRELL

RANDOM HOUSE AUSTRALIA

A Random House book
Published by Penguin Random House Australia Pty Ltd
Level 3, 100 Pacific Highway, North Sydney NSW 2060
www.randomhouse.com.au

Penguin
Random House
Australia

First published by Random House Australia in 2016

Addresses for the Penguin Random House group of companies can be found at
global.penguinrandomhouse.com/offices.

National Library of Australia
Cataloguing-in-Publication entry

Creator: Murrell, Belinda, author.
Title: The lost sapphire/Belinda Murrell.
ISBN: 978 1 92532 411 2 (paperback)
Target Audience: For primary school age.
Subjects: Nineteen twenties — Juvenile fiction.
      Melbourne (Vic.) — History — Juvenile fiction.
Dewey Number: A823.4

Cover design: book design by saso
Cover images: wren © Katarina Christenson/Shutterstock; mansion
© Jon Bilous/Shutterstock; wisteria © Valery Sidelnykov/Shutterstock;
flowers © Oleksandra Vasylenko/Shutterstock; girl © Aleshyn_Andrei/
Shutterstock
Internal design and typesetting by Midland Typesetters, Australia
Printed in Australia by Griffin Press, an accredited ISO AS/NZS 14001:2004
Environmental Management System printer

Penguin Random House Australia uses papers that are natural, renewable
and recyclable products and made from wood grown in sustainable forests.
The logging and manufacturing processes are expected to conform to the
environmental regulations of the country of origin.

To my beautiful family — Rob, Nick, Emily and Lachie,
who fill my life with love and joy.

1

Arrival

Melbourne, modern day

The plane skimmed high above the billowing white clouds. Marli peered out the window. She felt free, soaring so far above the earth. For a moment she forgot why she was there, where she was flying to. Then reality came back with a rush, and she felt her stomach sink.

As the plane wheeled and began its descent, Marli could see silver-roofed farmhouses scattered below, along with lush green paddocks bordered with darker hedges and dams that gleamed like shiny coins. The farmland looked like a magical miniature world. Despite herself, Marli felt a flicker of excitement.

Planes and airports always made her feel like that. They seemed to offer the promise of adventure, an escape from the everyday life of school, homework and soccer training.

But not this time, Marli told herself firmly. *This time, the plane is not taking me away on a journey to an exciting, exotic place. This time the plane is dragging me to the world's most boring summer.*

Marli turned away from the view, scowling, her arms firmly crossed. The flight attendant sashayed down the aisle, pausing beside Marli. Her uniform was crisp and bright, her face perfectly made up, her hair lacquered in a tight bun. Marli immediately felt scruffy and awkward in her grey jumper, ripped jeans and short black lace-up boots. Her mother had encouraged her to wear something pretty, but Marli had insisted she needed to wear something loose and comfortable for the trip.

'Coming home?' the flight attendant chirped.

'No.' Marli pushed a hank of auburn hair behind her ear. Her own bun was messy and unravelling. 'Just visiting.'

'Family or friends?' asked the flight attendant.

'My dad.' Marli fiddled with the engraved silver bangle on her wrist. 'For the school holidays. I don't see him often,' she confessed.

Why did I tell her that? thought Marli. *Too much information.* She hunched down in her seat.

'Well, have a wonderful holiday,' said the flight attendant. 'Melbourne is one of the most exciting cities in the world.' The flight attendant continued down the aisle, checking that all passengers were ready to land.

Marli's thoughts returned to her problems — there were several. The major problem was that Marli's mum had been offered an opportunity that was simply too good to refuse. She had been invited to England for eight weeks to lecture in history at Cambridge University and research a book she was writing on Celtic culture.

Several times in the past, Marli had accompanied her mum when she taught at interstate universities for a week or two. The best trip had been when Marli was twelve, and she and her mother had lived in Ireland for six months while her mother completed her PhD in Dublin and Marli attended a local school. She had come home with a broad Irish accent that had lasted for months.

However, this time Mum had decided that Marli should spend the summer holidays with her father in Melbourne. Marli had argued and sulked and begged, but to no avail. Her mother was adamant that it was the perfect opportunity for her to spend quality time with her father.

Marli's parents had separated four years ago, when she was ten. Dad had been offered a high-flying job in his home town of Melbourne while Marli and her mother had stayed behind in Brisbane. At first Marli had been devastated — she missed him terribly — but over time she became used to having the odd holiday with him or the occasional dinner when he came to town on business. They had gone from being close, with her dad teaching her about photography and coaching her soccer team, to having an awkward, intermittent relationship of hasty phone calls once a week. Now they only saw each other once or twice a year.

But she didn't want to spend a whole summer in a strange city where she didn't really know anyone. All her friends had been talking about their plans to have fun together. There would be parties and movies and picnics and beach trips. And Marli would miss everything.

She slumped further down in her seat and glared out the window. The colour of the sky had deepened and golden lights twinkled from the buildings below. The pilot made an announcement over the loudspeaker and the plane continued its descent.

Marli thought back to Mum's words as she'd dropped her at the airport. 'Marli, sweetheart, try to have fun. Your father is so looking forward to you coming. Please don't ruin it all by insisting on being miserable.'

'I'm not insisting on being miserable,' retorted Marli. 'I *am* miserable. I want to come to England with you, or stay at Evie's house so I can see my friends this summer.'

'Sweetie, we've been over this,' Mum said. 'You can't come to England with me because I have a really hectic work schedule. This is a huge chance for me. And I couldn't expect Evie's parents to have you for two whole months. Besides, Alex is your father and it's important you see him.'

Marli shook her head. 'It will be so *boring* staying with Dad,' she insisted. 'He'll be working all the time, and I won't know anyone in Melbourne.'

Mum had hugged her close, and Marli snuggled in against her, breathing in her warmth and the faint scent of citrus.

Mum abruptly pulled away and put her hands on Marli's shoulders. 'You'll make friends,' she assured her. 'Think of it as a great adventure.'

Marli felt her heart lift for a moment, then she frowned. She actually wanted to feel miserable. She was so angry with her mother for going off to England and making her go to Melbourne. She was angry with her father for leaving them in the first place. And she was angry with herself for not being able to persuade her mother to change her plans. She hoped Mum was worrying about her now and feeling sorry that she'd sent her away.

Marli felt her ears pop as the plane descended. Raindrops raced down the windows.

The plane thumped down and trundled along through the runway puddles towards the terminal before coming to a stop. Marli quickly switched her phone off airplane mode and checked for messages. Disappointingly, there were none from any of her friends. Just one from Mum: 'Love you. Have fun. M xxx'.

Marli grabbed her canvas backpack, heavy with books, from the overhead locker and shuffled up the aisle with the rest of the passengers, down the stairs and onto the tarmac. She shivered as a biting wind whipped around her, cutting through her thin jumper and tangling her hair. It had been summery and hot when she left home. Inside the airport, people waited to meet family and friends. Marli looked around, a knot of apprehension in her stomach. Would he be there?

'Marli-myshka,' called a familiar voice and Marli swung her head in its direction. There he was, her father, Alex Peterson, tall with dark hair and brown eyes, just like hers. He swept her up in a hug. 'I'm so glad you're here.'

For a moment Marli relaxed into the embrace, then she stiffened and pulled away. 'Hi, Dad.'

Her dad looked momentarily disappointed before schooling his face into one of warm welcome. 'Your grandfather can't wait to see you. He'll hardly recognise you — you're so grown up.'

Her father kept up a steady flow of chat as they queued to collect Marli's luggage, talking about his plans to take two weeks off over Christmas so they could drive along the Great Ocean Road.

'I thought we'd go out for dinner tonight, just the two of us,' he suggested as they made their way to the car park. 'There're some fantastic Vietnamese restaurants in Richmond near my place. That's if you're not too tired.'

Marli felt like saying yes, she was too tired to go out on a cold, drizzly night. But then she thought about the long evening ahead. Perhaps it would be better to be out in a noisy restaurant than sitting with Dad in his quiet apartment.

She nodded. 'That sounds good.'

'Great, then tomorrow we'll visit Didi. He says he has a special surprise for us.'

Marli felt a rush of anticipation at the thought of seeing her grandfather again. She hadn't seen him for two years. Memories came back of childhood games, reading by the fire and bushwalking with her grandparents.

It was a long, slow drive through peak-hour traffic to Victoria Street, Richmond, weaving through cars and trams. Pedestrians dashed across the road. Horns blared. Lights dazzled. Marli noticed that the streetscape changed drastically, becoming more exotic the farther they drove. Dad parked the car down a side street and they strolled along the crowded footpath.

Marli felt like they had been transported to a foreign country as they walked past vibrantly coloured buildings, a jumble of Asian signs and shopfronts crowded with mounds of vegetables, hanging barbecued ducks, baskets of shellfish and other unusual groceries.

'They call this area Little Saigon because there is such a large Vietnamese population living here,' explained Dad. 'Some time you must come down for the Moon Lantern Festival in autumn. It's great fun.'

Marli looked around with wide eyes, soaking up the sights and sounds of Little Saigon. The scent of mysterious spices and sizzling food wafted from the shopfronts. A Vietnamese woman in a quilted jacket stood beside a stall on the pavement selling fresh herbs, salad greens and golden mangoes.

Dad pointed further down Victoria Street. 'My favourite restaurant is just up here if you're happy with Vietnamese, or we could go to the Greek precinct in Swan Street, or there're Mexican, Chinese and Japanese eateries if you'd rather something else,' he said. 'I must confess, I don't cook much when there's so much amazing food right on my doorstep.'

'Vietnamese sounds great,' Marli said, suddenly feeling hungry.

Dad eased his way into a packed restaurant with crimson walls, simple wooden tables and chairs, and paper lanterns hanging from the ceiling. The proprietor hurried forward with a broad smile.

'Hi, Than,' said Dad. 'How are you?'

'Good, Alex,' replied Than. 'You're very early. We don't normally see you till nearly closing time. Are you eating in tonight?'

Dad beamed and gestured to Marli. 'Yes, I have a good incentive today. My beautiful daughter, Marli, has just flown in from Brisbane to spend a few weeks with me. I told my boss that neither fire nor high water would keep me in the office tonight.'

'Great to meet you finally,' said Than to Marli. 'Your father is our best customer, but he always comes very late. His boss works him hard.'

'I often pull up out the front and grab a quick takeaway,' Dad confessed with a rueful smile.

That must get rather lonely for Dad, eating takeaway on his own, Marli thought. Than chatted about business while he settled them at a table overlooking the bustling street. A babble of voices sounded from the kitchen, calling out in Vietnamese.

The two pored over the menu, sipped steaming green tea in tiny cups and discussed what to order. The food came quickly — delicate rice paper rolls stuffed with prawns, rice noodles and mint, lemongrass chilli chicken, barbecued spicy pork with fresh herbs and fluffy rice.

Dad asked Marli questions about school, soccer and who she was hanging out with. Marli told him about her best friends — Evie, Charlie, Max and Tess. She tried not to sound petulant as she talked about the movies they had seen, the soccer grand final and weekend excursions to the beach. It reminded her of what she would be missing out on over the summer.

'And how's your mother?' asked Dad. Was Marli imagining it or did he seem wistful?

Marli tossed her head, feeling the frustration welling up again as she thought of Mum winging her way to England without her.

'Fine,' replied Marli, stabbing a piece of chicken with her chopstick. 'She'll be in heaven in Cambridge, surrounded by all those grand, old buildings and dusty manuscripts. She'll forget all about us, discussing druids and burial rites with her students.'

When they had lived in Ireland, one of their favourite places had been the Long Room of Trinity College

Library, with its soaring arched ceilings, marble busts and galleries holding two hundred thousand books. Marli had loved to read or draw in one of the peaceful, silent library nooks. She still remembered the feeling of awe when Mum had shown her the famous Book of Kells, a collection of extravagantly illuminated manuscripts written twelve hundred years ago by the monks of Iona.

On weekends, they had travelled the countryside, staying in quaint cottages, grand country homes and ancient castles that had been turned into guesthouses. Mum had her guidebook in hand everywhere, telling Marli fascinating stories about the history of the buildings and the people who had lived there. It had been one of the happiest times of her life. Marli shook herself mentally. Mum would soon be in Cambridge, having an amazing time, and she was stuck here in Melbourne.

'Your mother's done brilliantly well,' Dad said, taking another spring roll and dunking it in the peanut sauce. 'It couldn't have been easy forging a career as an historical expert on Celtic culture while raising a child.'

'I guess so,' Marli replied, twisting the silver bangle on her arm. She hadn't thought about it from that angle before.

'I thought you might like to come into work with me one day next week,' said Dad, changing the subject. 'We're building an exciting new development down in the Docklands, a series of ultra-modern skyscrapers with apartments, offices, restaurants, cafés, shops and businesses. It will be a high-rise city with amazing views of the bay.'

'Sure,' said Marli. She didn't imagine it would be that interesting to spend the day on a big construction site, but what else was she going to do?

Dad frowned and rubbed his forehead. 'It's been a challenging project — we've had endless problems with environmental issues, delayed materials, unreliable suppliers and budget blowouts. I've been working day and night for months . . .'

As he spoke about work, Marli thought her father looked tired and worried. Dad was an architect. A few years ago he had his own small business in Brisbane, designing renovations for family homes, many of them old timber Queenslanders with ornate fretwork and wide verandahs. When Marli was young, her parents had spent every weekend sanding, painting, repairing and restoring their own hundred-year-old timber cottage in Paddington.

But while Dad had enjoyed renovating old homes, he had been offered a high-paying job with a national property developer, designing huge apartment blocks. Dad had said it was an offer too good to refuse — no more worrying about chasing up bills or looking for new clients. However, the corporate job had meant long hours, stressful deadlines and extensive trips away. Two years later, her parents had separated and Dad had been offered a promotion in Melbourne.

'It's been a *nightmare*,' Dad continued, then he grinned. 'I'll try and get home a lot earlier now that you're staying, and we'll have fun on the weekends. But enough about my boring work. What's your favourite thing to do with your mum on the weekend?'

Marli paused for a moment, feeling awkward talking to her dad about her mother. 'The local markets. Mum and I love rummaging through the second-hand stalls, finding bargains, like vintage clothes, or books, jewellery and knick-knacks. We have a pretty collection of antique cups and saucers that we've found over the years. Then we go out for brunch at our favourite café in Paddington for poached eggs and smashed avocado.'

Dad's face softened with nostalgia. 'Yes, I remember the markets. Well, there're some pretty cool vintage markets in Melbourne, too, you know. Maybe we can do a bit of rummaging ourselves.' He put his chopsticks down and smiled. 'It's so good to see you, myshka.'

The next morning Marli woke up to the sound of a coffee grinder. She sat up, disoriented, expecting to be at home in her own turquoise-and-white bedroom. But she realised she was in her dad's spare bedroom instead, which doubled as his home office, with shelves of files, piles of architectural magazines, her father's drawing board, computer and a pinboard covered with building plans and photographs.

The smell of freshly ground coffee wafted through the open door, making her feel hungry. Through the window, she had a view over the red rooftops of trendy Richmond to the parkland by the river and beyond to the leafy gardens of Hawthorn. The grey clouds had gone, replaced by blue sky, but it was still cool. Marli showered and dressed in her torn jeans, sloppy jumper and black boots.

She came out into the living room and looked around in the morning light. The apartment was very modern and sparse. Not at all like the charming, colourful clutter of the little timber cottage that she shared with Mum. There were arty black-and-white photographs that Dad had taken on the walls, a big flat-screen television and a small kitchen. The whole place was decorated like a spread in an architectural magazine – lots of black, white and grey. *It looks like a stylish hotel*, Marli decided.

'Good morning, myshka,' her dad said, standing at the stove with a spatula in one hand and a frypan in the other. The smell of sizzling butter filled the air. 'Did you sleep well?'

'Okay,' replied Marli, taking a seat at the bench. She pulled out her phone and checked for messages. There was just one from her mum, wishing her a good morning. Marli decided not to reply just yet.

'Coffee?' asked Dad.

Marli wrinkled her nose. 'I don't drink coffee, but I'd love a cup of tea, please.'

Dad raised his eyebrows in mock horror. 'Sorry, all out of tea. We'll get some this morning.'

He poured batter in the hot pan, swished it around, then flipped it. 'I've made pancakes, a special welcome breakfast.'

Marli remembered that her dad often used to make her pancakes when she was younger, served with sour cream and berry jam. It was her favourite breakfast as a child. She hadn't had them in years.

'That's nice, Dad,' said Marli. 'Do you have any muesli?'

Dad looked down at the tottering pile of fluffy, brown pancakes. 'No, I don't,' he replied. 'But we'll go to the shops later this morning and stock up on whatever you normally like to eat.'

Marli bit her lip. She didn't want to hurt her dad's feelings — it just slipped out. She was still feeling grumpy and cross.

'Thanks, Dad.'

The pancakes were as delicious as she remembered, but Marli pushed a forkful of pancake around her plate. She wondered what her friends were doing today back home. She imagined them all at the beach, laughing and splashing.

'You don't have to eat it,' said Dad, taking away her plate and scraping the leftovers into the bin. 'I'm a little out of practice. I usually just grab something on my way to work.'

He stacked the dishes in the half-size dishwasher. Marli checked her phone again.

'Are you ready to go?' asked Dad in a cheery voice. 'I spoke to Didi this morning, and he's mad keen for us to get there.'

2

The Abandoned House

It was a short drive from Dad's apartment, across the Yarra River to Didi's retirement unit in Hawthorn. After the bustling chaos of Richmond, it seemed serene and quiet in the back streets.

Dad knocked on the door and then used his key to enter the apartment. Marli followed him into the room. Her grandfather was sitting in a wing-backed chair by the window, reading a letter.

'Hello, Dad,' said her father. 'Look who I've brought to see you. It's our gorgeous Marli-myshka.'

As Didi struggled to his feet, Marli was surprised at how much frailer he looked from when she last saw him.

Didi's eyes misted up as he hugged her. 'Let me look at you, Marli.'

'Hello, Didi,' Marli replied. 'It's great to see you.'

'What a beautiful young lady you've become.'

'Hasn't she just?' Dad said proudly. 'And very clever, too. Your mother sent me a copy of your latest report, myshka. It's great to see you're doing so well.'

Marli laughed despite herself. 'Actually, Dad, I think most of my teachers said, "Marli is dreamy in class and could do better if she focused."'

Dad grinned. 'Just what my reports always said. The sign of a highly creative mind.'

Didi gazed at Marli as though memorising her features. 'Well, she would be creative. It's in her genes. You know, Marli, you have a very strong resemblance to my mother, Violet Hamilton Peterson. The same red-gold hair — although her eyes were green, not brown. I have a photo of her around here somewhere. She was exceptionally creative, like you and your father.'

Marli vaguely remembered her grandfather mentioning this when she was younger.

'I thought we'd go out to a café, Didi,' suggested Dad.

Didi assumed an air of great mystery. 'First, I have a surprise to tell you about.'

'What is it?' asked Marli.

'I've received a rather interesting letter,' he confided. 'Perhaps you could fetch it for me, please, Marli. It's there on my desk in the buff envelope.'

Marli found the envelope and brought it over. Didi extracted the letter with a flourish, and the three of them sat at the round dining table.

'It's from Macdonald, Mackenzie and Blakeney — a firm of lawyers,' Didi began.

'What do they want?' asked Dad.

Didi paused, reading the letter, then grinned broadly. 'It seems we have just inherited an abandoned house,' he announced theatrically. 'A grand old mansion, in fact.'

Marli leaned forward — an abandoned mansion sounded very intriguing.

Dad raised his eyebrows in surprise. 'Whoever would have left you a *house*?'

'Ms Blakeney has been a little sketchy, but it's the house where my mother, Violet, grew up, right here in Hawthorn on the banks of the Yarra,' explained Didi. 'It was called Riversleigh.'

The name sent a little shiver up Marli's spine. *Riversleigh.* Didi handed the letter to Dad, who quickly scanned it.

'Mmm. Nanna came from quite a wealthy family, if I remember correctly,' Dad said. 'Didn't she have some kind of tragic childhood?'

'She did, but Mum wouldn't talk about it very much,' replied Didi. 'There was some kind of falling out with her father. Albert didn't approve of her marriage to my father, and she was effectively disinherited.'

Dad stroked Marli's cheek. 'It's hard to believe that a parent would disown his daughter.'

'My grandfather was very traditional, like many of his generation.' Didi shook his head. 'He truly believed that duty to king, country and family came before personal happiness. My mother was expected to make a brilliant society match rather than follow her heart.'

'You mean marry for money rather than love?' Marli asked with dismay. 'That's crazy.'

Didi nodded. 'Many people felt that way before the wars. Anyway, Albert lost all his money and the house was given away to the government on a ninety-year lease. But now the house is empty and run-down. The government doesn't want the bother of it anymore, so the house is to revert back to the family early.'

'Can we go and see it?' asked Marli. 'It sounds exciting.'

'Of course we can. I thought perhaps we could go on an excursion this morning. That's if your poor father doesn't have to rush off to work.'

'But it's Saturday,' Marli replied.

'Yes,' said Didi with a twinkle in his eye, 'but your Dad's boss, Tony, has a habit of ringing constantly with dire emergencies, so your father seems to work six or seven days a week most of the time. But perhaps today will be an exception.'

Dad held up his hands in surrender. 'I wouldn't dare go to work and deprive us of a family excursion. In fact, I'm fascinated too.'

'Then let's go,' replied Didi.

Riversleigh Grove was a wide, curving street lined with mature oak trees, forming a leafy-green tunnel overhead. On either side of the road were grand heritage houses with tall fences and lush gardens. Dad drove, with Didi in the front passenger seat, leaning forward to check the house numbers. Marli sat in the back.

'Originally, in the 1880s, none of these houses were here, and this road was the driveway,' explained Didi.

'In the days of my great-grandfather, that little cottage was the gatehouse to the estate.'

Marli stared at the quaint gingerbread cottage they were passing, with its steep-pitched roof.

'There it is,' Didi said, pointing. 'Riversleigh.'

Dad pulled up and parked the car on the opposite side of the road. They all looked across to where a high, stone wall surrounded the property. A pair of ornate wrought-iron gates had been covered by a metal mesh barricade. A large sign read Keep Out. Behind the wall, Marli could see the tops of gnarled old trees — oaks, elms, conifers and magnolias with ivory flowers.

A thin boy with dark hair was ambling past the gate, his hands in the pockets of his black jeans, headphones on. A grey cat came to greet him, winding around his legs, arching her back to be patted. The boy scooped the cat up in his arms and stared curiously at Marli and her family in the car before glancing away. He turned into the neighbouring driveway and disappeared.

'It's looking rather forlorn,' said Dad, frowning.

'The house has been abandoned for nearly ten years,' Didi explained. 'I think at one stage squatters were living there. Before that it was a nursing home, a school and a convalescent home for soldiers during the Second World War. It's nearly ninety years since the Hamilton family lived here.'

They all climbed out of the car and walked towards the barricaded and padlocked gate. Through the bars, they could see extensive overgrown gardens with waist-high grass and thick weeds. A circular bitumen driveway surrounded a broken marble fountain. Behind that was the two-storey house.

It must have been beautiful once: cream-coloured with graceful arches across the upper and lower loggias, arched windows in the rounded bays. On the left-hand side was a three-storey square tower with a rooftop terrace enclosed by a balustrade. Yet closer inspection showed dirty, peeling paint, boarded-up windows and cracked glass.

'It's a bit of a dump,' said Marli, wrinkling her nose.

'But you can see how grand it once was,' said Dad. 'The Italianate style of architecture was very popular in the late nineteenth century. Many wealthy families built these huge, extravagant mansions in the boom years after the gold rush to demonstrate their prosperity.'

'That's why they called it Marvellous Melbourne,' Didi added. 'There were lots more of these grand mansions around all over the city when I was young. But so many of them have been demolished for development in the last fifty years.'

'Can we go in and have a look around?' Marli asked. She pressed her face against the mesh barricade to get a closer look.

Didi shook his head. 'We won't get access for a couple of weeks.'

'Perhaps we can find a way into the garden,' Marli said.

Dad peered through the gate. 'It looks like the wall completely surrounds the property. I'll ask the lawyer if we can get early access. We'll have to decide what we're going to do with it.'

Didi stared dreamily at the mansion. 'My mother said that when she was a girl her family owned all the land along the banks of the Yarra River here. The land was gradually subdivided during the early twentieth century.'

'They must have been very rich,' said Marli. 'Did you ever visit the house when you were young, Didi?'

'No, the house was turned over to the state government before I was born,' Didi said. 'I remember my mother bringing me here a couple of times when it was a soldier's convalescent hospital. We walked around the gardens, and there were lots of soldiers in wheelchairs.'

Didi turned to Marli. 'I think it made her quite sad coming back here — too many painful memories.'

'It's a large block of land,' Dad said. 'It would be worth a lot of money to a developer. We could build a dozen townhouses, or a multi-storey block of ultra-modern apartments.' Dad gazed up, visualising the development he would design.

'I'd hate to see Riversleigh demolished,' said Didi. 'The house was built by my great-grandfather back in the 1880s. That makes him your great-great-great-grandfather, Marli.'

'But Marli's right — the house is pretty derelict,' Dad said. 'It would take a lot of hard work to restore it.'

Didi shook his head. 'So much history is being lost.'

Marli's phone beeped as a message came in. She eagerly grabbed it from her pocket, hoping the text might be from one of her friends with news of what they were all doing. But instead it was Mum, saying she was boarding her plane and would phone once she got to England. Marli thought about replying but decided she was still too annoyed. She'd answer later.

A flash of colour caught her eye. It was a small bird with vibrant bands of blue, brown and black plumage. It darted above her head and sat for a moment on top of the wall, examining her with bright, beady eyes. It chirruped a song then hopped over the wall into the wilderness of the over-grown garden.

'A fairy wren,' Didi said. 'The males are so pretty with that bright blue colouring.'

Marli scuffed the toe of her boot on the footpath. The old abandoned house made her feel sad. It looked so for-gotten, so unloved.

'Should we go now?' Marli asked. 'There's not much to see if we can't go in.'

Didi looked disappointed.

'Yes, of course,' Dad replied. 'I thought we could go up to Burwood Road. There's a little café there that serves a great brunch. Marli, you must be starving.'

Sunday was grey and drizzly, so Marli and Dad had caught a tram into the city centre and wandered around, getting thoroughly drenched. Dad bought her a black jacket with a hood to keep her warm and dry. They ate souvlaki in Lonsdale Street, took photographs of the graffiti art in the laneways, then came home to watch an old movie.

On Monday morning, Marli slept in late and woke to find that Dad had already gone to work. There was a note written in his neat architect's handwriting:

Good morning, myshka. Hope you slept well. Food in fridge. Keys on bench. Bike in garage if you want it. I'll be home early. Promise! Ring if you need me. Love, Dad ☺ xx

Marli took a photo of herself crashed back on the sofa, pulling a funny face, and sent it to her friends.

Nice pad. Having an AWESOME time in Melbourne all by myself. Miss you guys. xxx

She made herself some breakfast, cleaned up, had long phone conversations with Evie and Tess, then read her book. After a couple of hours, she put the book down and wandered restlessly from perfect room to perfect room. *I could watch a movie*, Marli thought, noting the neat row of DVDs stored in the cupboard under the television, but nothing took her fancy.

Marli went out onto the balcony and looked out at the view. In the distance to the west were the tall, silver skyscrapers of the city centre, glittering in the sun. To the east was the river, with parkland and walking paths wending along beside it. Cyclists raced past, overtaking mothers pushing prams and couples walking dogs.

I have to get out or I'll go mad with boredom, thought Marli. *How on earth am I going to survive two months living down here?*

She packed her backpack with a bottle of water, an apple, her book and phone, then grabbed the keys from the bench.

In a few minutes she had a helmet on and was off cycling, winding her way through the busy Richmond roads towards the river. Marli felt so much better when she was out doing something. It was peaceful riding the bike along the main trail through the picturesque parkland beside the river. Sunlight glimmered through the leaves, dappling the ground and glinting off the water. Marli crossed over a bridge and followed her nose through the quiet streets of Hawthorn.

It wasn't until she found herself cruising down Riversleigh Grove towards the wrought-iron gates that Marli realised where she was heading. She padlocked the bike to a telegraph pole, grabbed her backpack and set off to explore. The old house and its high-walled garden had captured her imagination. There must be some way of getting in.

Next door to the walls of the property on the southern side was a small block of Art Deco apartments with a low brick fence across the front. Looking down the driveway, she could see the stone wall of Riversleigh stretching towards the river. On the northern side was a large Federation house. An old man was pottering in the garden and waved to her as she hovered.

A trilling warble sounded. The cheerful fairy wren, with his iridescent blue bands, was back. He swooped down over Marli's head, then alighted on top of the wall. The bird danced along, cocking his head from side to side, observing Marli. He trilled again, then flew off into the garden beyond, as though enticing Marli to follow. This made her even more determined to find a way in.

On her second prowl, Marli peered into the garden of the block of flats. The fairy wren appeared again, skimming over her head, then alighted on a branch of a tree growing beside the wall. He watched Marli with his bright, beady eyes, then hopped from the branch onto the wall. He cocked his head to the side and flitted down into the garden.

The fairy wren had shown her a way in. Marli glanced around, hoping no-one was watching. Then she quickly shimmied up the tree and onto the top of the two-metre high wall. She didn't hesitate, dropping over the other side, breaking her fall by bending her knees.

It was only once she was in the garden that she suddenly wondered if she'd be able to get out again. Marli gazed around. She hoped there weren't any snakes lurking nearby in the waist-high grass — luckily she was wearing jeans and sturdy boots. Marli set off, wading through the vegetation, feeling like an explorer in another world. The scent of sun-warmed stone, crushed grass and sweet blossom floated around her as she wandered.

On the southern side of the house was a massive, dark-green hedge that must once have been clipped but now grew rampant. The belvedere tower was on this side also, jutting above the dense foliage like a fairytale turret. Marli headed towards the front of the house, which faced east.

The going was easier once she reached the crumbling circular driveway. The marble fountain in the centre of the circle had a cracked rim and its three basins were filled with slimy green water. Dragonflies flitted above the basins, their wings a silvery blur. Marli felt nervous as she crept up the stone front steps, past the smashed urns on either side and onto the front verandah.

The windows were boarded up, as was the arched front door. Graffiti was scrawled across the peeling paintwork; ivy crept up the walls.

Marli continued around the house, past the protruding bay window with its three arches. A stone-flagged terrace, crazed and cracked, ran along the northern and western sides. The doors along the terraces were also boarded up. One of the hoardings was loose, so Marli prised it away, revealing French doors. Sunlight flooded through the glass and Marli could see a dusty parquet floor and a vast room. She tried the handle but it was locked.

The phone in her backpack rang, making her jump. She quickly pulled it out and checked the screen. It was Mum, calling from England. Marli sighed. *Should I answer it?*

'Hi, Mum,' said Marli. 'How was your flight?'

'Long.' Mum's familiar voice sounded far away over the phone. 'But I'm here now in Cambridge. I was worried because you didn't reply to my texts. Is everything all right?'

The sound of Mum's voice made Marli feel sad and homesick.

'Sorry, Mum,' replied Marli, 'there wasn't really anything to say. It's been pretty boring. I don't know anyone down here and Dad's at work all day. So what am I supposed to do?'

Marli felt a twinge of guilt because of course there had been things happening, but she wasn't going to tell her mum that.

'Perhaps you should think about taking some photos?' Mum suggested. 'You haven't taken any for a while, and it might be a good chance to practise. And you could post them online; I could see what you're doing.'

Marli huffed. 'I might have had lots to photograph if I was in Cambridge with you, but there's not much worth photographing *here*.'

'Well, I'm glad you're all right,' said Mum, trying to sound patient. 'I'll call you again in a few days, but in the meantime could you please text me so I know everything is all right?'

'Okay, Mum,' Marli groaned. 'I promise.'

Marli felt uneasy because she was hardly ever in disagreement with her mother. For years it had been just the two of them, so they usually loved spending time together — watching movies, making dinner, walking and reading. She didn't like arguing with her mother, even if she'd gone off on an adventure without her.

Marli said goodbye and stashed the phone into her backpack. She looked down over the gardens towards the thick shrubbery that hid the river below. To the left was a sunken area that, despite decades of neglect, was filled with rambling roses in shades of pink, cream, white and yellow, filling the air with their rich scent. Marble benches, spotted with lichen, were set on each side of the square, facing the roses.

A path led right across the garden towards a tumbledown summerhouse on the right. Its roof was weighed down with wisteria vines that twisted and twined around the posts, their tendrils bursting through the wooden shingles. A pair of swallows had made a small mud nest under the eaves. They darted above the ground, chasing whirring insects.

A sudden hacking cough made Marli jump. She swung around, her heart thudding.

A thin, dark-haired boy about her own age was standing on the terrace, hands on hips, staring at her. Marli recognised him as the boy she'd seen walking past the house on Saturday. He still had the earphones hanging around his neck.

'What are you doing?' he demanded, his face flushed. 'You shouldn't be here. It's private property.'

Marli immediately felt guilty, but that quickly turned to anger. 'What are *you* doing here?' she retorted. 'You're the one trespassing.'

'I'm not,' insisted the boy, his voice rising petulantly. 'Leave, or I'll . . . I'll call the police.'

Marli mirrored the boy's stance: hands on hips, glowering. All the anger and frustration that she had been trying to keep bottled up over the last few days bubbled to the surface. This boy was being rude, and she wasn't going to let him bully her.

'You do that,' she snapped. 'I'm not leaving.'

The boy glared at her. Marli glared back. The silence stretched out. The boy was the first to break the impasse.

'My grandfather keeps an eye on the place,' he explained grumpily. 'Nonno hates it when people break in and graffiti the house and break windows. Someone tried to set fire to it a few years ago.'

'This house belongs to my family,' Marli explained.

The boy shook his head. 'No it doesn't — it's been owned by the government for years. It was a nursing home when I was younger, but no-one's used it for ages.'

Marli decided he was a most unpleasant boy. 'It was only leased to the government,' she retorted. 'But they've released it, and it belongs to my grandfather, Michael Peterson. So I have every right to be here.'

The boy looked discomfited. 'Oh,' he said. 'My name's Luca Costa, and I live in the flats next door.'

'I'm Amalia Peterson, Marli for short. I usually live in Brisbane, but I'm down here for a few weeks.'

'I saw you climb the tree in our front yard,' Luca explained. 'So I followed you in.'

Marli had the grace to look embarrassed. 'Well, I probably was trespassing in your garden, but I couldn't work out how else to get over the wall.'

'My bedroom looks out over the garden here at the back,' Luca said. 'I've never been in here before, and I've always wanted to know what it was like.' The boy coughed harshly, making him breathless.

'Why would your grandfather keep an eye on the place? Is he some sort of caretaker?' Marli asked.

'We live next door, but my great-grandfather used to work here many years ago.'

'What a coincidence,' said Marli, feeling rather prickly about Luca's connection to the estate. 'Did he work here when it was a hospital?'

Luca shook his head. 'No, he was a gardener here when it was owned by the Hamilton family. You know, the old cursed family who lived here.'

Marli felt a shiver run up her spine. 'Cursed?'

'Yes, my grandfather's parents knew the family and said that some terrible things happened to them. My great-grandfather was sure that someone had cursed them with the *malocchio* — that's Italian for "evil eye",' Luca explained.

Marli thought that, with its rose brambles, wild shrubbery and weeds, the garden looked like it could belong to a cursed castle.

'Really?' she replied. 'That sounds sinister. My grandfather said it was his mother, Violet Hamilton Peterson, who lived here — and it made her sad to come back.'

The two started walking down the steps and into the garden, back towards the tree where they had climbed in.

'Ouch,' cried Marli, bashing her shin on something buried in the long grass. It was a fallen statue of Cupid, the god of love, his nose chipped, staring sightlessly up at the sky.

'Give me a hand,' Luca suggested.

Together, the two wrestled the statue upright on its plinth, facing back towards the house. The effort made the boy cough into his hand.

'That's better,' said Marli, rubbing Cupid's marble curls.

Her mind was bubbling with curiosity and unanswered questions. Was the family really cursed? What had happened to the Hamilton family to make them give up this beautiful house? Marli was determined to find some answers.

3

Early Morning

Riversleigh, 6 November 1922

Violet Hamilton woke at a slight sound and burrowed deeper under her coverlet. *It can't be time to wake up yet,* she thought. *Just a few more minutes.* Next, she heard the sound of the heavy curtains being pulled back. Early-morning light flooded the room. Violet sighed, rolled over and opened her eyes. A steaming cup of milky tea had been placed on the bedside table.

Violet sat up, leaned against the pillows, lifted the cup and took a long sip.

Silhouetted against the sunlight of the window was a young maid in a blue floral dress and starched apron, tying back the grey silk curtains. Her brown hair was pulled back into a tight bun, hidden under a frilled cap, her nose sprinkled with freckles.

'Good morning, Sally,' said Violet, resting the pale aqua cup in its saucer. 'Thanks for the tea.'

Sally bobbed a curtsey. 'Mornin', miss. Would you like anythin'?' Sally was an Australian-born working-class girl, but her accent hinted at her parents' Irish heritage.

Violet took another sip, savouring the invigorating warmth of the tea. Through the window she could see the wide blue sky scudded with fluffy clouds and the vivid green sea of the treetops. It was a glorious morning, perfect for a swim. Could she manage it? Could she sneak away? Violet's eyes sparkled with mischief.

'Do you think you could come back, please, Sally?' asked Violet. 'In about fifteen minutes?'

The maid nodded. 'Very good, Miss Violet.' Sally padded away, her footsteps silent on the plush carpet, and closed the door behind her.

Violet threw back the white coverlet on her wrought-iron bed and jumped up. If she was going for a swim, she would need to be quick to make it before her father came down to breakfast. Violet flung open the armoire door and searched through the drawers, tugging out the items she needed.

She tossed her nightgown on the rumpled bed and wriggled into a navy swimsuit dress, slipping a colourful silk kimono wrap over everything. She didn't bother with the canvas slippers or the matching cap, preferring to leave her hair hanging down her back in a long braid.

Violet took a towel from the hanging rail, pulled open the creaky, white-panelled door and peeked into the hallway. Her sister Imogen's door was firmly closed. She might not be up for hours if she'd been out the night before. At the front of the house, the doors to her father's room and dressing room were also tightly shut.

Perfect, thought Violet. *No-one up yet.*

She escaped down the sweeping staircase to the entry hall. The house was eerily quiet. Beside the staircase, a narrow corridor led towards the servants' wing. It was hard to believe that behind the green baize door was a hive of activity where the cook, housemaids and footmen would be busying themselves with preparing breakfast, making tea and polishing silver.

To the left of the stairs was the rear of the house, with its darkened billiard room, sunny morning room and the vast ballroom that ran across much of the back, overlooking the river. Violet, however, went straight ahead down the short corridor that led out onto the northern stone terrace, down the steps and onto the croquet lawn.

The house was surrounded on three sides by formal lawns and flowerbeds. The southern side was the service quadrangle, hidden from view. The old stables and carriage house had recently been converted into a garage with the male servants' quarters above.

Violet was greeted on the lawn by her boisterous dog, a black-and-white Dalmatian called Romeo. The dog pranced on his paws then reared up on his hind legs, dancing backwards, his pink tongue lolling in welcome.

'Hello, boy,' said Violet, scratching Romeo's head. 'Want to come walkies?'

Romeo bounded around her in circles, licking her hand, ecstatic to be accompanying her on an early-morning adventure. Violet stopped to give him a good rub under his chin.

The two headed towards the river, down paved terraces with wide, shallow steps. Stone urns were bursting with white primula, blue hyacinths and sweetly scented freesias.

In the centre of the lawn was a sunken rose garden, filled with a profusion of blooms of ivory, cream, yellows and blushing pinks. Wider beds, perfectly weeded and mulched, were filled with flowers in every shade of blue, mauve and white — daphne, daisies, forget-me-nots, aga-panthus, lupins, gardenias and hydrangeas. Violet stopped to breathe in the scent, enjoying the sunshine on her face and the feathery grass under her bare feet.

Two gardeners in flat caps, one balancing precariously on a ladder, clipped the tall camellia hedges. They tipped their caps as she walked past.

'Good morning, Alf. Good morning, Joseph,' Violet called.

'Morning, miss,' they replied in unison, in their thick accents.

Violet crunched down the gravel path flanked with box hedges, past the summerhouse. From here, the path zigzagged down the bank, hidden from above by dense shrubbery. A fairy wren darted above her head.

Once out of sight of the house, Violet began to run, hurtling downhill towards the boathouse, Romeo chasing her. The green-brown water of the Yarra rippled past, carrying swirling leaves and small twigs. The banks were lined with weeping willows, feathery ferns and tall gums.

She looked around to see if anyone was about, then dropped her wrap and towel on the timber decking. Violet's father, Albert Hamilton, didn't approve of his daughters swimming in the river, and she was definitely not supposed to venture down here on her own. The river looked tranquil from above, but its depths had many hidden dangers — tangled roots, submerged logs and jagged rocks.

She dived — a clean, shallow curve — into the deepest pool. The water was freezing, making her gasp. Romeo preferred to scrabble down the steep bank and launch himself into the water from the river's edge. He paddled next to her, head held high above the water.

Violet faced upriver and swam hard against the current, propelling herself with powerful strokes. At the northern bend she stopped and turned, treading water. From here she could see the house — her house. Riversleigh.

With its cream arches, shady loggias and graceful tower, it was perched high on the riverbank, surrounded by greenery. The morning sun bathed the house in a rosy golden glow. Overhead soared a deep-blue sky with pale wisps of cloud. The beauty made her catch her breath.

Riversleigh looked so solid, so safe. Like an Italianate castle, guarded by high walls and forest, it had sheltered her family for generations, a haven from the turmoil of the outside world. At least that's what she'd thought as a child.

Violet lay back, staring at the sky, letting the river carry her back downstream. Romeo's bark woke her from her reverie. She'd better hurry or she'd be late for breakfast, and late for school. That would definitely make her father cross.

She scrambled up the metal ladder and grabbed the towel to dry herself and squeeze the water out of her long hair, then twisted the towel up in a turban. Flinging her silk kimono around her shoulders, she hastened back up through the shrubbery.

Violet was cautious as she sped across the lawn with Romeo. Her father could be down from his bedroom now, sitting in the morning room, or he could be upstairs watching from his bedroom window. But there was so sign of him as she crept back into the house, leaving Romeo outside to dry in the sun. Violet made it back to her bed-chamber without being detected. She pushed open her door and went in, leaning her back against the door in relief. Or was it disappointment?

She looked around. It was a pretty room — dove-grey walls, white woodwork, a French writing desk by the window and a rose-pink velvet armchair beside the fire-place. While Violet had been swimming, Sally had made the bed, tied back its filmy muslin curtains and tidied away the belongings Violet had strewn around.

Sally was laying out Violet's school uniform on the bed — silk underwear and dark stockings, white shirt, navy box-pleat tunic and tie, with black buckle shoes. Violet let out a little sigh. Sally looked up and bobbed her head.

'Thanks, Sally,' said Violet. 'I'm running terribly late, but it was worth it.' Violet stripped off her sodden wrap and costume, passing them to the maid.

'Yes, miss,' replied Sally, handing her the fresh under-wear and uniform, piece by piece. 'Was the water cold?'

'Freezing,' Violet said, 'but refreshing.'

Sally helped Violet with the buttons and knotting the tie while they chatted. Violet sat down on the stool in front of the dressing table, regarding her reflection: pale skin, green eyes and a sprinkling of freckles across her nose. She glanced away. She thought her school uniform hung like a sack on her slight frame, and her long, wet hair made her look half-drowned. It was Imogen who was the renowned beauty of the family.

'How's your family, Sally?' asked Violet. 'You went home to Richmond yesterday?'

'Mmm,' Sally agreed, her mouth full of bobby pins. She put the pins down on a crystal tray and unbraided Violet's hair. 'Ma made lovely scones for us all, an' it was good to see the kiddies. Billy has grown so much in a month, an' Maisie is as cheeky as a barrel full of monkeys.'

Violet nodded, trying to imagine Sally's mother's house full of children. She thought it must be a rowdy, warm and loving place.

'Did your mother like the basket of goodies from Mrs Darling?' asked Violet.

Sally nodded vigorously. 'Oh yes. The kiddies were so excited about the apple cake an' the meat pie. They scoffed the lot in no time at all.'

Violet could imagine the merry scene. She glanced wistfully at her image in the mirror. 'One day I'd like to come and visit your ma, and all your brothers and sisters. It would be lovely to meet them.'

Sally looked a little embarrassed. 'Oh no, miss. You wouldn't like to come to my place. It's not right for the likes of you. It's too noisy an' crowded.'

'It sounds charming.'

'Yes, miss.'

There was silence as Sally pulled long, sweeping strokes through Violet's wet hair with a silver-backed brush. When it was dry, Violet's hair was thick and curly, hanging to her waist. Her father used to say that both his girls were true Scottish lassies with their rich auburn tresses with hints of gold through it. Violet flicked a hank of hair behind her ear in irritation.

'What else is news in the kitchen?' she asked, changing the subject. 'Has Monsieur Dufour been throwing any pots this morning?'

Sally shook her head as she continued to work the brush through the knots. 'Only a little one, an' it was empty.'

Violet laughed. The French chef was very temperamental and seemed to think that it was part of his job description to hurl pots and pans around the kitchen when his fellow workers annoyed him with their stupidity. When they were younger, Violet and Imogen had loved to venture into the kitchen to beg titbits from the kitchen maids, but when Monsieur Dufour had taken charge of the kitchen last year, he had swiftly declared that his domain was definitely out of bounds for the misses of the house.

'The new chauffeur started today, miss,' said Sally after a moment's thought.

'Oh, I'll miss Ellis,' Violet said. 'And the horses.'

Mr Ellis had worked for the Hamilton family for decades, first as a carriage driver and then as chauffeur, though his first love had always been the horses. He had driven Violet to school each day and ferried Imogen around to her social engagements.

Violet smiled as she remembered the furious scolding Ellis had given her when she was twelve. One of the grooms had left the buggy, hitched to a pair of horses, tied up outside the carriage house. When she spied them, Violet had decided to take the buggy for a joy ride. She had urged the horses into a canter and had taken the corner too fast. The left-side horse shied and the buggy overturned, throwing Violet into the hydrangea bushes.

Ellis had come chasing after her, calmed the horses, then checked that she was not too badly hurt. Violet had been scratched and bruised, but that was nothing compared to the tongue lashing she received for endangering his precious horses. Ellis then told her that the consequences would be dire if she ever did anything so foolish again, but he never told her father about the accident, and that week he taught Violet how to drive the buggy properly. That was the beginning of a firm friendship between the two.

'It broke Mr Ellis's heart when your father sold all the horses, an' he said it's better to go now while he can still find another place,' explained Sally. 'He's gone to a big house in Toorak that still keep horses and carriages.'

'Dad decided the horses weren't being used enough and he finds the motor car more convenient for longer trips,' said Violet. 'But I loved riding Sultan and driving the buggy. It's not the same being driven everywhere.'

Violet suspected that the real reason her father had decided he no longer needed horses was so he could sell the paddock. The neighbouring houses were creeping closer every year as parts of the estate had been sold off.

'The new chauffeur's a foreigner,' Sally continued, wrinkling her nose. 'A Russian. Maybe he's one of those Bolshies.'

Violet smiled at the thought of her father having a comunist revolutionary driving his beloved automobile. That was totally incongruous.

'I don't think Father would employ a Bolshevik,' said Violet. 'The Bolshevik threat to the world order is one of his favourite topics at dinner parties.'

Sally nodded. 'They say the Russians are starvin'. Those Bolshies are a murderous lot, killin' their emperor an' his poor family.'

Tsar Nicholas II of Russia, his wife Tsarina Alexandra and their five children had been executed in 1918 by Bolshevik soldiers during the Russian Civil War.

'It was very sad,' Violet agreed, 'but I don't think our chauffeur will be murderous.'

'He's young an' charmin'. An' a bit of a looker, if you like foreign types.'

There was something about Sally's repressed air of excitement that piqued Violet's curiosity.

'Oh? And does this chauffeur have a name?' Violet asked.

Sally concentrated as she untangled a knot. 'Nikolai,' she said. 'Nikolai Khakovsky.' Sally stumbled a little over the unfamiliar surname.

Violet smiled at Sally in the mirror. 'I look forward to meeting him.'

Sally finished the braid and pinned back the loose wisps of hair. 'Best head down for breakfast, miss,' she said. 'The bell rang quite a few minutes ago.'

Violet nodded. It was time to face her family.

Breakfast was laid out downstairs, in the morning room, on the small round table near the French doors that opened to the terrace. A vase of blue hydrangeas, sweet-scented freesias and white roses nodded in the centre. Golden toast stood upright in its silver toast rack beside the silver domed butter dish and crystal dishes of citrus marmalade and berry jam. Boiled eggs were nestled in delicate silver egg cups at each place.

Mr Hamilton was already seated, dressed in a grey three-piece suit, reading his newspaper. The remains of his breakfast lay on the plate in front of him. To Violet's surprise, Imogen was also there, eating half a grapefruit. She raised her eyebrows at her sister.

'Good morning, Violet,' her father said, not looking up. 'You're late.'

Saunders, the butler, pulled Violet's chair back for her then stepped over near the sideboard, his face impassive. He was dressed in his black livery of tailcoat, tie, vest and trousers with a white wing-collar shirt. Romeo was lying beside the French doors. He thumped his tail on the floor as Violet walked towards the table.

'Good morning, Dad,' replied Violet, slipping into her chair and placing her napkin in her lap. 'It's the most glorious morning.' She pushed her damp braid over her shoulder.

Imogen shook her head and gently waggled her finger. She had noticed the damp hair and assumed it meant an illicit swim in the river. Violet screwed up her nose in defiance and stuck out her tongue.

The silver teapot, jug and sugar bowl were placed beside Imogen. She poured tea and milk into a rosebud teacup and passed it to Violet.

'Thanks,' Violet replied as she helped herself to toast and a curl of butter. She chipped at her boiled egg with a silver teaspoon.

Her father huffed and shook his paper, still reading. 'Steel stocks are down again.'

On the sideboard stood various dishes of stewed fruit and silver salvers of bacon, mushrooms and sausages. The footman, Harry, brought fresh hot toast and tea from the kitchen.

'More strikes,' her father commented. 'Utterly ridiculous nonsense. Don't these workers realise that the trade unions are being stirred up by communist agitators? They should throw the lot of them into prison. That would solve the problem.'

Violet rolled her eyes at Imogen, who patted her lips in a fake yawn. Their father's breakfast conversation was drearily familiar.

'Why are you up so early today?' Violet asked her sister. 'You're hardly ever up before noon these days. Too many late nights out at dinners and balls.'

'No time for sleep when there's fun to be had,' Imogen replied with a grin before turning to her father, her blue eyes wide with innocence. 'Daddy, could I please have the car today? We've a meeting of the ball fundraising committee this morning at Audrey's, then a gang of us are playing tennis there this afternoon. That is, if you don't need it?'

Her father looked up. His face softened as he looked at his elder daughter. She was undeniably pretty, with her red hair pinned up in a low bun and her ivory skin. Imogen was dressed in the height of fashion in a loose-fitting pale-blue dress, which emphasised the colour of her eyes.

He thought for a moment then nodded. 'The new chauffeur can drive you there, after he takes Violet to school,' he decided. 'The car can come back for me mid-morning and take me to the factory. I have a meeting with my foreman, but that can wait.'

Imogen looked delighted. 'Thank you, Daddy.'

Violet felt annoyed. How did her sister get her way so often, when her father hardly seemed to acknowledge Violet's own existence? Imogen was Dad's favourite, no doubt about it. Violet flicked her damp plait over her shoulder again, willing her father to ask why her hair was wet. He didn't notice, turning back to his newspaper instead.

Violet put her spoon down — she didn't feel hungry anymore — and gazed out the French doors onto the terrace. The grey cat, Juliet, sat on the flagging, delicately licking her paw.

'Excuse me, Miss Violet,' said Saunders. 'The chauffeur has brought the car around.'

4

The New Chauffeur

'Don't forget to wait for me,' Imogen reminded Violet as she headed down the hall towards the front door, which Saunders was holding open. 'I won't be long. Could you bring my bags down for me, Harry?'

The ruby-coloured glass in the fanlight and sidelights above and beside the door glowed in the early morning sunshine.

'Goodbye, Saunders,' Violet said as she popped her white straw hat on and pulled up her gloves.

'Have a pleasant day, Miss Violet,' the butler replied.

The buttercup yellow Daimler was parked at the bottom of the terrace steps, and a tall young man was standing to attention beside it — the new chauffeur. *Sally's right*, thought Violet. *He is handsome . . . in a stiff, military sort of way.*

He looked about eighteen and wore the usual grey chauffeur's uniform of baggy breeches and double-breasted jacket with tan driving gloves and knee-high black boots. A black peaked cap sat neatly over his carefully slicked back dark hair. As Violet approached, he saluted and opened the rear car door.

'Good morning,' Violet said. 'You must be Nikolai.'

'Yes, miss,' he said. 'Nikolai Petrovich Khakovsky.'

His English seemed very good, with a slight Russian accent mostly revealed by his long vowels and rolling r's. Violet smiled at his serious face and the formality with which he delivered his three names. It made her want to tease him.

'Welcome to Riversleigh, Nikolai Petrovich Khakovsky,' she said in her best hostess voice. 'I hope you are happy here with us.'

'Thank you, miss,' he replied.

Nikolai glanced at her briefly then stared off into the distance. In that moment, Violet was struck by his startling golden brown eyes the colour of toffee, fringed with thick black lashes. Exotic, Byzantine eyes.

'My sister, Imogen, will be here eventually,' Violet explained. 'She is *always* running late.'

He nodded. 'Yes, miss. I don't mind waiting.'

Violet felt a surge of curiosity about this young man. His manner was quiet and reserved, as befitted a servant, yet there was something about his stance that didn't fit with the servants she had known. His bearing was tall and proud, yet he was too young to have been a soldier during the war. *I don't mind waiting.* Violet had never thought to wonder if a servant minded waiting for her or anyone in her family. That was what servants *did*.

She realised that she was staring, and that was behaviour

44

definitely not befitting a well brought up young lady. She hurriedly glanced away.

Violet slid onto the back seat of the Daimler, breathing in the scent of leather polish and beeswax. Imogen, of course, took ages to come down. When she eventually descended, she was wearing a wide-brimmed, dark-blue hat to match her tailored overcoat. Harry followed behind, carrying a carpet bag and a tennis racket, which he stowed in the front seat.

'I hope it's not too hot for tennis this afternoon,' said Imogen to Violet as she settled into the seat beside her sister. Nikolai closed the door. 'Audrey's asked quite a crowd.'

Imogen pulled a gold compact case out of her handbag and began to powder her nose with a puff, then smudged her lips with lipstick into a crimson bow as she peered into the compact mirror. Imogen didn't usually wear make-up at home in front of her father — he definitely did not approve of young ladies painting their faces. Since the war, he hardly noticed anything, but Imogen always thought it was better to be cautious.

Imogen chatted about her plans for the day, while Nikolai drove carefully round the carriage circle, past the cascading three-tiered marble fountain and down the long gravel driveway to the heavy wrought-iron double gates. Joseph, the gardener, stood by the open gate, ready to lock it behind them. The whole garden was surrounded by a high stone wall, except for the riverfront, giving the estate total privacy.

Violet only half-listened to Imogen's chatter. She was thinking about the day ahead — school lessons, gossiping with her friends about their weekends and then ballroom dancing class in the afternoon. Ten minutes later, as they drove up towards the bluestone towers of Rothbury Ladies' College, Violet realised that something was different. Standing outside the school was the headmistress, Miss Parker, wearing her long old-fashioned clothes and pince-nez spectacles.

A line of automobiles and horse-drawn buggies crawled along the street towards the school gates. But instead of dropping the students off there, they paused for a minute, speaking with the headmistress, before driving off again.

'I wonder what's happening?' asked Violet, peering out the side window. 'No-one's going in.'

'Maybe old Parker's gone on strike,' Imogen joked. 'Now, wouldn't that be glorious?'

'Unthinkable,' Violet declared. 'Miss Parker could be dying of pneumonia, and she'd *still* be out the front there, welcoming the girls each day.'

Imogen had attended the small Rothbury Ladies' College until a year ago, so she was quite familiar with the formidable headmistress, with her strict discipline, focus on academic study and genteel manners. Violet was always getting into trouble for running between classes or jumping the flower beds, instead of walking sedately with a straight spine and her straw hat perched at the correct angle.

'Thank goodness I'm free of there,' said Imogen. 'I'm half-convinced that old Parker will chide me now for wearing my skirt this short or daring to wear lipstick.'

'Utterly disgraceful,' Violet agreed cheerily. 'I'm sure she'll order you to detention at once, although I seem to remember you were always the *perfect* Hamilton sister!

The one who studied hard and always managed to get straight A's. I don't think you ever had a detention in your life.'

'That's because I actually did what I was supposed to do, instead of staring dreamily out the window like someone else we know,' Imogen retorted.

Violet took that as a cue to stare dreamily out the window of the Daimler, at the manicured gardens of Rothbury Ladies' College. The Daimler crawled forward another few metres.

'Do you remember the time I hid Gertie and Myrtle in my pocket?' asked Violet. Gertie and Myrtle had been pet mice that Violet often carried around with her. 'And then somehow they escaped when I wasn't paying attention and ran round and around the class-room? Mademoiselle Moreau jumped up on the chair and screamed as though she was being stuck with hot pins, until Miss Parker came in and stared at us all with that terrifying glare of hers.'

Imogen raised her eyebrows. 'How could I forget? The whole school was talking about it! I think that was the prank that made Mademoiselle Moreau decide to go back to Paris.'

'Yes, and the prank that made Miss Parker suggest to Dad that perhaps I would be happier at a different school,' added Violet. 'Luckily Dad had made a large donation to the building fund the year before, so Miss Parker agreed I should have a second chance.'

'Perhaps that's what Miss Parker is doing now,' Imogen joked. 'Expelling all the girls who have run out of second chances.'

Violet chose to ignore this jibe. The car rolled forward another few metres, but when Nikolai parked the car outside the school gates, Miss Parker merely stepped forward to speak to them.

'Good morning, Miss Hamilton and Violet,' Miss Parker said through the open window, looking unusually harried. 'My apologies — I did try to telephone all the students this morning but could not contact everyone in time. I am sorry to inform you that we have to close Rothbury for the summer.'

Violet glanced at Imogen in disbelief.

'Why, Miss Parker?' Imogen asked. 'Whatever's the matter?'

Miss Parker frowned. 'Unfortunately we've had an outbreak of scarlet fever amongst the boarders over the weekend,' she explained. 'The doctor has placed them all in quarantine, and the school will be closed from now until the summer break. All the boarders must stay inside, and no day girls are allowed in.'

Violet felt her stomach twist with worry. Scarlet fever was a disease that was often fatal — sometimes families could lose several siblings in a severe epidemic.

'Are the girls all right?' asked Violet, thinking of her best friends in the boarding house — Cecily, Hen and Bea.

'The doctor says that none of them are gravely ill,' Miss Parker assured her. 'But all the boarders will be in quarantine for at least four weeks, then they will be sent home in early December. In any case, Rothbury will be closed from now until February.'

'So no exams?' asked Violet, barely containing her

delight. What a heavenly thought — no school for three whole months!

'And no school concert, dances or picnics,' Imogen reminded her.

'Is there anything we can do for the girls?' asked Violet. 'Can we send some food baskets or sweets?'

Miss Parker shook her head. 'No. They are all too ill for that, but perhaps you could write to them.'

She turned her head to see another car pulling up behind them. 'Enjoy your long holiday, Violet,' said Miss Parker. 'But remember to keep up with your reading and your study, and use the time wisely. We will have make-up examinations in February.'

'Goodbye, Miss Parker,' Violet replied. February was a very long time away.

'Well, it looks like you had better come along with me to Audrey's, darling,' said Imogen. 'I don't have time to take you home first, and we do need some more helpers for our Russian Famine Relief Fund Ball.'

Violet thought about objecting. Perhaps she could go home and swim or draw — and she definitely needed to change out of her school uniform. She glanced at Nikolai in the driver's seat and thought she saw his shoulders stiffen at the mention of the Russian Famine Relief Fund.

Violet paused. The thought of exotic Russia suddenly intrigued her. 'All right then — why not?'

Imogen settled back into the comfort of the deep leather seat. 'Glorious. We need someone artistic to guide the decoration committee,' she added. 'I can't think of anyone better. We want the ballroom to look heavenly.'

Nikolai drove them to Audrey Williams's villa at Kew, dropping them at the front door, while he returned to drive their father to work at his glove factory in Richmond.

Like the Hamiltons, Audrey lived in a spacious mansion surrounded by acres of landscaped gardens. There were already six young ladies gathered in the drawing room, all wearing wide-brimmed hats decorated with a variety of feathers, ribbons and flowers. They were drinking tea, laughing and chattering about their social calendars.

'Imogen, do come in, *cherie*,' called their hostess as they were shown in by the maid. She rose to greet them, the only one not wearing a hat. 'And who is this young lovely?'

A few years older than Imogen, Audrey was fashionably thin, with her hair cut into a very short black bob that was carefully sculpted onto her cheekbones, with a thick, straight fringe cut just above her eyebrows. Her grey silk dress draped to mid-calf, and she moved with languorous, feline grace.

'Audrey, this is my younger sister, Violet,' Imogen said. 'Her school, Rothbury College, has been closed due to an outbreak of scarlet fever, so Violet is free for the summer. She's very artistic and I thought she might be able to help us with decorations for the ball.'

Violet felt a thrill of pleasure at this uncommon praise from her elder sister.

'Perfect,' said Audrey. 'I'm sure you will be far more useful than most of these chattering parakeets.'

Audrey introduced everyone. Violet recognised two of the girls, Dodo and Edie, as old school friends of Imogen's. Violet sat on the window seat while Imogen chose a chintz-covered armchair.

Audrey held up her hand for attention. 'May I remind you, ladies,' she said, 'we are here on a serious mission. There are millions of Russian children who are in danger of *starving* to death over the winter. The idea is that our ball will raise loads of money to send over to feed those poor children.'

'It's awfully sad,' said Imogen. Everyone murmured in agreement.

'And don't forget that we want to organise the best ball of the season,' added Dodo. 'I plan on making the social pages with my outrageous costume.'

Audrey turned to Imogen and Violet. 'These frivolous flappers have made hardly any progress yet on organising our ball, other than picking a date and venue. We have decided on Thursday, December the fourteenth, at the Hawthorn Town Hall. We want to hold it before everyone disappears to the country for Christmas. But at this rate, summer will be over before we decide anything.'

Edie tutted at Audrey. 'Oh, very harsh. We've chatted endlessly about themes as well. We've been arguing over whether we should have a Cinderella dance or perhaps a Venetian masquerade.'

'I vote for an underwater theme, where we dress as nymphs,' Dodo suggested, beaming at everyone. 'We can dangle silver fish from fishing line and make seaweed streamers from crepe paper.'

'I can see you as King Neptune,' teased Imogen. 'Just be careful you don't knock anyone over with your golden trident!'

Violet suppressed a giggle. She remembered that Dodo had a reputation for being endlessly clumsy but always cheerful.

'Or we could have a costume ball,' added Edie. 'I rather fancy being Marie Antoinette.' She spread her imaginary pannier skirts wide and curtseyed regally, fluttering an invisible fan.

Audrey raised her eyebrows at Violet in mock despair. She picked up a sheaf of leaflets from the side table and showed photographs of stick-thin, emaciated children with big, dark eyes. Violet felt a lump rise in her throat.

'Just like during the French Revolution, peasants are dying of starvation,' Audrey explained to Violet. 'After years of war and revolution, the crops have failed and people are reduced to eating bread made of bark and grass.'

Violet thought of the four beautiful meals produced each day by Monsieur Dufour. She couldn't imagine ever eating bark and grass.

'Every pound we raise will save a child's life,' Audrey continued, 'so we're hoping to have six hundred people at the ball for supper and dancing. If we sell the tickets for twelve shillings six pence each, then we should take over three hundred and fifty pounds.'

'That's an awful lot of people to invite and loads of food to provide,' Imogen added.

Audrey fanned herself with the leaflets. 'That's why, *cherie*, I've put you and Edie in charge of advertising.'

Violet glanced from Imogen to Audrey, thoughts tumbling through her mind.

'If the ball is to raise money for the Russian Famine Relief Fund, why don't you have a Russian theme?' Violet suggested.

'That sounds a bit grim,' said Dodo, pulling a face of

distaste. 'Poor peasants in rags and Bolshevik revolution-aries in uniform?'

Violet shook her head. 'No, I was thinking something far more exotic. You know, Cossack dancing and gypsy violins, and the grand old balls of Imperial Russia.'

Audrey sat up straight and nodded her approval. 'Now that sounds more glamorous. You were absolutely right, Imogen — I can already see that Violet will be a *huge* help. Welcome to our Russian Ball committee, *cherie*.'

Violet couldn't help but feel a thrill of pleasure. The Russian Ball would be a fun project to fill the days now that she couldn't go to school. She imagined the Town Hall glittering with golden candles and filled with dancers in their evening dresses. She listened as the girls around her discussed music, costumes, refreshments, caterers and posters, while Imogen took notes and Audrey allocated jobs.

'So we need to decide on a Russian-themed dinner menu,' Audrey said. 'And Violet needs to come back with decoration ideas to suit our theme, plus a plan to make it happen.'

Violet nodded, her mind buzzing with possibilities.

Just then the doorbell rang. Audrey stood up, twitching her grey silk skirts. 'It sounds like the gentlemen are starting to arrive. We are going to have lunch in the garden under the trees, followed by a few games of tennis.'

The other ladies began to follow the footman out into the garden. As Violet stood, Audrey noticed that she was still wearing her navy-blue serge school uniform.

Audrey took Violet by the arm and whispered, 'Why don't you come upstairs and let me find you something to change into. I'm sure you don't want to wear your awful school uniform on your first day of freedom.'

Violet grimaced. 'They are definitely not designed to be flattering, are they?'

'Perfect for playing hockey and memorising Latin verbs, but not very stylish for a garden party,' Imogen agreed. 'I'm sure Audrey will have something much more fashionable.'

Violet and Imogen followed Audrey upstairs into her bedroom. Audrey pushed the electric bell to summon a maidservant. 'I have a couple of frocks you might like to wear,' she explained. 'Marthe can help you.'

Audrey explained to Marthe what she wanted, and the maid showed Violet next door into the dressing room. Marthe pulled two dresses out of the wardrobe. The first was a pale-green dress, loose and softly draped to mid-calf. Marthe loosened Violet's hair, coaxing it into long, heavy ringlets, with the front segments twisted up behind, and threaded a pale-green silk ribbon across the top of her head twice to make a headband.

Violet walked back into Audrey's bedroom to show the girls. 'What a beautiful dress,' she said, admiring her grown-up and surprisingly elegant reflection in the long mirror. 'I don't have anything half as pretty as this.'

'It brings out the green of your eyes,' said Audrey. 'I thought it would look divine on you.'

'Thanks awfully, Audrey. It's so kind of you to lend me something lovely to wear.'

'It's no trouble at all.' Audrey picked up Violet's heavy hair. 'You have beautiful hair — have you ever thought of bobbing it?'

Violet looked dubious.

'Daddy would have an absolute fit,' Imogen said. 'No offence intended, Audrey, but Daddy doesn't approve of the flapper style. He can't understand why the young women of today insist on, as he puts it, dressing like children.'

Audrey waved her hand dismissively. 'I chopped all my hair off during the war. It was the only way to deal with the lice.'

'Lice?' asked Violet, wrinkling her nose in disgust.

'Audrey was an ambulance driver in France during the Great War,' Imogen explained. 'She was over there for two years.'

Violet felt a hollow in the pit of her stomach. Mention of the war always made her feel sick with sadness. 'You must have been very brave.'

Audrey waved her hand as though swishing away a bothersome fly. 'It had nothing to do with bravery. I just wanted to do something useful with my life. I thought I'd die of boredom staying here and knitting socks while the men went off and had all the adventures.'

Audrey pulled a face, mocking her own naivety. 'Of course the reality was vastly different — dirty, danger-ous and despicable. Our adventures included no water for washing, barely any food, never enough sleep and driving at great speed over the most impossibly rough roads, all the while getting shot at.'

Violet shivered. 'That sounds terrifying.'

'Many of the poor men I ferried back to the hospitals had terrible injuries, and all of them were infected with lice,' Audrey explained, frowning at the painful memories.

She paused then shook her head. 'So most of the nurses and drivers cut off their own hair. I must say it is a lot easier to maintain.'

Imogen smiled. 'Not to mention extremely fashionable — it makes you look like a film star!'

Audrey pursed her lips and bunched up Violet's hair. 'Not as short as mine, perhaps. Your hair is so curly, but perhaps just mid-cheek. It would be *très chic*.'

Violet stared at her image in the mirror and wondered if she'd look as chic as Audrey with short hair. She couldn't imagine cutting off her hair. But she could imagine what her father would have to say about it.

'How about you, Violet?' asked Audrey. 'Are you going to do something useful with your life? Or are you going to be like your sister, Imogen, and marry a wealthy grazier and spend your life organising bridge and tennis parties and having loads of deliciously beautiful but naughty little scamps?'

'I . . . I'm not sure,' Violet stammered. What did she want to do with her life? It was unheard of for girls from her background to work. Most of them finished school, were presented into Melbourne society, enjoyed a whirlwind season of balls and parties, then were married as soon as possible to a respectable young man from a wealthy family. Only poor girls worked.

Imogen flushed slightly at Audrey's teasing. 'Who says I'm going to marry a wealthy grazier? I might choose to marry a . . . a poor medical student. Or not get married at all!'

Violet looked from one to the other. Audrey patted Imogen on the arm with a knowing look. 'Come on then, *cherie*. Let's go down and see if we can rustle up a handsome but impoverished young medical student for you.' Audrey drew one arm through Imogen's and the other through Violet's. 'We live in a modern new world with endless possibilities. Life will never be the same again — so let's go and have some fun!'

Under the trees stood a long trestle table covered with a crisp, white cloth and set with silverware, glasses and orange-and-black china plates. The other guests were already seated on an odd assortment of chairs, chatting, laughing and drinking lemonade. There were seven young men dressed in white tennis flannels and striped jackets, who all stood up as Audrey and the girls approached.

Audrey rattled off another string of names, but Violet only caught Jim Fitzgerald, Tommy O'Byrne and Theodore Ramsay. Violet realised she had met Theodore Ramsay at the Henley-on-Yarra rowing regatta the previous weekend, which she'd attended with her father and Imogen. Theodore's father was one of Albert Hamilton's business associates, and Theodore looked particularly pleased to see the girls again.

Everyone exchanged pleasantries. Imogen and Violet sat in the vacant chairs on either side of Tommy.

Three maids dressed in black dresses, snowy starched aprons and caps circulated with jugs of lemonade and platters of sandwiches, oysters with lemon and slices of baked ham.

Violet quickly realised that her sister and Tommy seemed to know each other quite well. Imogen smiled a lot as she chatted to him about the regatta.

'It was so colourful with all the decorated barges and punts,' Imogen said. 'But such a crush — I heard there were nearly twenty thousand people there watching.'

Tommy whispered something low in Imogen's ear. She flushed and smacked him lightly on his fingers.

'Nonsense, Tommy,' she said, but she looked as though she had enjoyed whatever it was he had said.

'It was almost impossible to push through the crowd,' Violet added, taking a chicken, mayonnaise and lettuce finger sandwich from a silver tray. 'I thought we'd never get to the river. And of course, Imogen being Imogen, we were running terribly late.'

The sandwiches were dainty and delicious, the chilled oysters salty and creamy.

'*Pfff.*' Imogen waggled her fingers to reject this slander. She turned to Theodore Ramsay lounging beside her. He was dressed like the other young men, but somehow he looked smarter, with his black hair neatly parted and slicked back. Violet thought he had the air of a Hollywood film star, like the handsome Rudolph Valentino, who her friends loved to swoon over.

'Violet and I were very lucky that Theodore's family invited us to be guests on their barge,' added Imogen. 'Otherwise we couldn't have seen a thing.'

'Lucky indeed,' Tommy agreed, glancing over at his rival. 'We poor peasants were stuck jostling on the banks. I ended up climbing a tree in desperation. At least I didn't fall out of it like the young urchins in the tree beside me.'

Theodore looked gratified to be included in the conversation and leaned forward, putting down his silver fork. 'By Jove, we had a good mooring spot,' he said. 'I made sure my crew was there several days before, and the weather was perfect for it. Although, the only disappointment was that I was certain that Hawthorn would beat Melbourne University in the eights this year.'

'Absolute bosh,' said Tommy. 'Melbourne Uni was always going to win. Only a numbskull would have thought differently.'

Theodore scowled momentarily and then leaned in to murmur something to a laughing Imogen. They began chatting about the horses racing in the Melbourne Cup the next day.

For a moment, Tommy looked disappointed at the interruption, then he turned to Violet with a warm smile. 'So you're Imogen's younger sis? There is certainly something of a family resemblance.'

Violet shook her head. She wasn't the one who had two young men obviously jousting to hold her attention.

'Yes, perhaps. However, according to our housekeeper, Mrs Darling, Imogen is the perfect, pretty one, who always does the proper thing. I'm the wild, rambunctious sister, who should probably be locked up until I'm fit to be seen in polite company. She constantly reminds me of the time when I was nine and insisted on taking my pet lamb, Bianca, to Sunday church.'

Tommy laughed, throwing back his blond head. 'No wonder she wants to incarcerate you. I thought Imogen said you were still at school?'

Violet nodded and explained about the scarlet fever outbreak. 'So it's awfully hard luck for my poor sick friends, but I'm looking forward to a heavenly three months away from school. Absolute bliss!'

Tommy nodded thoughtfully. 'Nasty disease, scarlet fever, but for some reason it doesn't seem to be as deadly as it was a few years ago. Funny how diseases seem to evolve over time, becoming either more or less virulent.'

Violet looked at him in surprise.

'Oh, terribly sorry,' said Tommy. 'I'm a third-year medical student at Melbourne University, and we all tend to get a bit carried away with nasty diseases. I'm always surprised that no-one else seems to share my utter fascination! I offered to take your sister on a tour of the Alfred Hospital, and she made up some bosh about having to tidy her glove drawer.'

Violet laughed. Tommy seemed so funny and natural. It was no wonder that Imogen seemed to be listening in on their conversation with half an ear while she chatted to Theodore.

'Well, I'd be happy to come on a tour of the hospital,' Violet assured him, although the thought had never crossed her mind before. 'And I'll make sure we drag Imogen along as well. She spends far too much time having fun.'

'Speaking of fun,' said Audrey from across the table, 'it's high time we dusted off the tennis racquets and fought it out for the Williams Championship Cup. Are you up for it?'

'Absolutely,' replied Imogen.

'How about some mixed doubles?' Theodore suggested. 'I'll take you on, O'Byrne. How about I pair with Imogen, while you go with Violet?'

Violet thought that Tommy might have been hoping to pair with Imogen himself, but he laughed good-naturedly and fetched a pair of tennis rackets for a serious, fast-paced game.

The afternoon was spent playing doubles tennis and chatting on the sidelines. A group, including Imogen and Tommy, went walking in the gardens.

In the mid-afternoon, Marthe came out to find Violet. 'The motor has arrived for you and your sister, *mademoiselle*,' the maid informed her in her charming French accent. 'It is waiting out the front.'

Marthe went to fetch Imogen, who was still in the gardens with Tommy.

'Thanks so much for having me,' Violet said to Audrey. 'I had a perfectly lovely afternoon. Much better than practising awful Latin verbs at school.'

'A pleasure,' replied Audrey. 'It was splendid to meet you. And don't forget to dream up some concepts for our Russian Ball. We're meeting again in a few days to finalise the details, so I'm expecting lots of fabulous ideas from you.'

Violet walked out to the car. Nikolai was waiting, standing to attention as before. Violet checked back towards the large red-brick villa, with its steep terracotta roof and white dormers. Storm clouds had begun to roll in from the south, and the temperature had dropped. It felt like rain was on its way. Of course there was so sign of Imogen.

'What part of Russia did you come from, Nikolai?' Violet asked on impulse.

Nikolai glanced at her in surprise. 'Petrograd, Miss Violet,' he replied. 'Or St Petersburg, as it was called before the war. We still can't get used to calling it Petrograd.'

Violet leaned against the yellow car, looking out over the manicured lawns. Three gardeners were clipping the shrubs into perfect spheres in the distance. Violet could hear the rhythmic *click-click* of their shears. Bees hummed in the warm air.

'Tell me about St Petersburg,' said Violet. 'What's it like?'

A look of pain crossed Nikolai's face. For a moment, Violet thought he might not answer her.

'It was once the most beautiful city in the world,' Nikolai replied, turning to Violet, his face alight with enthusiasm. 'Imagine a city of extravagant gilded palaces and ornate bridges, surrounded by parks and crisscrossed with canals and rivers. In summer, there are the white nights, when the sun never quite sets. In winter, the rivers freeze over and the whole city is mounded with thick white snow. It is dazzling.'

Violet felt a shiver. 'It sounds wonderful. I wish I could see it.'

'It *was* – before the war,' said Nikolai, looking despondent. 'Perhaps not so wonderful now.'

'When did you leave?' asked Violet. Nikolai looked away and didn't answer. Violet felt a rush of remorse. 'I'm sorry. I shouldn't have asked. You must think I'm being frightfully nosy, but Russia sounds like a fascinating country.'

Nikolai shook his head and lifted his chin. 'No, it's all right. It's just something I try not to think about very often. My family and I left Russia three years ago, in 1919, and we came to Australia just recently. We are trying to start a new life here, which can be . . . fraught.' His r's rolled more than usual on the last word.

'I'm so sorry,' said Violet. 'You must miss your home.'

Nikolai lifted his chin and stared into the distance. 'We are lucky to be here in Australia.'

Violet was thinking of dozens more questions that she would like to ask Nikolai. Where had he lived in St Petersburg? What was his life like there? How did they come to Australia? What did he miss about Russia? Did he have family back there who were starving like so many of their countrymen? But as the questions bubbled on her tongue, Violet saw Imogen walking towards the car, escorted by Tommy. Violet reluctantly repressed the tantalising questions and, instead, slid into the back seat, waiting as they said their goodbyes. Imogen hopped in the car. Nikolai tipped his cap and closed the back door.

'Nikolai, would you mind taking us back via Glenferrie Road?' Imogen asked.

'Yes, miss,' Nikolai replied in a toneless voice with little trace of his foreign accent.

Imogen turned to Violet. 'I've changed my mind about my hat for tomorrow's Melbourne Cup. I think ostrich feathers would be more stylish than flowers.' She pulled out her compact and touched up her lipstick.

'So, did you have a lovely *long* stroll with Tommy in the shrubbery?' asked Violet with a wicked grin. 'You didn't happen to get lost?'

Imogen flushed and looked up quickly. 'We were with Edie and Jim,' she said defensively. 'Edie and I were talking about how to advertise the ball.'

Violet swatted her sister on the shoulder and chuckled, leaning back against the leather seat. 'Of course you were. I'm sure Tommy was keen to hear all about Edie's posters.'

Imogen laughed as well and shook her head. 'I don't think so, but the boys did say they could help. What did you think of Tommy? Isn't he a honey?'

Violet smiled affectionately at her sister. 'He seemed very nice. I think he was rather keen on you.'

Imogen glowed. 'Do you think so?'

'Ab-so-lutely! Head over heels,' Violet assured her.

'Did he tell you that he's studying medicine at Melbourne University?' Imogen asked. 'He's halfway through his studies. Audrey does charity work at the hospital, and she met him there a few months ago, so she's invited him to lots of our parties.'

'Aha!' Violet crowed. 'I was right — Tommy *is* the mysterious, romantic, poor medical student!'

Imogen dropped her eyes into her lap. 'Don't be such a silly. We're friends and nothing more.'

5

The Peacock Box

Hawthorn, modern day

Marli was sitting at the round dining table in Didi's apartment, drinking a cup of tea. Her grandfather smiled at her across his teacup.

'What a lovely surprise,' he said. 'I was hoping to see lots of you while you're down here.'

'Dad's at work so I thought it was a nice day for a cycle,' Marli said. 'I've been exploring.'

Didi nodded. 'I hope your father takes some time off work while you're here. It would be good for him.'

Marli changed the conversation to why she had really come. 'Could you tell me some more about your mother, Violet Hamilton, and her family? Someone told me that the family was cursed.'

Didi raised his shaggy, grey eyebrows. 'I don't know about cursed, but they certainly had their fair share of tragedy. Who told you that?'

'Just some kid I met,' Marli replied. She thought about Luca and his surly manner. 'He was probably making it up.'

'I've been thinking about my mother a lot since I got the letter,' said Didi. 'She was always very adventurous and never seemed afraid of anything. My parents were passionate about travelling to exotic, faraway places all their lives. But she was also kind and compassionate, always helping other people.' He stood up and fetched a large oval box from the sideboard. It was decorated with peacocks, flowers and ferns in a faded swirl of turquoise, green and lavender. 'I finally remembered where I hid Mother's old hatbox. She stored some of her treasures in here, including her scrapbook from 1922 — it must have been a special year for her.'

Marli felt jittery with anticipation as Didi untied the turquoise ribbon around the box. He pulled out a black leather scrapbook with the words *My Memories* embossed on the cover.

Didi opened it to the first page and showed her the inscription in neat, loopy handwriting:

Violet Hamilton
Riversleigh, Riversleigh Grove, Hawthorn
November 1922

There were two black-and-white photographs on the front page. The first showed a girl, aged about fifteen, with long, wavy hair hanging loose, wearing a white dress. The second was the same girl, with her hair cut short in a curly bob, wearing a stylish 1920s evening dress. A caption underneath read, *December 14, 1922 — The Russian Ball.*

'What a beautiful photo,' Marli said, taking a closer look. 'She was just a year older than me when this was taken. She certainly looks very glamorous.'

'The 1920s was a glamorous time,' Didi replied. 'Especially for the wealthy families of Melbourne like the Hamiltons. But it was also a time of huge social change after the First World War.'

Didi turned the pages carefully. The scrapbook was crammed with invitations, newspaper articles, sketches, tickets, menus, dance cards and black-and-white photographs with captions written in the same neat calligraphy. There were informal shots of a spotted Dalmatian and an aristocratic cat in Riversleigh's garden, and more formal photos of garden parties, dinners and balls. It was a fascinating insight into a long-ago life.

'These photos are amazing,' Marli said. 'Look at that fantastic old car.'

Didi turned the page. 'Here's a photo of the house in the grand old days. Wouldn't it be nice to be able to see it like that?'

'And look at all the servants in their uniforms, lined up out the front in a reception line.'

'They probably had lots more servants than that before the war,' Didi replied with a laugh. 'Those grand houses needed a lot of staff to run them in the old days.'

'There are *ten* of them,' Marli said. She pored over a photograph of a factory that had a large sign painted on the wall: Hamilton's Fine Gloves and Bags.

'I thought you might like to take the box home and go through it, Marli,' Didi suggested. 'I always meant to give it to you.'

Marli felt a thrill of excitement. It was like being a detective trying to solve the mysteries of the past by sifting through the evidence. 'I'd love that, Didi. I promise I'll take good care of everything.'

'I have some of Violet's jewellery in the safe too,' Didi added. 'There are some beautiful pieces, but you might find them too old-fashioned now. I was saving them for when you get a bit older.'

'Thanks so much, Didi,' Marli replied enthusiastically. 'I actually love old jewellery. Mum and I look at antique pieces at the markets and imagine who might have owned them and what their stories might be.'

Marli showed Didi the engraved silver bangle that she always wore on her wrist.

'That's pretty,' said Didi. 'You don't often see crafts-manship that fine these days.'

'Mum gave it to me for my fourteenth birthday. We found it, tarnished black, in a box of junk at the op-shop for a few dollars. Mum polished it until it gleamed. We took it to a jeweller and he told us it's from the 1920s — it's actually quite valuable. So I'd love to see my own great-grandmother's jewellery.'

Marli closed the scrapbook and reached for the hatbox.

Didi frowned. 'The only thing that's worrying me is that I can't find my mother's sapphire engagement ring. It was stunning and had a fascinating history, and it's worth a king's ransom. I can't think what could have happened to it — I hope it's not lost.'

'That's a shame,' said Marli as she peered inside the hatbox. There was a jumble of items at the bottom. Marli pulled out a large, old-fashioned key with ornate fretwork on the bow. It was hanging on a faded velvet ribbon. It was such a beautiful key that Marli felt sure it must open something special. She laid it down on top of the scrapbook.

Next, she pulled out an antique Kodak Brownie folding camera.

'That must have been Violet's first camera. Isn't it quaint?' Didi took it from Marli and flicked a lever, revealing a lens that folded out like an accordion. 'Did I tell you that Violet was a professional photographer? She started taking photos when she was not much older than you. It was a much more complicated hobby back then.'

'I love taking photos too,' said Marli. 'Dad and I used to do it together. But I haven't really had time lately.'

Didi closed the lens back up and carefully replaced the camera inside the box. 'It was Violet who encouraged your Dad to take up photography when he was a teenager.'

'What was your mother like when she was a girl?' Marli asked.

Didi gazed down at the scrapbook, searching back through the mists of time. 'Violet was quite unconventional, really. She always taught me to fight for what I believed in. I imagine her poor father, Albert Hamilton, found her rather a handful . . .'

6

The Hidden Key

Riversleigh, 7 November 1922

A storm came in late in the afternoon, buffeting the house with wind and rain. Violet rummaged through her desk drawers, looking for a fountain pen and note-paper to scrawl letters to her sick friends at school. She was annoyed to find that her fountain pen was dry and her paper stocks low. Sally was meant to keep the writing desk stocked with pens, ink and paper.

For a moment, Violet thought about ringing the servants' bell to order fresh supplies, but she decided instead to fetch a pen and fresh paper from her father's desk in the library. It would be quicker.

Violet hurried towards the stairs. For a moment her eye was drawn to the white panelled door that led to the tower halfway along the southern side of the house. The door had been locked for the last four years. Violet barely thought about it anymore. It was like so much else in her life that was never talked about, and hardly even thought about, anymore. She ran downstairs.

The dark library, with its thousands of books, was at the very front of the house, on the south-east corner. The room smelled of old leather, beeswax and pipe tobacco. Violet ran her fingertips across the gilt-etched book spines. Two deep velvet armchairs stood before the black marble fireplace, while her father's large roll-top desk stood in the centre of the room, facing towards the terrace.

Juliet, the grey cat, was asleep in one of the armchairs. She yawned and stretched, begging Violet for a tummy rub. When Violet obliged, she purred with contentment, four paws in the air.

Violet opened the bottom drawer, where her father kept the spare stationery, searching for what she needed. As she rifled through the drawer, she felt something cold and sharp that was hidden right at the very back. Pulling it out, she saw it was a key with an ornate bow, hanging from a purple velvet ribbon. Violet looked at it for a moment then returned it to the back of the drawer. It was only as she was picking up her pile of paper and pens that she wondered which door the key might open. A memory stirred from long ago.

Could it be the missing key to the tower? Violet wondered. She picked the key up again and weighed it in the palm of her hand.

On the ground floor, the square tower held a small guest powder room, but above that were a further two rooms, one on top of the other, accessible from the first floor of the house. These rooms had been locked up for years. Violet suddenly had an overwhelming urge to see if this key would fit that lock.

Back upstairs, she checked around carefully. The servants had cleaned all the bedrooms in the morning and were now occupied in the servants' quarters. Violet crept towards the locked tower door, her heart thudding.

She glanced around once more to check that no-one was around, then pushed the key in the lock and turned. For a moment the lock refused to budge, sticky with lack of use. Then it gave suddenly, turning with a loud creak. Violet pushed open the door and went inside, still holding her breath.

Violet quickly closed the door behind her and leaned against it. She was in a small square room with windows on three sides, looking out over the treetops. To her right, a narrow spiral staircase led up to the room on the third level of the tower. Violet looked around, her throat tight.

This had been her mother's study. Did she imagine it, or did it still smell, warm and familiar, of her mother's floral perfume? No, the air smelled merely of hot, stale air.

The tower room was simply furnished with a white painted writing desk and chair, and a duck-egg blue velvet armchair by the western window, next to a side table piled with books. A tall bookcase was against the wall on her left. Everything was covered in a thick layer of dust.

On her mother's desk was a collection of photographs in tarnished silver frames. Violet walked over slowly, as if in a dream. There was a formal portrait taken on the front steps of Riversleigh. Violet, Imogen, her father and mother — and the two boys. Tears sprang to Violet's eyes. It was her family, before the war that changed everything.

There were old photographs that Mamma had taken of Violet's brothers, Lawrence and Archie, dressed in knickerbockers, riding hobby horses in the garden. Imogen and Violet were dressed in white pinafores over their cotton dresses, playing with Romeo as a wrinkly, spotted puppy.

Beside these were framed portraits of the two boys — Lawrence at eighteen years old and Archie at seventeen, dressed in their Australian Imperial Forces uniforms, just before they were sent to the Western Front in France. The two boys had run off together to enlist, with Archie convincing the recruitment officers that he was old enough. The first that their desperately worried parents had known of it was when the photographs arrived in the mail with their farewell letters.

Their faces looked so young, so serious. The boys had disembarked just a few short months before the war ended. Later, the newspaper stories said that the battle for the town of Villers-Bretonneux had been a crucial turning point in the war. It had certainly been a crucial turning point in Violet's life — in a matter of weeks she lost two brothers and a mother. And her grief-stricken father had never been the same again.

Violet sank down to the dusty rug. Hot, thick tears flowed as the memories rose up — memories she had tried to suppress. How could her world be ripped apart so savagely? How could she lose nearly everything she held most dear? Violet wept as though her heart was breaking all over again. She imagined it glued together, like a smashed plate that could never be made properly whole again.

Eventually the tears stopped. She rubbed her eyes and slowly stood. It was best that the tower room stayed locked, hiding away all the painful memories. Violet shuffled slowly towards the door, but instead of leaving and locking the memories behind her, she couldn't resist climbing the spiral staircase to the room above.

At the very top of the tower was Mamma's studio, an eyrie above the rest of the house, with views on four sides of the river, lawns and gardens. Over the high stone wall she could see to the paddocks and estates beyond. Rain dribbled down the window now, the wind rattling the glass. A ladder led from the studio up to a rooftop terrace, but the weather was too wild to go up there today.

An easel in the corner held an unfinished painting — a vase filled with blue and white flowers from the gardens. Other canvases were stacked against the walls. A table held dried-up oil paints, a pot of brushes and a crumpled ball of tissue paper, as though her mother had just tossed it there, before she left the room forever.

Violet could see her mother as though she were a ghost, wearing a paint-spattered smock, frowning in concentration as she dabbed at the canvas, or smiling at Violet as she taught her how to draw. Violet had spent many, many happy hours in this studio painting beside her mother.

'Mamma,' Violet sobbed jaggedly. 'Mamma, why did you leave us?'

It was too much — the rush of emotion and memories. Violet felt she had to flee the studio at once.

As she stumbled back towards the stairs, she noticed her mother's Brownie folding camera sitting on the side table in its brown leather case. She had been a keen photographer as well as an artist, taking many candid photos around the house and garden, as well as family picnics, birthdays, holidays and games.

Violet picked up the case and took out the camera, caressing it lovingly. She unlatched the lock at the top and unfurled the lens. A hazy memory darted into her mind, like a silvery fish: herself as a child of ten or eleven and Mamma in her long, swishing skirts and wispy chignon. Mamma stood at Violet's back, her arms encircling her, holding the camera at Violet's waist. Her mother's breath tickled her ear as she whispered the instructions: *Look down through the viewfinder at the top, just here. Think about your picture. Make it beautiful — a perfect balance of sky and land and subject. Then when the shot is perfect, hold your breath, stay still and push the shutter button. And it's magic — a moment of truth frozen forever.*

Violet made a quick decision and took the camera with her as she slipped down the stairs and out the door, locking it firmly behind her. Her father must never know she had found the key to the tower. Her father must never know that she had found Mamma's camera. It was a secret she must keep safe.

Back in her room, Violet folded out the accordion lens and cleaned the camera carefully, polishing the lens with a small brush and a soft cloth.

At first Violet merely thought of keeping the camera concealed in her room, like a memento of happier times. But she couldn't keep it hidden. She kept taking it out of her cupboard, holding it, stroking it. There was an old film still in the camera, a film from before. Violet yearned to use the camera to make her own magical photographs, her own moments of truth.

The first few days of the unexpected holiday flew by. It was the height of Melbourne's social season, so Imogen was busy with a whirl of engagements — the Melbourne Cup, the Lord Mayor's dinner, a garden party at Federal Government House with Lord and Lady Forster, dances, luncheons and visits to the theatre. Violet was left to her own devices — books, drawing, dancing classes, illicit swims in the river.

Violet also researched menu and design ideas for the Russian Ball. She borrowed books from her father's library and doodled in her sketchbook. Most of all, Violet wondered about her mother's camera and how she could learn to take photographs without raising her father's suspicion.

On Thursday afternoon, on the way home from dancing class, Violet asked Nikolai to drive her to Hawthorn's main shopping strip on Burwood Road, where there was a small camera shop that sold film cartridges and printed photographs. Nikolai parked the car and waited out the front while she went inside.

The shop was filled with glass cases displaying cameras and various accessories. Large prints of Melbourne landmarks and buildings were hanging on the walls. A male shop assistant stood behind the long timber counter, polishing the glass lens of a professional-looking camera.

'Good morning, miss,' he said, laying the cloth and camera down. 'Can I help you?'

Violet carefully drew her mother's camera out of her handbag and took it out of its case. 'Yes, please. I would like to buy some film for this camera.'

The assistant pulled open a drawer under the bench and pulled out a yellow cardboard box. 'How many would you like? Each roll takes six photographs.'

'Could I have three rolls, please?' Violet asked, pulling out her purse.

The assistant placed the boxes of film in a bag and Violet paid for them from her pocket money.

'Thanks,' Violet said, hesitating. 'I was wondering if you might be able to show me how to use the camera, please? It was my mother's and I'd like to learn how to take particularly good photographs with it.'

The assistant's face lit up. 'Let's see. What you have here is a Kodak Autographic Folding Brownie, about five years old.' He took the camera from her and clicked the lever so the front opened to release the lens.

'It's easy to use,' he assured her. 'You hold the camera about waist high and against your body, like this, and look down through this viewfinder on top to see how your photograph will look. It's worthwhile taking the time to frame your photograph carefully. You want to make sure your subject is in the centre of the frame and that the photograph is nicely composed and balanced. You don't want too much sky or too much ground.'

Violet nodded to show she understood. Her mother and her drawing teacher at school had taught her about composition and balance in art.

The assistant explained how to set the aperture and shutter speed for the amount of light available, and how to focus the camera, demonstrating the various levers and settings.

'Once you have the settings and composition right, you push the shutter release here to take the photograph,' he said. 'I suggest that you hold your breath while you take the shot to make sure the camera stays completely still. If you or the subject moves while the shutter is open, the photograph will be blurry.'

He took a similar camera out of a display case. 'Why don't you have a quick practice on this one? It doesn't have any film in it. Imagine we're outside on a sunny day, and your subject is standing there. Make sure the sun is behind you, shining on the person.'

Violet took her gloves off and worked through each step of the setting-up process, moving the various levers then clicking the shutter. She had to concentrate to remember which shutter speed she should use and exactly how to focus.

'Is that right?' she asked.

'You've got it.'

'Wonderful.' Violet felt elated. 'Let's hope I can remember it all.'

The assistant showed her how to load a new film into the camera. 'Don't take too many snapshots until you've had one of your films developed. That way you can check the prints and make sure you're doing everything right. Bring it back in if you have any questions.'

'Thank you so much,' Violet replied. 'I do appreciate your help.'

Violet had a spring in her step as she went back outside with the camera and rolls of film in her handbag. Instead of waiting by the car, as he usually was, Nikolai was sitting in the front seat reading a book. He was so engrossed in what he was reading that he didn't realise that Violet had come out until she was right beside the car, peering in the front window.

Nikolai, flushed with mortification, hurriedly placed the large book aside and jumped out of the car.

'Sorry, Miss Violet,' said Nikolai, saluting as he opened the rear door. 'I didn't see you come out.'

'That's all right, Nikolai,' Violet said with a smile. 'I lose track of everything too when I'm reading a good book. What're you reading?'

Nikolai looked uncomfortable and averted his eyes. 'Nothing in particular.'

Violet's curiosity was piqued. The book she had glimpsed was battered, but it looked like a beautifully bound textbook, not a cheap thriller.

'I'm reading *My Brilliant Career* by Miles Franklin for the third time,' said Violet. 'But I feel I should read Tolstoy's *Anna Karenina* so I can get some ideas for the Russian Ball.'

Violet chatted on about the books she had read recently, and Nikolai murmured short replies when necessary as he drove slowly through the afternoon traffic. Burwood Road was teeming with horse-drawn buggies, automobiles, motorbikes and pedestrians. A crowded electric tram rattled down the main street, with shoppers and workers hanging out of the doors.

'I haven't read many Australian books,' said Nikolai. 'We had to leave all our books behind when we left Russia, except one. So we don't have a very extensive library here.'

Violet sat forward, intrigued to finally get Nikolai talking. 'Which book did you bring?' she asked.

Nikolai looked embarrassed. 'It was a book of old Russian fairytales. It was our favourite book when we were children, and we couldn't bear to leave it behind.'

'Is your family in Melbourne with you?' Violet asked.

'Yes, I have three sisters — Tatiana, Katya and Anastacia — who live with my mother here. My father died four years ago during the civil war.'

'Four years ago? In 1918?' *How strange — just like Mamma, Lawrence and Archie*, Violet thought.

'Yes,' Nikolai replied, staring ahead through the windscreen as he concentrated on overtaking a horse-drawn baker's cart. 'We left Russia the following year. It became too difficult for us there. We went to Paris, then to London, but it was hard to get work there so we came to Melbourne. We were told if you work hard in Australia there are many opportunities.'

'I guess it's much better here than war-torn Russia at the moment,' Violet mused. She thought for a moment. 'I don't suppose you've ever been to one of the old Imperial Balls in St Petersburg? I'm planning the supper menu for our ball and wanted to think of some truly Russian dishes. What should we have?'

Nikolai glanced at her in the mirror, his tawny eyes flashing with humour. 'Russian food? Oh, that's easy. Nothing less than seven or eight courses will do.' His voice lost its usual formal tone. He held up his fingers on the wheel as he counted off the courses.

'Of course you must have hors d'oeuvres, such as *pâté de foie gras* and *petit* pastries, and piles of black caviar with blinis,' continued Nikolai, his French accent sounding perfect. 'The entree should be lobster or *saumon* with a hollandaise sauce, followed by the main course — stuffed poultry with truffles and *filet de boeuf* served with asparagus and *salades à la francaise*. All washed down with lots of champagne and French wines.'

'Mmmm. You're making me hungry, but it all sounds rather more French than Russian,' Violet said.

Nikolai laughed. 'Well, just like your Monsieur Dufour, the best chefs in Russia were always French.'

Violet nodded. '*Naturellement.*'

'Of course, for a true Russian supper, the highlight is always the dessert table,' Nikolai said. 'It should be a sumptuous spread — a work of art. With ice sculptures of animals and everything from ice-cream, chocolate and compotes to *petit fours* and *meringues à la chantilly*.'

Violet grabbed a small notebook and pen out of her handbag and began to scribble down Nikolai's suggestions. She could imagine a vast table piled with sweet delicacies and decorated with golden ornaments.

'That all sounds marvellous, especially the ice sculptures. But if the food is mostly French, how can we make the ball more Russian?'

Nikolai thought for a few moments. 'The old aristocratic balls usually began with a Grand Polonaise, with all the couples promenading with great ceremony around the ballroom. Then the usual dances, like waltzes and quadrilles, were mixed with colourful Russian folk dances, like the mazurka, which are very energetic and lively. Nothing like a mazurka to get your heart pumping!'

Violet was fascinated. 'Nowadays everyone is more interested in jazzing. So perhaps we could start with some traditional dances, and then move onto the one-step, shimmy and foxtrot as the night goes on. And what about decorations?'

'The balls in St Petersburg always had masses of flowers, potted palms and hundreds of candles,' Nikolai said, his voice alight with enthusiasm. 'And we always finished the evening with fireworks, lighting up the night sky with thousands of coloured falling stars.'

Nikolai paused before continuing. 'But perhaps you could re-create some typical Russian scenes, like ice skaters or horse-drawn troikas, or you could dress the waiters as colourful Cossacks with baggy crimson trousers, sashes and vests.'

'Yes. That would be brilliant.' Violet scribbled down these suggestions, her mind bubbling with ideas. 'I'm sure we could find some Russian folk dancers to perform. Perhaps you might know of some?'

Nikolai turned left, heading off the main road into a quieter, tree-lined suburban street. Out the window Violet could see the familiar houses, gardens and paddocks flash by.

'All Russians love to dance,' Nikolai said. 'The winters are so long and cold that without music, dance and good books, we'd all go mad. In St Petersburg, before the war, there were dances and balls and dinners every night, as well as opera, theatre and ballet.'

'It sounds marvellous,' Violet said. 'I suppose your parents were in service back in Russia. Did they work for one of the big aristocratic families?'

Violet could see the muscles in the back of Nikolai's neck stiffen. He didn't answer for a moment.

'Yes. I suppose they did,' Nikolai said quietly. 'But all the Russian aristocratic families are gone now. Dead, or scattered to the far corners of the world.'

Violet felt as though she had touched a raw nerve. 'I'm sorry, Nikolai. I didn't mean to upset you. It must be very difficult to be so far from your home and your old life.'

'Yes, miss,' Nikolai said in his old voice — the formal one he reserved for speaking to his employers — and Violet felt inexplicably disappointed.

7

Journey to the Slums

A week later, Nikolai was driving Violet home from a ball committee meeting. The members of the committee had met at the Hawthorn Town Hall to inspect the venue and meet the caterers. Audrey, Imogen and Edie had gone on to see the printer to get the invitations and posters organised. Everything was coming together well.

Violet sat back, watching the shadows of the trees flash past, then the familiar high stone wall of her own garden appeared, partially hiding the cream-coloured tower and graceful arches of her home. The car slowed down as they neared the front gates, with their stone-capped pillars and the name *Riversleigh* scrolled in brass letters on a black plate.

As Nikolai stopped the car, Violet noticed Sally hurrying towards them across the gravel driveway, her head down. She was wearing her daytime uniform — a demure blue floral dress, but with a black straw hat instead of her usual starched white apron and cap.

'Nikolai, would you mind checking if everything is all right, please?' asked Violet. 'Sally looks bothered about something.'

Nikolai jumped out of the car and opened the gate. He chatted to Sally and then Sally came over and leaned through the open driver's window.

'Pardon me, miss,' Sally said. 'But Mrs Darling has given me a couple of hours off. My brother brought a note to say me ma is sick, so I'm goin' to visit her. Is there anythin' you need me to do?'

'I'm so sorry to hear that, Sally,' Violet replied. 'Is she very ill?'

Sally frowned. 'She's been workin' awful hard since me da took sick. My brother said she can't get out of bed, so I thought I'd better check.'

Violet glanced at her wristwatch. She knew that Imogen had gone to stay at Edie's house overnight for dinner and an evening dance. 'Is my father home yet?'

'No, he's not,' Sally said.

'Mr Hamilton asked me to pick him up from the factory at five o'clock, Miss Violet,' Nikolai said.

'Perfect. Why don't we give you a lift then, Sally?' Violet suggested. 'Your mother lives in Richmond, so it's a long walk. Then we can pick up my father on the way home.'

'Oh, that's kind of you, but I can take the tram from Burwood Road,' Sally said.

'Nonsense,' replied Violet. 'You only have two hours off, so please let us drive you. That way you won't waste most of the time walking there and back.'

Sally gave a huge grin. 'Thanks awfully, miss. That would be lovely.'

Nikolai opened the front passenger door for her, and Sally settled back into the comfortable leather seat with a sigh of satisfaction.

'Which part of Richmond are we driving to?' Nikolai asked.

'If you cross the river at Hawthorn Bridge then drive north to Victoria Street, I'll direct you from there,' Sally said.

As Nikolai drove, following Sally's directions, Violet leaned forward to stare out the open window at the passing landscape. Immediately the view changed from leafy, spacious parks and gardens to grimy-grey, tightly packed shops, cottages, tramsheds and factories.

On the western riverbank were the tanneries and wool scouring warehouses, with their jumble of smokestacks and sheds. Violet could smell the industry — belching smoke, the foul tanneries and the underlying stink of sewage. She pulled a lacy handkerchief from her bag and covered her nose. Violet had rarely ventured across the bridge into Richmond, and she was intrigued to explore. It truly was a different world. The newspapers called it 'Struggletown'.

Driving up Burnley Street, the shops were smaller and close together, their windows filled with a jumble of colourful goods. A warren of narrow streets and laneways ran off on either side. Trams clattered and jangled back and forth, the bells clanging. Cars and motorbikes battled with horse-drawn delivery carts, buggies and two-wheeled jinkers. Violet felt a rush of exhilaration at the chaotic scene.

Victoria Street was narrow and dingy, hemmed in by ramshackle buildings. There was barely room for traffic to pass in each direction. Pedestrians took their lives in their hands as they tried to cross the congested thoroughfare.

Violet gave a start of recognition when she saw the red-brick, two-storey factory belonging to her father, and the large sign painted over the arched doorway: Hamilton's Fine Gloves and Bags.

Many of her father's wealthy friends, who lived on large estates in Hawthorn or Kew, just on the other side of the river, also had factories and businesses in busy Richmond. There were boot factories, furniture-makers, breweries, clothes workshops and tanneries, all surrounded by cramped workers' cottages and tiny terraces.

Directed by Sally, Nikolai continued further down Victoria Street, then turned left and left again down a narrow laneway barely wider than the car. It was cobbled with bluestone, and a gutter ran down the centre. A gang of barefooted, grubby young urchins were playing cricket in the lane, using a fruit crate as a wicket, a homemade ball and a bat made from two fence posts spliced together with twine. One girl had crutches and a twisted, withered leg, but she hopped around, chasing the ball with the others.

'Freddy's out,' yelled one of the boys as the fruit crate was knocked over by the flying ball.

'I ain't,' cried Freddy, refusing to hand over the bat. 'The motor car put me off.'

Nikolai honked the horn and the kids reluctantly packed up their game and moved to the side of the laneway, staring curiously inside the yellow Daimler.

'That's a bloomin' fancy car,' called one of the girls with tangled hair, carrying a baby on her hip. 'Is that Maisie Burke's sister in the front seat?'

Violet sank back against the rear seat as the dirty faces peered in on each side, the boys' faces shadowed by their oversized flat caps. She felt vaguely afraid, although they were only children no older than twelve. Perhaps it was because she could see the hunger in their eyes and gaunt faces. Her father's luxurious buttercup motor car cost more money than most working families would earn over years.

'Get on with the lot of you,' Sally yelled out the window.

The children jeered and taunted, but soon lost interest and went back to their game.

Nikolai parked the Daimler outside Sally's family home. It was a tiny timber place, one of a row of six terraces built right on the laneway. There was only a narrow, rickety porch and a low picket fence between the cobbled lane and the front door. The door flew open and a scrawny boy raced out and through the front gate. He was closely followed by a sister and a brother.

'Sally, is that you?' The boy was wearing a darned shirt and shorts that were too big for him, with clumpy, battered boots and grey socks that had fallen around his ankles. 'Ma'll be pleased to see you.'

Sally climbed out of the car to meet him. 'How is she, Frank?' Her voice sounded strained.

'She's in bed,' Frank replied. He looked over his shoulder towards the front door and lowered his voice. 'Ma says she's fine an' will get up later, but she's as weak as a kitten. She just has her head turned to the wall. I made her some tea but she wouldn't drink it.'

'I'll come an' see her,' Sally said. She leaned in the car window. 'It's awfully good of you bringin' me here. It saved a lot of time.'

'Is there anything I can do?' Violet asked.

'Oh no, miss,' Sally said hurriedly. 'I'm sure she'll be better soon. It's more 'n likely just exhaustion. Ma works real hard to feed four kids an' pay the rent, now that me da's too sick to work. He's never been the same since the Great War.'

'Should we get a doctor?' asked Violet.

'That's good of you, miss, but we can't afford a doctor,' Sally replied tersely. She turned to go inside. Her siblings stayed outside, milling around with the other kids in the street.

Violet felt helpless.

'What would you like to do, Miss Violet?' asked Nikolai. 'We have an hour before I need to pick up your father. Shall I take you home?'

Violet shook her head. 'No, we'll stay here for a little while, Nikolai. Then we can give Sally a lift home so she can spend more time with her mother.'

'Very well, Miss Violet.'

They sat in silence for a few moments. Outside, the local children continued their game of cricket, with Sally's siblings joining in. Nikolai sat still, staring through the windscreen, his book beside him on the seat. Of course he couldn't read while Violet was sitting in the car.

'Let's get out and stretch our legs,' Violet suggested.

Nikolai opened the door for her and tipped his cap. Violet wandered up and down the laneway, watching the children play and examining the tiny terraces, with their peeling paint and falling down fences. They looked like abandoned cubbyhouses.

Fortunately the stench from the tanneries was fainter

here, but Violet could still smell the whiff of coal smoke, mixed with rotting garbage and the outdoor lavatories behind the terraces. A woman sat on the narrow porch of one terrace house, shelling a basin of peas. A baby sat in a push-chair beside her, waving a wooden spoon. Violet called a friendly good afternoon, but the woman only replied with a surly nod.

The cricket ball skidded up beside her, and Violet leaned down to pick it up. It was made of tightly rolled rags tied with string. Of course a rag ball didn't bounce, so it had to be bowled on the full. She threw it back towards the wicketkeeper, who caught it easily and hurled it at the fruit crate, sending it flying. The kids threw their arms in the air and cheered.

Violet remembered her Brownie tucked away in her bag on the back seat of the car. This would be an excellent opportunity to practise using it. She had already taken some photographs when her father was out — of the house and garden, of Romeo and Juliet, but she was keen to try taking some more natural photographs.

She fetched the camera and took it out of its brown leather case, folding the lens out. For a few minutes she wandered up and down the street, stopping every now and again to practise framing up a shot, even though she didn't actually take any photographs.

She moved back and forth, checking the framing through the viewfinder to see if it looked better close up or further away, or as a portrait or landscape shot. Violet fiddled with the shutter, aperture and focus and pretended to take shots, the camera at her waist, holding her breath to keep it totally still.

Sally's sister finally noticed what Violet was doing. 'Look, she's takin' our photo!'

'No,' Violet replied hurriedly. She felt it might be impolite to take people's photographs without asking permission. 'I didn't take any. I was just practising.'

'Oh,' groaned Sally's brother, disappointed. 'I've never 'ad my picture taken.'

'Would you like to me to take your photograph?' Violet asked the children.

A buzz of enthusiasm rippled through the gang as they crowded around her.

'Yes. Yes,' came a cacophony of exuberant shouts.

Nikolai moved closer from where he had been waiting beside the car. Violet felt more confident with his tall frame and authoritative uniform behind her.

'So you're Sally's brother, aren't you?' Violet asked, trying to remember which of the children in the crowd were Sally's family.

'Yes, I'm Frank, an' this is my brother Billy — he's ten — an' little sister Maisie, who's eight,' Frank replied. 'My other sister Peggy is fourteen, but she's at work — she just started at Hamilton's Gloves as an apprentice machinist.'

'At Hamilton's Fine Gloves? My father's factory?' Violet asked, wondering at the coincidence that both sisters worked for him. Frank nodded.

'She didn't want to go into borin' old service like Sally,' Billy explained, jostling for attention. 'The hours are too long an' 'ard, an' Peggy wanted to stay close to help Ma.'

Violet was a little taken aback by Billy's brutal honesty. She had never considered that Sally might find the hours as a Riversleigh maidservant long and difficult.

'Oh?' said Violet. 'I hope Peggy enjoys working at the factory?'

'No. It 'urts her back, but Ma says she'll get used to it,' Maisie said, a tiny, barefooted girl who looked much younger than her eight years.

Frank glared at his siblings and their indiscretion. 'It's all right. Peggy likes the money an' most of the workers are nice. I'm goin' to start work next week too,' he boasted. 'I got a job trainin' as a strainer at Ramsay's Tannery by the river.'

Violet was shocked. The boy in front of her was a mere child, with his oversized clothes and snub nose with freckles.

'How old are you, Frank?' Violet asked. 'Shouldn't you be still at school?'

Frank drew himself up tall. 'I'm thirteen, but they ain't too fussy at Ramsay's, as long as I work hard,' he objected. 'I'll get ten shillings a week to start an' thirteen shillings after three months.'

Ten shillings for a week's work, thought Violet. *We're charging more than twelve shillings for a ticket to our Russian Ball.*

'Frank, perhaps it might be better if you stayed at school,' Violet said. 'Then you could get a better job in a few years.'

Frank looked at Violet as though she were crazy. 'With Da not workin', me ma works day an' night, an' we still can't pay the rent. Sally an' Peggy give all the money they earn, but it's still not enough. Now Ma's sick — how're we to eat?'

Violet felt sick to her stomach. She had been shocked when she'd seen the photos of the starving Russian children on the other side of the world, but these hungry children were right here — just a ten-minute drive from her grand home on the other side of the Yarra River.

The children around her were losing interest in the conversation. Talk of how to pay the rent or feed the family was all too common for them. Some began to drift back towards the abandoned cricket game, while others argued over whether to play skipping or hopscotch.

'Let's take that photograph,' Violet suggested. 'But first, tell me all your names.'

Violet looked up to see the sun's position and arranged the nine children in the centre of the laneway, the light falling on their faces. The smaller children were gathered at the front, Paddy holding the cricket bat and Freddy the ball. Helen held Bubby on her hip and smiled shyly, while Ruthie with the withered leg stood beside her, trying to hide her crutches.

'Remember, you'll have to hold completely still while I take the photograph,' Violet reminded them. 'If you move, it will be blurry.'

The children obediently held themselves still. Maisie hid behind her brother Frank, her face peeking out from behind the safety of his protective body. Billy looked solemn, as though he were engaged in the most serious business of his young life. Frank, however, twitched his cap to a jaunty angle and grinned broadly with delight.

Violet set the shutter speed, aperture and focus, and wound on the film. Looking down through the viewfinder at waist height, she checked the framing and positioning. 'Maisie, can you just move forward a bit so I can see you? Billy, stand closer to your brother.'

Maisie shrank further back behind the others, while Billy moved a mere centimetre closer to his brother. Frank put his arm around his little sister, drawing her out. 'It's all right, Maisie. It won't bite you.'

Nikolai stepped behind Violet and pulled some crazy faces to distract the children. Maisie and Billy forgot their nervousness at the novelty of having their photograph taken and moved forward, giggling.

'Splendid, that's better. On my count,' warned Violet. 'One, two, three . . .' She held her breath and pushed the button. She felt a huge sense of exhilaration as she took the photo — she'd done it! — and there were two more shots she was keen to experiment with.

'Can I take some photographs of you playing?' Violet asked the children, who happily agreed. 'You might just need to stay still for a moment when I tell you.'

Next Violet took a photograph of Ruthie bowling, while Frank aimed the bat in front of the fruit case. The other kids gathered around as fielders in the narrow laneway. The last shot was of Maisie and Billy, crouched in the gutter, rolling marbles down the grimy channel towards Nikolai, who was out of the shot.

'Is your father sick as well?' Violet asked the two siblings.

'It was the Great War,' Billy said. 'Ma says he's got shell shock. He was a soldier, but he lost his arm. When he came home, he couldn't get work. Now he has funny turns where he trembles an' gets angry.'

'Ma says it's the nightmares,' Maisie added.

'Poor man,' said Violet. 'Your father must have had a difficult time fighting in the Great War.'

'Yes, but I wish he'd get better,' said Billy. 'He's been sick for a bloomin' long time.'

'Ma says it's *habominable*,' said Maisie. 'He fought four years for his King and country, an' now he's treated like dirt.'

'Your ma's right,' Violet said. 'I think it's abominable too.'

A minute later Sally came out to call her siblings. She looked surprised when she saw the car still parked and Violet chatting to them. Nikolai by this stage was deep in conversation with the other children. They all had their heads buried under the bonnet of the Daimler while Nikolai explained the various parts of the engine and what they did.

'What're you still doin' here, miss?' asked Sally, confused.

'Nikolai and I decided to stay here and play with the kids while we waited for you,' Violet explained with a laughing glance at Nikolai. 'I've been taking photographs.'

'Oh, you shouldn't have waited, miss,' Sally replied. 'I can walk back.'

Violet shook her head. 'Truly, it's no trouble — but what about your mother? How is she?'

Sally sighed. 'She's pretty crook. But hopefully a day or two in bed will fix her right up.'

Violet checked her watch. 'We need to go in about fifteen minutes to pick up Father, so you can come with us then. Or if you'd rather stay with your mother, I'll explain it to Mrs Darling.'

Sally glanced back over her shoulder towards the house. 'I'll come back with you, miss. I've just made the kiddies some boiled potatoes for tea, but I want to do a quick tidy up. Ma tries so hard to keep the place spick an' span, but with four kiddies running riot, it's turned into a right mess.'

'That's fine. I'll send Frank in when it's time for us to go,' said Violet.

Just before they left, Violet loaded a new film into the camera and set up a family portrait of Sally with Frank, Billy and Maisie against the picket fence outside their home.

8

Hamilton's Fine Gloves Factory

Nikolai parked outside the Hamilton's Fine Gloves factory a few minutes before five o'clock.

'I'm going to visit my father,' Violet announced. 'I'd like to see the factory — it's been so long.'

'Very well, Miss Violet,' Nikolai replied. Sally and Nikolai settled back to chat.

The factory had lots of tall, airy windows and double-arched doors on the lower floor, which stood open. Violet took a photograph of the outside of the factory. She would have loved to take the camera inside, but she didn't want her father to see it.

She tucked the camera away and went through the entrance and into a wide hallway. To her left were the two offices, guarded by a fierce-looking secretary sitting at a long desk in a small anteroom at the front. To her right was the showroom filled with glass cases and display shelves. Violet turned into the anteroom.

The secretary looked her up and down critically. 'Yes, can I help you, miss?' she asked briskly, with the manner of one used to dealing with underlings and nuisances.

Violet felt momentarily uncomfortable and worried that her hat was crooked or her stockings stained from kneeling in the laneway. She pulled herself tall and projected her voice, speaking in her best Rothbury College accent. 'Hello. My name is Violet Hamilton. I'm here to visit my father.'

The secretary's demeanour immediately became more attentive. 'Welcome, Miss Hamilton. How nice to see you here. I'm Mrs Clarkson, your father's secretary. Let me check if Mr Hamilton is available.'

'Thank you. That would be splendid, Mrs Clarkson.'

Mrs Clarkson bustled to one of the doors behind her and went into the office beyond. Violet could hear the murmur of low voices, then Mrs Clarkson beckoned for her to come through.

The office was pleasant, lined with bookshelves. Albert Hamilton was sitting in a commodious leather armchair behind his broad oak desk, talking on the candlestick telephone. A pair of smaller visitors' chairs were drawn up in front of the desk while a side table held piles of papers and ledgers. On the wall behind him was a large gilt-framed oil portrait of Violet's Scottish grandfather, Lachlan Hamilton, looking successful and stern.

It was Lachlan who had started Hamilton's Fine Gloves in 1870. He had arrived in the colony with thousands of others during the Victorian gold rushes, hoping to strike it rich. His first fortune had been made, not through mining, but from selling tools and clothes to the miners from the back of his travelling horse-drawn dray.

Later, Lachlan settled in Melbourne with his wife and young family and, with substantial capital behind him, began with a small workshop in the back streets of Richmond, making gloves. As his wealth grew, he bought a large estate at Hawthorn across the river and built Riversleigh in the 1880s.

With the changes in technology in the early twentieth century, he built this new factory on the main road, expanding his range to include leather helmets and coats for motorcyclists, automobile drivers and aviators. Lachlan Hamilton always had a knack for business.

'Just one moment, Mr Ramsay,' said Albert Hamilton. He looked worried, covering the black mouthpiece with one hand. 'Violet. What are you doing here? Is there anything wrong?'

He looked her up and down. Violet pulled her skirt self-consciously. She had grown so much in recent months that it was a little short. Mrs Clarkson hovered behind her, waiting for orders.

'No, no,' said Violet. 'Nikolai collected me from dance class and said he had to pick you up at five, so I thought I'd pop by to see you.'

Mr Hamilton looked relieved. 'Right, well, I'm a little busy now, Violet. Would you like Mrs Clarkson to make you a cup of tea while I finish these telephone calls?'

'I . . . I thought perhaps I could take a look around the factory,' said Violet. 'I haven't been here for ages.'

Her father looked distracted, glancing back at Mrs Clarkson, as though seeking help.

'Would you like me to take Miss Hamilton on a little tour of the factory while you finish up, Mr Hamilton?' asked Mrs Clarkson.

Mr Hamilton waved his hand, shooing them away. 'Good idea, Mrs Clarkson. I'll only be ten minutes, Violet, but I do need to get this done.'

Violet swallowed her disappointment. She had actually hoped to look around the factory with her father so she could ask him questions. She'd imagined him explaining the process to her, their heads bent together, the way he had when she was a little girl.

'Come this way,' urged Mrs Clarkson, ushering Violet out of the office like a mother hen herding a chick. 'Now these, of course, are the offices — your father's here and the accountant's there. And across the hall is the showroom, where buyers can examine our whole range.'

Mrs Clarkson didn't give Violet time to look at the goods on display, hurrying her past the lavatories and kitchen to the loading dock and warehouse at the rear. Men were unloading a truck filled with rolls of soft leather in many colours. The side of the truck was emblazoned with Ramsay's Tannery. The workers shot a glance towards Violet but, with the formidable Mrs Clarkson there, they didn't dare pause for a moment.

'A new delivery from Ramsay's,' explained Mrs Clarkson. 'The skins are cured at the tannery a few blocks away, in River Street, then brought here for cutting and machining upstairs.'

Violet followed Mrs Clarkson up the narrow stairs on the left-hand wall. The second floor of the factory was one big room, roughly divided in half by a long wooden workbench. Large windows let in plenty of light and air, while extra illumination was provided by several electric bulbs dangling from the high, vaulted ceiling. Dust motes danced in the air, while scraps of leather and silk offcuts littered the floor and benches.

'And this is our workshop,' Mrs Clarkson explained. 'To the right is the cutting area. The men cut out the shapes for each item. The skill is to make sure there is as little wastage of material as possible.'

Violet wandered around the room, watching the cutters work. Mrs Clarkson followed her, explaining the process as she went.

Ten men stood at high benches, tracing and cutting out glove and bag shapes on leather hides, using metal patterns and sharp blades. Tables were piled high with rolled leather hides of various colours from white kid, to fawn, dark tan, navy, crimson and black. The air smelled of leather and strong glue.

A tall, skinny foreman with a bobbing Adam's apple walked back and forth, supervising the workers. The leather shapes were gathered up from each cutter by a young apprentice, about Frank's age, and delivered to the central dividing bench. Another boy delivered fresh hides to the men and periodically swept up the leather offcuts from the benches and floor.

'To the left is the machining area,' Mrs Clarkson continued. 'The women assemble and sew the garments together.'

About forty women sat on either side of long tables, perched on round stools behind their sewing machines, stitching seams. The noise of the whirring machines was deafening. A group of older women sat together, working on the more elaborate and decorative gloves.

'The workers at this table are our most experienced machinists who do the fancy work,' Mrs Clarkson said. 'While over there are our apprentices.'

Two teenage girls ran back and forth, keeping the machinists supplied with cut-outs and taking the finished garments away. Another group of girls worked at a separate table, tying on labels and packing the finished gloves into tissue paper.

'Is there a girl at that table called Peggy Burke?' asked Violet.

One of the girls, who looked remarkably like her older sister, turned around. Violet walked over. 'I'm Violet Hamilton, and your sister Sally works at our house.'

The other girls and women slowed their sewing to listen in.

'Hello, Miss Hamilton,' Peggy replied. 'Nice to meet you.'

'I'm sorry to hear about your mother,' Violet said. 'Sally says she thinks she just needs a good rest.'

A look of concern crossed Peggy's face. 'She's been poorly for a few weeks.'

Violet chatted to Peggy for a moment about her work. Then her father came in. Violet noticed that all the workers quickened their pace.

'Dad, did you know that Peggy is Sally's younger sister?' Violet asked. Mr Hamilton looked momentarily confused, looking at his latest employee. 'Our maid at home, Sally Burke. Peggy is her sister.'

'Oh, truly?' Mr Hamilton said. 'Well, I hope you've settled in well, Peggy, and become as dedicated a worker as your sister.'

'Yes, sir,' Peggy replied, looking down at the floor.

'Now, Violet,' said Mr Hamilton, changing the subject, 'seeing you're here, I thought you might like a little present.'

Mr Hamilton led the way to the work table where the completed items were being labelled and wrapped. There was a range of beautiful leather handbags in a variety of colours and sizes, as well as gloves and other goods.

'We've just made a new selection of bags in the very latest fashion for the Myer Emporium's summer collection. So why don't you choose one you like?'

Violet looked up at her father with delight. 'Thanks so much, Dad. That'd be marvellous.'

After a few minutes' deliberation, Violet chose a large chocolate tote bag with a gold clasp. Mr Hamilton opened a side cupboard and pulled out a rectangular-shaped cardboard box and offered it to Violet. 'And this is also something new that we've recently added to our range.'

Inside the box was a black leather book with *My Memories* embossed on the cover and thick blank pages inside.

'I'm not certain if you'd use it, but apparently scrapbooks are very popular now,' her father said gruffly. 'You stick invitations and dance cards and photographs inside. It might give you something to do now that you are on an extended holiday.'

Violet rifled through the pages, touched by his thoughtfulness. 'It's beautiful, thanks, Dad. I'd love to keep a scrapbook.'

'My pleasure, Violet. Let's take you home.'

The next day Imogen came home from her stay at Edie's, just in time for afternoon tea.

It was such a gorgeous afternoon that Violet had given orders for tea to be served in the summerhouse. The round, open-air structure was draped with wisteria vines and surrounded by gardenia shrubs; it looked out over the river to the west and the sunken garden to the south. A gentle breeze wafted sweet scents from the rose bushes. Violet sat in a white wicker chair, wearing a large straw sunhat. Romeo lay at her feet, and he whined with pleasure as she tickled him under the chin.

Imogen threw herself back into one of the wicker armchairs theatrically, pulling off her gloves and hat and tossing them onto a spare chair.

'We had the most marvellous time at Edie's last night,' Imogen declared, her eyes sparkling. 'We danced and laughed and chatted until three in the morning.'

'Did you dance with anyone special?' Violet teased. 'Any poor young medical students, for example?'

'I danced with countless young men,' boasted Imogen. 'Now that you mention it, though, I think one of them might have been a medical student. What was his name?'

'Would that be Tommy O'Byrne, by any chance?' Violet asked, raising her eyebrows.

'Yes, that does sound familiar,' Imogen agreed nonchalantly. 'It was quite ridiculous because Tommy kept cutting in on whoever I was dancing with, and then Theodore would cut in on Tommy, then someone else. But Tommy had to leave to go home early — he had university today — so that took some of the fun out of it.'

'I imagine Theodore was happy about that.'

'Blissfully,' Imogen said. 'Daddy has actually invited Theodore and his parents for a cosy dinner tonight. Apparently they have some boring business to discuss.'

'Bother — I'd forgotten we were having people to dinner tonight,' Violet said. 'I'm not sure what to wear. Everything I own seems to be shrinking.'

'Time for a shopping trip, Vivi. And we need to start thinking about getting our gowns made for the Russian Ball. I'm determined to have something absolutely adorable.'

Violet nodded. 'I wonder where the tea is. It seems to be taking an awfully long time.'

Violet glanced towards the house and saw Sally picking her way down the steps and across the lawn, carrying a heavy tray. Romeo sat up at once, tongue lolling. He knew what the tea tray meant.

Joseph the gardener was clipping the box hedges. He said something as Sally passed, and she stopped for a moment to talk to him before hurrying forward.

'Here she is,' said Violet, stroking Romeo's soft, velvety ears.

Sally stepped into the summerhouse and carefully unloaded each item onto the white tablecloth — the silver tea pot, milk jug, hot water jug, and plates of scones, sand-wiches, biscuits and fruitcake.

'Thank you, Sally,' Imogen said, pouring milk into two dainty cups. 'I'm dying for a cup of tea.'

Violet took a ham sandwich and tossed it to Romeo, who swallowed it in one bite.

'Yes, Miss Hamilton,' Sally said. 'Mrs Darling asked me to apologise for it takin' so long, but the kitchen is in a-whirl with the dinner party tonight. Monsieur Dufour is shoutin' in French an' throwing pans again.'

Imogen laughed as she poured tea into Violet's cup, then her own. 'Thank goodness we're having a cosy little dinner and not a formal banquet. But at least we all know the meal will be heavenly.'

Violet took a sip of her tea then glanced up at Sally. Something about her voice sounded strained, her eyes were red-rimmed and her face looked pinched. 'Are you all right? Has Monsieur been shouting at you?'

Sally shook her head. 'No, miss. It's just . . . It's just that Frank came by this afternoon to say that Ma is worse . . . But Mrs Darling says it's far too busy with the dinner party tonight, so I can't check on her until tomorrow. We still have so much to do.'

Violet set her teacup down in its saucer. 'But of course you must go to your mother.'

'I can't, miss,' Sally repeated. 'I've hours of work to do yet. Mrs Darling says I can have an hour off tomorrow afternoon.'

Violet thought for a moment then stood up, her chin in the air. 'Sorry, Imogen, old thing, but I've just remem-bered there's something I need to do.' She turned to Sally.

'Come along. Imogen doesn't want anything to eat, so bring all that food back to the kitchen. I'm going to have a word with Mrs Darling.'

'What do you mean?' Imogen demanded. 'I'm starving.'

'No, you're not,' Violet insisted. 'Think of that lovely new dress you want to have made for our Russian Ball. Remember, the latest fashion is to look like a skinny boy.'

Imogen grabbed two triangles of ham-and-lettuce sandwich from the plate. 'If you'd spent all night dancing, you'd be starving too.'

'Come on, Sally,' Violet ordered. 'There's no time to waste.'

Sally obediently took the plates of food from the table and loaded them back on the tray, following Violet back across the lawn, up onto the terrace, in through the servants' entrance and into the service wing. Romeo followed hopefully, but stopped at the servants' door — he knew better than to brave the wrath of Monsieur Dufour.

The back corridor led past the scullery, where a teenage girl was scrubbing a huge pile of greasy saucepans, her arms elbow-deep in grimy water. Further along were the pantry, storerooms and laundry, then the maids' sitting room. A narrow, steep stairway climbed up to the maids' bedrooms and provided the servants with access to the family bedrooms at the front of the house. A laundry maid bustled past, hefting a basket almost as big as she was.

Unlike the front of the house, the servants' quarters were painted a utilitarian grey, with small, high windows and bare timber floors. Before she reached it, Violet could hear the sounds of the kitchen — oil sizzling, pans clattering and banging, Monsieur Dufour shouting in French, '*Allez, vite. Vite!*'

Rich buttery smells drifted out the door, and the fresh, tangy scent of fresh herbs from the kitchen garden. Above the door were the servants' bells, each a different size for every room, so the servants would know where to go when summoned.

Violet turned into the kitchen, which was hot and stuffy, despite being the only spacious room in the back quarters. Monsieur Dufour, sweat beading on his forehead, was chopping thyme, rosemary and parsley, his long steel knife flashing with great speed. He threw chopped onions and garlic into the sizzling butter and tossed them in the air, flamboyantly stirring them with a wooden spoon.

The housekeeper, Mrs Darling, was sitting at the scrubbed pine table with Annie, one of the other maids. They were counting and polishing the silver cutlery with soft rags before stacking them back in the timber canteen. Mrs Darling saw Violet and rose quickly, nudging Annie to do the same.

'Miss Violet, can I help you with anything?' Mrs Darling asked.

'Yes, please, Mrs Darling,' Violet replied. 'I have an important errand that I need to run just now, and I need Sally to accompany me. We won't be very long.'

Mrs Darling glanced at Violet and then at Sally behind her. 'Sally has lots of work to do to get ready for tonight,' Mrs Darling explained. 'We're expecting seven guests for dinner, and your father has instructed that he would like an exceptional meal.'

Monsieur Dufour slammed a pot down on the table. His knife chopped the ends off a pile of asparagus in one quick motion.

Violet smiled winningly. 'Yes, I understand that, and I'm sure Sally can catch up when we return, but I do need her for a little while.'

Mrs Darling crossed her hands in front of her chest and nodded. 'Then of course, Miss Violet.'

'Sally, could you please run to the carriage house and tell Nikolai that I need the car immediately?' asked Violet. 'I'll meet you and Nikolai out front.'

Violet quickly looked around the kitchen, noticing the large leg of ham that had been carved to make the sandwiches. She turned to the other maidservant. 'Annie, could you please pack up all this leftover food into a basket for me, please? And assuming that Monsieur Dufour doesn't need it for this evening's meal, can you please put that ham in a bag as well, along with any fruit, potatoes and bread we can spare?'

Mrs Darling hesitated for a moment and then reached for a wicker shopping basket on the sideboard. 'There's also half a chocolate cake, a dozen scones, a bottle of milk and a packet of tea. Would you like those as well?'

Monsieur Dufour huffed loudly and muttered something that Violet translated to mean 'spoiled daughter of a pig'. Violet smiled sweetly at the chef and murmured back, '*Merci beaucoup, Monsieur.*'

He flushed, forgetting that both Violet and Imogen spoke quite passable French, and Violet had just said, 'Thank you very much, sir.'

Annie and Mrs Darling began wrapping the food in

tea towels and packing it into the basket. 'Perfect,' said Violet. 'Would you mind putting that in the car for me, please? I'll just dash upstairs and fetch my handbag, hat and gloves.'

When Violet hurtled back downstairs, Nikolai was waiting with the back door of the car open. Sally sat in the front with the huge basket on her lap.

'Could you drive us to Sally's house as quickly as you can, please Nikolai?' asked Violet. 'We don't have much time.'

Nikolai saluted. 'It would be my pleasure, Miss Violet.'

'I just have to grab one more thing,' Violet said.

Inside the garage on a back shelf was a box of old sporting equipment that had belonged to Archie and Lawrence. Violet rummaged around and pulled out a cricket bat and a leather ball. She hesitated for a moment, the bat heavy in her hand as memories crowded in of backyard games with her brothers. She pushed the memories away and hurried to join the others.

Nikolai was as good as his word, driving quickly but safely through the crowded streets of Richmond. Once again he parked outside the little row of terraces where the gang of children were playing football, using a ball made from crumpled newspapers tied with twine. This time they were boisterous and welcoming when they saw the bright yellow car.

'The food is for your family, of course, Sally,' said Violet. 'It's not much, but it's something.' She fumbled around in her handbag and pulled out a small paper bag. 'I didn't know if you'd have any medicine for your mother, so I brought some things from our medicine chest — aspirin, cough wafers and Mrs Darling's chest rub. I hope they help.'

Sally's eyes welled with tears, and she tried to blink them away as she took the package. 'You're too kind, miss.'

'Not at all. I only wish I could do more,' said Violet. 'Now hurry — we need to head back in about ten or fifteen minutes.'

Nikolai helped Sally with the heavy basket as she climbed out of the car.

'Would you like to come inside, miss?' Sally asked. 'You could look at Ma and see what you think is wrong. She made me promise not to get a doctor, because we can't afford it, but she doesn't seem to be getting any better.'

Violet hesitated. She knew nothing about illness, and for all she knew it might be highly contagious. The newspapers were always full of stories of the dreadful diseases that festered in the slums. She saw the hope in Sally's face.

'Of course I will.' Violet turned to the children crowding around the car. 'But first I have a little present for you all to share.' She handed the cricket bat to Ruthie, the girl with the withered leg, and the leather ball to Paddy. 'Have fun.'

The children squealed with joy as they all squabbled to touch the new treasures. Violet took a brown paper bag of fruit from the basket over Sally's arm and passed it to Nikolai to distribute to the children.

'It's a very simple house, miss,' Sally explained as she led the way onto the porch. 'It's a little crowded when everyone is home.'

Maisie answered the knock at the door. Violet followed Sally down a narrow hallway, with paint peeling from the ceiling and walls. There were two tiny, dark bedrooms at the front of the house, which were crowded with beds and belongings. The third room was a kitchen overlooking a small, dusty yard.

In the corner, a gaunt, grey-haired man was sitting on a chair, staring at the floor and absently stroking a tabby cat on his lap. He looked up, rather confused, as they came into the room. Violet suddenly realised that one shirtsleeve was empty — he was missing his right arm.

Sally leaned over and kissed him on top of his head. 'Can I make you a cup of tea, Da? Have you had anythin' to eat?'

'Sal, my girl,' he said in a hoarse voice, as though he rarely spoke. 'What're you doin' here? Is it Sunday already?'

Sally heaved the basket onto the kitchen table. 'No. It's Thursday. I'm just here to check on Ma, and Miss Hamilton has brought us all some food from Riversleigh.'

Violet shook his limp, listless left hand. 'Glad to meet you, Mr Burke.'

Sally took a triangle of sandwich from one of the cloth packages and gave it to her father, who nibbled at the crust.

The atmosphere of sickness and squalor saddened Violet. Sally had often chatted to her about her family and the cheery meals they had whenever she went home on her afternoons off, and Violet had imagined an idyllic, cosy cottage with roses around the door. The reality was much bleaker.

On the wood stove was a large, black kettle that Sally took outside to fill with water from the tap near the outdoor washhouse. Sally stoked the fire with kindling from a bucket and put the kettle on to boil.

'Ma's in the second room,' said Sally. 'I'll just check on her an' straighten up a little.'

'Why don't I make the tea?' Violet suggested. She had never made tea at home, but how difficult could it be?

Sally smiled back at her, as though at a helpless child. 'No, that's all right, miss. It might be best if I might make the tea. I know how Ma likes it.'

Violet looked out the back door at the courtyard with its washhouse, single tap and rope washing line laden with drying clothes. A stack of firewood was piled against the sagging fence. A makeshift table held iron buckets and a bar of soap for washing. Another tabby cat ran across the paving and jumped up onto the roof of the lean-to next door.

Sally came back to the kitchen after a few minutes to make the tea in a big enamel teapot. She poured an earthenware mug for her father, and his one hand trembled so violently as he held it that the hot liquid slopped over the sides.

'Leave it till it cools down a little, Pa, or you'll burn yourself,' Sally suggested, calmly wiping up the mess.

Violet declined the offer of a mug of tea, following Sally back into the bedroom. Mrs Burke was sitting up in a dishevelled bed, the sheets tangled around her. Under her grey nightie she was very thin, and when she coughed her whole body was wracked with spasms.

'I'm fine, Sally, don't fuss,' Mrs Burke said, her voice raspy and breathless. 'It's lovely to see you, but I'll be better after a couple more days in bed.'

Sally handed her mother the mug of tea. 'Well, I'd feel better if you ate somethin'. Miss Hamilton brought you a basket of good food to help you get better.'

Mrs Burke shook her head weakly. 'Maybe later. I'm not hungry now, but I'll take a sip of this tea.'

Violet wanted to help, but she felt rather useless as Sally straightened the sheets and tucked them in. She was not used to doing any domestic chores. Finally, Violet hung back near the door, out of the way.

'I'm sorry, Sally,' Violet said, checking her wristwatch, 'but we can't stay any longer. Mrs Darling will be furious if I don't get you back in time to help with the dinner.'

Mrs Burke nodded at the girls. 'You go, Sal. We can't have you losin' your job right now.'

Sally hugged her mother. 'Everythin'll be all right, Ma. We'll muddle through.'

9

The Scrapbook

Hawthorn, modern day

Marli chained up her bicycle to the pole outside the gates of Riversleigh and peered through the bars. The house seemed more beautiful to her now that she had seen the photographs of what it looked like in its heyday. Marli was determined to explore the estate more thoroughly. Perhaps she could even find a way into the house.

Violet's scrapbook was stowed safely inside her backpack, along with her dad's digital camera and its long zoom lens, which she'd borrowed to take photographs of the house and garden. Hearing Didi talk about her great-grandmother's love of photography had reminded Marli how much she loved taking photos. Marli pulled the camera out and took a photograph of the wrought-iron gate with the Keep Out sign.

There was no-one around, so she crept into Luca's

front garden, scrambled up the tree and onto the wall. She felt a buzz of exhilaration as she dropped over to the other side.

She waded through the thigh-high grass, photographing the summerhouse almost swallowed by the wisteria vine and the rose garden with its snub-nosed cherub statue. She tried to take a photograph of the fairy wren chasing insects through the waving grass, but he was far too quick and the photo was just a blue-and-brown blur.

While grass and weeds had overtaken many of the formal beds, there were still some flowers that bloomed regardless — a ragged hedge of pink hydrangeas, a bank of blue agapanthus and a drift of white freesias under a spreading oak tree. It was so different to her tropical garden in Brisbane, which was filled with frangipanis, hibiscus, palms, birds-of-paradise and an ancient mango tree.

A familiar hacking cough sounded behind her. It was Luca, once more wearing his uniform — black jeans, grey T-shirt, white earphones — and walking around the side of the terrace.

'Hi,' he said. 'Hope you don't mind, but I saw you from my bedroom window and thought I'd come over.'

Marli wasn't sure if she was annoyed at the interruption or happy to have someone to talk to. 'Sure,' she replied. 'I'm just poking around.'

Luca came closer. 'I talked to Nonno about the gardens. He said this area here, to the north, used to be the croquet lawn.'

Marli looked around. She tried to imagine it as a smooth rectangle of manicured lawn, but it was impossible.

'There used to be a boathouse down near the river,' Luca continued, 'but it was swept away in the big floods of 1934.'

'What a shame,' Marli said.

Luca gestured to the left. 'Our block used to be the horse paddocks, then our apartments were built in 1923. There's still a door that leads from the old carriage house into our garden, but it's locked now.'

'It must have been gorgeous, surrounded by paddocks,' said Marli. 'I have some photos here of the house and the garden as it was. Would you like to see them?'

Luca's face lit up. 'Sure. That'd be great.'

Marli thought it was the first time he had looked friendly. 'Why don't we go and sit on the steps?'

They wandered back towards the house. Luca stooped and pulled a few clumps of grass from between the freesias. He began to cough severely and had to lean over until the spasm passed.

'Are you all right?' asked Marli, feeling concerned.

Luca didn't answer for a moment, his face red with the effort of breathing. 'Sorry,' he replied in a raspy voice. 'I have whooping cough.'

'That sounds nasty,' Marli said, inadvertently stepping back. Didi's younger sister had died of whooping cough as a baby.

'I'm not contagious anymore, but the cough goes on for ages. It's exhausting. The Chinese call it "the hundred-day cough". So the doctor said I had to stay home for the rest of term to build up my strength.'

Marli felt a wave of sympathy for the thin, pale boy. 'So you're missing school too,' she replied. 'I'm down here to spend "quality time" with my father while Mum's away overseas. But Dad's at work all the time, so I hardly see him.' She explained about her mum's trip to Cambridge and missing all her friends.

'I know what you mean,' he replied. 'My sisters and all my friends are at school every day. Now that Mum's gone back to work, I've just been hanging around, visiting my grandparents and watching TV. It sounds like fun, but it's dead boring after a while.'

'Tell me about it,' said Marli, rolling her eyes.

The two sat on the stone steps in the sun. Marli carefully took out the old scrapbook from her backpack.

'It's Violet's scrapbook from 1922,' Marli explained. 'My grandfather gave it to me.'

The two pored over the pictures of the house and garden, and the servants lined up on the driveway.

'I wonder if one of them might be my great-grandfather?' Luca said, examining the photo. 'Perhaps Nonno could tell us?'

'We can ask him,' Marli said. She turned the page. 'There're some incredible shots of barefoot children in the slums here.'

'It must have been a very hard life to be poor in those days,' Luca added.

'A huge contrast to life at Riversleigh.' Marli hesitated, then looked behind her at the boarded-up doors of the house. 'I was thinking, it would be pretty awesome if we could get inside and explore.'

Luca looked uncertain. 'You mean break in somehow?'

'It's not trespassing,' Marli assured him. 'Didi will get the key in a couple of weeks, but I can't bear to wait that long. We might be lucky; there could be a window or something open. Shall we take a look?'

Luca laughed. 'I've lived next door to this house all my life, and I've always been curious about it. I'd love to see inside.'

The two circled the house to see if any of the doors or windows might open, but all were securely boarded up. On the southern side of the house was a bluestone cobbled courtyard, a collection of outhouses and a large, two-storey garage with a set of stairs on the outside.

'The old carriage house and stables,' said Marli.

'I think the door that leads to our garden is in there,' said Luca. 'The door's locked, but perhaps we can open it from this side.'

The carriage house had an old-fashioned arched doorway with blue timber double doors, one of which was hanging lopsided from its hinges. Luca dragged it open.

Light flooded inside, revealing rusty tools, an old mower, paint cans, a pile of musty furniture and a jumble of milk crates. Right at the very back was another set of double doors with peeling blue paint, which were locked with a wooden crossbar.

Luca pulled away some of the junk to make a path through to the back wall. Marli dragged back the crossbar and the door creaked open, revealing a glimpse into Luca's garden.

'We can get in and out now without breaking our necks,' Marli joked.

Luca rummaged through the carriage house, setting aside two wooden chairs and an old chest. 'I wonder if this stuff belonged to your family, or if it was just hospital junk?'

'It all looks really old,' Marli said. 'And look, there's an old gramophone. I bet that didn't belong to the hospital.'

The brass horn of the gramophone was tarnished and blackened with age. Marli rubbed at the dust.

'I wonder if there're any old records in here?' Luca said. 'This place is like a time capsule.'

Marli picked up a cracked china doll with one arm. 'Maybe this belonged to my great-grandmother.'

Luca reached for a rusty rake with a snapped handle and brandished it in the air. 'Perhaps this was used by my great-grandfather.'

Marli laughed and put the doll aside. 'I wonder what happened here. Do you think the Hamiltons were really cursed? It all sounds so mysterious.'

'Perhaps we should try and find out,' Luca suggested, sitting backwards on one of the chairs. 'We could search the internet to find out some of the history. There must be newspaper articles or records that will tell us something.'

'That would be brilliant,' Marli agreed. 'Would you really help me?'

'Try and stop me,' Luca said, his eyes alight with enthusiasm. 'It'll be an adventure.'

10

The Dinner Party

Riversleigh, 17 November 1922

At seven o'clock the dressing gong sounded from the hall to remind the family to prepare for dinner. Violet bathed and dressed in an ivory silk teddy, white silk stockings and white Mary Jane shoes, with a kimono dressing gown over the top in shimmering peacock colours of turquoise, emerald and amethyst. She sat at the dressing table, thinking about all she had seen in her visits to Richmond over the last two days.

It seemed such a contrast to be sitting here, in her exquisite bedroom, surrounded by luxury, while children just a mile away were living in abject poverty. She mentally shook herself — now was not the time to think about that. She had to be on her best, sparkling behaviour for Dad and his business associates. With her mother gone, it was Imogen's role to be the charming hostess for their dinner guests, and it was Violet's job to help her.

Violet pulled the lever for the servants' bell, signalling Sally to come up and help her finish dressing. She sprayed on some perfume and began to lightly powder her face. Imogen had lent her some make-up to wear but warned her to be very subtle or 'Daddy will have a fit'. Lastly, she blackened her eyelashes with a smudge of mascara and added a slick of crimson lip colour.

Sally huffed in, wearing her black evening uniform with starched white collar, cuffs, cross-over apron and ruffled cap. 'Pardon, miss. Mrs Darling wouldn't let me come until she'd checked the table settings an' all the flowers. Lucky Joseph did such a good job with the roses.'

Sally began brushing Violet's long, wavy hair with a silver hairbrush.

'That's fine,' Violet replied. 'I hope Mrs Darling wasn't too cross about me stealing you away.'

Sally chatted on as she worked, twisting Violet's copper-red hair up into an elaborate chignon at the base of her neck. Then Violet stood and Sally slipped the evening dress over her head and carefully did up the buttons at the back. Violet had borrowed the dress from Imogen, as she had nothing suitable of her own to wear. Imogen had bought a wardrobe of stylish new clothes for her first social season after finishing school.

The ankle-length dress was filmy turquoise silk with crushed velvet detailing at the waist and hem. She wore no jewellery, but simply pinned a creamy gardenia flower above her right ear.

'You look a treat, miss,' Sally said as she pinned the last stray curl into place.

'Thank you, Sally,' Violet replied. 'You've achieved wonders.'

'S'all right, miss,' Sally said, then paused. 'I want to say thanks to *you* for helpin' me today. Some of my friends in service, their mistresses treat 'em like dirt. But not you — you've a good heart.'

Violet felt her heart sing. It felt good helping Sally and her family. Although it had been confronting, Violet had enjoyed her trips to Richmond more than anything she could remember in a long while.

Imogen popped her head around the door as she passed. 'Come on, Violet. Time to go down.'

Imogen and Violet walked down the stairs. Their father, Albert, was already waiting in the drawing room, wearing his black tailcoat, winged shirt and white bow tie. He glanced up as the girls walked in together, a look of surprise sweeping over his face.

'My dears,' he said, his voice catching. 'You look . . . you both look so beautiful, so grown-up.'

Imogen inclined her head, pulled her rose-pink skirt out and curtseyed, as though being presented to royalty. 'Thank you, Daddy. I had to lend Violet a dress, as she has nothing suitable to wear. Doesn't she look adorable?'

'Yes, she does,' said Mr Hamilton, looking at Violet tenderly. 'I have never seen her look prettier.'

Violet felt warmed by the unusual praise. She couldn't help taking a quick glance at herself in the gilt-framed mirror above the marble fireplace. The reflection reassured her that she did look very grown-up and stylish.

'Now that Violet is on holidays, I do think she needs some new clothes,' Imogen continued as she took a seat on the linen sofa. 'We can't have her looking like a raga-muffin, can we?'

'I never look like a ragamuffin,' Violet objected, perching on the edge of the rose chaise longue. 'It's just that I seem to have grown taller.'

Imogen raised her eyebrows and laughed. 'We don't want the neighbours thinking that Daddy and I don't take care of you.'

Deep down Violet knew that her father loved her, but ever since her brothers and mother had died, he had been different — distant and distracted, even cold. He had buried himself in work and golf, and seemed so ravaged by his grief that he hardly noticed what the girls were doing, let alone what they wore.

At Imogen's comment he looked taken aback. 'Definitely not. Of course Violet must get some new clothes. Just order a few things and have the invoices sent to me. But please try not to go completely overboard — I don't want to be sent into *total* bankruptcy.'

'Thank you, Dad,' said Violet, touched. 'That would be terrific.'

Violet glanced around the drawing room. It was one of her favourite rooms in the house, with its bay window overlooking the fountain, soft ivory walls, large Chinese rug, crystal chandeliers and furnishings in muted shades of rose silk and blue velvet. Pastel paintings of flowers and Italian landscapes in gilt frames adorned the walls. Her mother had collected many treasures during the family's trips to Europe before the war.

The grandfather clock in the hall marked the hour with eight resounding clangs.

The servants had all taken up their positions. Joseph had unlocked the double gates, ready for their guests' arrival. Nikolai was stationed at the bottom of the front steps to open the car doors for each guest. The front door was open, with the butler and the footman in their white ties and tail-coats standing by in the hall to collect the coats, top hats and canes, while the maids were in the kitchen preparing to serve the meal at precisely twenty minutes past eight.

Violet heard the crunch of the gravel driveway and the purr of a motor.

The butler, Saunders, soon showed the guests in, announcing each one as they entered. 'Mr and Mrs Ramsay. Mr Theodore Ramsay.'

There was a commotion of greetings as Theodore and his parents were served drinks and seated in the drawing room. Next to arrive was one of her father's business friends and golf partners, Mr Marchant, with his wife, who was wearing an ostentatious headdress featuring glittering diamonds and ostrich feathers.

Finally, Saunders announced Miss Audrey Williams and Mr Thomas O'Byrne, whom Imogen had invited to provide some younger company for Theodore. Audrey, as always, looked elegant in a heavily beaded and embroidered black dress. Violet thought that Tommy looked especially handsome in his white tie and tails. He shook hands with her and asked if she was enjoying her holidays.

As hostess, Imogen chatted dutifully to the older ladies and gentlemen until Saunders stood in the doorway and announced, 'Dinner is served, Miss Hamilton.' Everyone finished their drinks and followed him next door into the dining room.

Crystal and silver sparkled in the light of dozens of candles, while the air was scented from the bowls of pale-pink roses scattered around the room. The long table was set with a white damask cloth and starched napkins, cobalt-and-gold-rimmed fine bone china and five crystal glasses at every place. Silver cruets, cutlery and candelabra, polished to perfection, were precisely spaced.

Saunders and Harry pulled out chairs and helped seat the ladies, while Mr Hamilton took his place at the head. At one end of the table, the talk was all about business and investments, while at the other end, the young people talked about tennis and dances and summer excursions to the beach.

'You must come down to our house at Sorrento in January,' Audrey insisted. 'I'm planning on inviting a crowd of us for a few days. We'll have a heavenly time.'

'We'd love to, wouldn't we, Violet?' Imogen replied.

'Absolutely,' Violet said, tucking her gloves away on her lap. But she was distracted by Theodore's father's talk of property development and construction times.

'Do you mean to say that you plan to build flats there?' asked Mr Hamilton. 'I thought you were planning a large house, one in keeping with the area.'

'No, flats are a much better investment,' Mr Ramsay said. 'We have to move with the times. No-one wants to build big houses like this anymore. They're too expensive and you need an army of servants to run them. And as we all know, it's impossible to find decent servants since the war.'

Saunders and Harry remained impassive as they continued to pass the platters of oysters and fill the glasses with ice-cold champagne.

As Mr Ramsay talked, Violet realised with a sinking heart that he was talking about building several blocks of flats right next door on the horse paddock. The horse paddock was the last remaining part of the Riversleigh estate, outside the gardens. Last year, her father had gradually sold off the orchard and most of the surrounding paddocks, and several large homes had already been built on them.

At the time he had muttered something about a post-war slump and the collapse of import prices, which had made little sense to Violet and Imogen. It wasn't until he'd sold the horses that Violet had really been upset. Now it seemed that the latest sale of Riversleigh land had been to the Ramsay family, and that their new neighbours would be flat-dwellers.

Mr Hamilton looked shocked and struggled to regain his composure.

Theodore turned towards him. 'You needn't worry, sir. They'll be priced so that only the better sort of families will be able to afford them — you won't have any uncouth, working-class neighbours.'

Saunders and Harry cleared the oyster plates and served the soup course — a clear, golden-brown consommé.

Mrs Marchant changed the subject to one of her favourites: the degeneracy of today's youth. 'Have you seen Bessie Douglas lately?' she asked, directing her comment at the whole table. Her feather headdress jiggled with outrage. 'The girl has bobbed her hair as short as a boy's and has announced to her parents that she is getting a job!'

Imogen caught Violet's glance and raised her eyes.

'*No*,' Audrey murmured, pushing a strand of her own short bob back into place. 'How dreadful.'

Violet, Imogen and Tommy grinned at Audrey over their soup spoons.

'What on earth is she going to do?' asked Mrs Ramsay, her voice thick with horror. 'Don't tell me she is going to become one of those typists.'

Mrs Marchant shook her head. 'Worse than that . . . She is going to get an apprenticeship at Alice Anderson's garage and learn to drive a car. She's going to be a *chauffeur* and a *mechanic*!'

'Apparently Miss Anderson is teaching lots of the local ladies how to drive,' said Violet.

Mr Ramsay chortled. 'Remind me not to go driving near Miss Anderson's garage! Women generally don't make very good drivers. They get too easily distracted.'

Theodore laughed. 'I've heard they have the prettiest chauffeurs at Alice Anderson's. They're all the rage in Kew.'

'Yes, but they wear *breeches*,' his mother objected. 'Now, you wouldn't let your daughters do anything so vulgar, would you, Albert?'

Mr Hamilton shook his head. 'Under no circumstances would my daughters do any such thing. It was different during the war, when everyone had to do their bit. For example, Imogen tells me Miss Williams was an ambulance driver in France. I'm sure she did an excellent job, but now she's home and settled down.'

Audrey looked around the table. 'Driving in France during the war was one of the hardest things I've ever done, and I saw some terrible sights. But coming home again to the life of a leisured lady, I think perhaps it is even harder to sit around doing nothing. Well, nothing truly *meaningful*. I much prefer to be busy, and I don't want to live my life feeling like I've wasted it.'

Mrs Ramsay looked shocked. 'But Miss Williams, Theodore told me that you girls are working hard on organising a little charity ball to raise money for some worthy cause or another. Surely that's doing something meaningful.'

Audrey arched her eyebrows. 'Just a *little* ball. But we hope it will save lives.'

'It's for the Russian War Relief Fund,' Imogen added quickly. 'We're hoping to raise two hundred pounds for the starving Russian children. Violet has come up with some wonderful ideas for decorations.'

Mrs Marchant nodded her head in approval. 'A very suitable project for young ladies, something to do until you get married.'

Theodore glanced proprietorially at Imogen. 'Indeed. You'll be busy soon enough with a husband and household to look after.' Tommy bristled beside Violet.

Saunders and Harry cleared the soup bowls then walked around the table offering guests portions of poached white fish fillet with lemon-and-parsley sauce, served with a finely sliced cucumber salad.

'I'd like to do something for the children who live in poverty just a mile away from here, across the river,' Violet said, thinking of the barefoot slum children with their stunted growth and hungry eyes.

'We see some very sad cases at the hospital,' Tommy added. 'Children with terrible diseases, like poliomyelitis, diphtheria and typhoid, which spread like wildfire in the slums, especially when you have four or five children sleeping in one bed. Yet they could be so easily prevented with clean water, nourishing food and decent housing. It's a disgrace that poverty like this exists in Melbourne in the twentieth century.'

Mr Marchant shook his head as he helped himself to a large serving of fish and sauce. 'Charity just encourages the workingman to stick out his hand to get something for nothing. We don't want to crush the spirit of independence in the workers — they'll just sit around doing nothing, expecting to be fed.'

'By Jove, I agree,' Mr Ramsay boomed. 'Like the workers at my tannery who are constantly wanting more pay and fewer hours. Yet to make the tannery more profitable, we need to reduce wages and increase production. You must have the same at yours, Hamilton. The workers are like recalcitrant children who need a firm hand.'

'We've not had a strike at Hamilton's for many years,' Mr Hamilton replied, frowning. 'Our workers are happy and fairly paid, and I think if the staff are content with their working conditions, they don't cause problems.'

Theodore leaned forward to join in the conversation. 'We had some of those Bolshevik types sniffing around the tannery earlier this year, trying to cause trouble. The police said there was a Russian spy here in Melbourne, posing as a Norwegian, who'd been sent to Australia with the express purpose of fostering a communist revolution. He was discovered, of course, and deported a few weeks ago, but not before he'd spoken at a number of workers' meetings.'

'The police think there is a ring of Bolshevik spies here in Melbourne, continuing with his work of inciting workers to strike and overthrow their bosses,' Mr Ramsay said. 'I tell you, I'll bring down the full force of the law if they try causing trouble at Ramsay's again.'

Mr Hamilton glanced down the table, taking a sip of his white wine. 'Yes, I read about the trial of the Russian Bolshevik, but let's not bore the ladies by talking about business and politics. We can save that for after dinner, when the ladies retire.'

Violet put down her silver fish knife and fork. Her temper had risen during the conversation. The poor families she had met in the slums didn't look like they were revolutionaries trying to cause trouble. They looked like they were sick and hungry.

'Our maid Sally's mother is very ill, and they can't afford a doctor,' Violet said, her voice high with emotion. 'Mrs Burke usually works as a cleaning lady. She takes in washing as well as running the house, so she's exhausted. They have five children, aged eight to fifteen, and the three eldest are working in jobs that pay just a few shillings a week. They hardly have enough to eat, and Sally is worried they'll be evicted if they can't pay the rent.'

'They will be fine, Violet,' said her father soothingly. He shot her a glance that meant young ladies should be seen and not heard at adult dinner parties.

Mrs Marchant sniffed disapprovingly. 'She's probably Catholic. Catholic families always have far too many children. They bring it on themselves.'

Mr Ramsay looked at Violet patronisingly. 'Maid-servants are very good at spinning sob stories for their mistresses to get out of work. I'm sure a little investigation would show that their situation is not so dire.'

'I've been to the slums in Richmond,' Violet insisted, her voice rising. 'I've seen the poverty myself.'

Mr Hamilton now glared openly at Violet. 'I should certainly hope that you have not been to the slums. That is no place for a respectable young lady. There are all sorts of criminals and thugs there. It is simply not safe.'

'Especially with that dreadful gangster Squizzy Taylor on the loose again!' Mrs Marchant exclaimed dramatically. 'I can't believe he's out on bail. Didn't he grow up in Richmond? Certainly no decent girl would be seen there.'

'Do you understand me, Violet?' her father demanded. 'I expressly forbid you from visiting the slums.'

Violet lowered her eyes to the napkin in her lap and took a sip of her water. She felt like bursting into tears.

Imogen signalled Saunders to clear the fish course and begin serving the main course of roast chicken with creamy mushroom sauce, buttered French beans and sautéed potato.

The elder end of the table changed the subject to a shot-by-shot description of the latest competition game at the golf club. Theodore took the chance to tell Imogen and Audrey about his own recent golf game.

Tommy leaned over and spoke quietly to Violet. 'Would you like me to go and examine your maid's mother to see how she is?'

'Oh, yes, please, Tommy,' Violet replied, her eyes sparkling. 'Could you?'

'I'm not a qualified doctor yet,' Tommy reminded her,

'but I'm in my third year, and I've been working as an assistant at Alfred Hospital.'

'That would be wonderful, Tommy. I'd be so grateful.'

'We'll talk later and arrange for me to visit her first thing in the morning.'

Audrey smiled at Violet over the roses. 'Have courage, Violet. Don't let the old fogeys get you down.'

Theodore turned to Violet. 'Things will never change. There will always be poverty amongst the great unwashed, and there will always be a few whose good fortune is to be very, very wealthy. Thank goodness we're amongst the lucky ones.' Theodore shot a triumphant look at Imogen.

Violet twisted and scrunched the napkin in her lap. 'No, I disagree — it's not right that so many should have so little.'

Theodore patted her on the arm. 'Look at the revolution in Russia. The Bolsheviks rose up and slaughtered the aristocracy, seizing their land and wealth, and now the Bolshevik leaders are living like kings while the poor old peasants are starving to death. One could argue that the peasants were far better off under the autocratic rule of the Tsar.'

Audrey rolled her eyes.

'Social change is never easy, especially when it is achieved through violence,' Tommy said. 'But surely it is our duty to improve the situation of the poor, through health care, education and legal reform if necessary.'

Theodore put his knife and fork down and leaned back in his chair. 'Pretty words . . . but unrealistic. Most working men are like sheep and need firm guidance from their betters.'

Violet swallowed another sip of her water. 'I think Tommy's right — we *must* do something to make society change.'

Mrs Ramsay gave Violet a disapproving glare.

Theodore laughed and turned to Imogen. 'Your sister is quite the fierce little warrior. Are all the women in your family so revolutionary?'

Imogen smiled fondly at Violet. 'I'm sure we come from a long line of Celtic warriors, stretching all the way back to Queen Boadicea.'

The servants cleared the main course and served home-grown garden salad dressed with vinaigrette.

'Here's to Queen Boadicea,' said Audrey, lifting her wine glass. 'Long may she battle the forces of injustice.'

Mrs Ramsay exchanged a horrified glance with Mrs Marchant. Mr Hamilton quickly changed the subject to progress in the international cricket match.

The sixth and final course was pudding — vanilla ice-cream served with raspberries and strawberries from the kitchen garden. Once everyone had finally finished, Imogen caught Violet's eye and rose gracefully to her feet.

'Ladies, shall we retire to the drawing room and leave the gentlemen to their coffee and cigars?' Imogen suggested.

Violet wondered what serious business the gentlemen would discuss over their cigars, while the ladies and their delicate sensibilities were safely removed. It annoyed her that as a female her thoughts and opinions were so easily dismissed.

It was nearly midnight by the time all the guests had left, and Violet rang the bell for Sally to come and help her undress. Sally looked sleepy as she hung the evening dress on a hanger, unbound Violet's hair and laid out her nightdress.

'Don't worry, Sally,' Violet said. 'I have a plan for tomorrow. Everything will be all right.'

Sally didn't look convinced, but she nodded her head dutifully. 'That's good, miss.'

But Violet lay awake for many hours feeling jittery and sick. Her anger bubbled up — anger at the smug complacency of people like her father's business associates and their wives. Anger that she felt so helpless. Anger that there seemed to be so many things wrong with the world and no way to fix them. Violet tossed and turned all night, thinking of ideas then rejecting them, thinking of more ideas, each one more outlandish than the one before.

It was very late when she finally fell into a feverish sleep.

11

The Secret Plan

The next morning, Violet implemented the best plan that had come to her in the early hours of the morning. She saw no option but to return to the slums that her father had forbidden her from visiting.

After breakfast, Nikolai drove Mr Hamilton to work at the factory as usual. Imogen was sleeping in after the late night. As soon as her father had left, Violet telephoned Tommy to arrange a meeting point, then visited Mrs Darling in the kitchen and Joseph, the gardener, to beg for more food to take to Sally's family. By the time Nikolai returned, Violet and Sally were ready to go with a basket of supplies.

Leaving Riversleigh, Nikolai drove them back across the Yarra River and into Richmond. Violet examined the now familiar streets, framing up potential photographs as they passed the many colourful sights. A rabbit vendor, pushing a small handcart, held up a fistful of fluffy carcasses, calling out 'Rabbitoh! Rabbitoh! Buy your fresh rabbits.' A cheeky newsboy, with his flat cap and leather satchel, darted into the traffic selling newspapers. A tram rattled past, laden with passengers hanging out the doorways. A young girl of about ten pushed a wicker pram with three smaller siblings crammed inside. Violet promised herself that she would come back later to take the real photographs.

They passed a number of small shops and businesses, and lots of large advertising posters for films, products and remedies. One sign caught her eye — an old-fashioned black-and-white sketch of a woman with a pompadour hairstyle.

They pulled up at a tram stop in Victoria Street, near Sally's house. Tommy was waiting there, carrying a black leather medical bag. The locals stared at the buttercup yellow Daimler, with its uniformed chauffeur and well-dressed occupants. It obviously belonged to a wealthy family from across the river.

'Thank you so much for coming, Tommy,' Violet said as he climbed in the back seat beside her. 'This is Sally; it's her mother who's sick. And this is Nikolai, our chauffeur who is helping us. Sally and Nikolai, this is Mr O'Byrne.'

Tommy greeted everyone then looked at her sternly. 'Well, Violet. What are you doing here? I thought your father forbade you from coming to Richmond.'

Violet glanced at him guiltily. 'Please don't tell him, Tommy. I just want to help, and I'm perfectly safe with you and Nikolai.'

Tommy smiled reassuringly. 'I can keep a secret. Especially when it's for a good cause.'

At Sally's house, Violet and Nikolai waited outside while Sally took Tommy in to examine her mother. Once again, the gang of children were playing in the street. Helen, who should have been at school, had Bubby on one hip while the others were fiddling around a homemade billycart, which was missing a wheel. Paddy kicked the cobblestones in frustration.

'Would you mind if I take a look at the cart while we're waiting, Miss Violet?' asked Nikolai. 'I might be able to fix it for them.'

'No, of course not, Nikolai,' Violet replied. 'At least you can do something for the poor little mites.'

Nikolai wandered over to check the billycart. In a moment he had his coat and hat off, and was crouched down, fixing the wheel with a spanner he kept in the toolkit. Violet pulled out her camera and took a photograph of the scene. By the time Tommy returned, the billycart was repaired and the children were taking turns pulling each other along, screeching with delight.

'What's wrong with her, Tommy?' Violet asked, packing her camera away. 'Will Mrs Burke be all right?'

Tommy put his medical bag on the back seat of the car. 'I'd like to take her into hospital for a second opinion, but I think she has tuberculosis. She's coughing up blood and she's very weak.'

Violet's stomach clenched with worry. 'That's terrible news. What should we do?'

'I want to call for an ambulance to take her to Alfred Hospital, but there's no telephone here, and Sally says none of the neighbours have one either. So perhaps we should set off in search of a telephone?'

'Why don't we drive her ourselves?' Violet suggested. 'By the time we find somewhere to call and wait for the ambulance, it will take ages. It's not that far to the hospital.'

Tommy frowned as he thought. 'Good idea, but we do need to be careful of infection. Tuberculosis is highly contagious. When the patient coughs, they exhale the tuberculosis bacteria, which are then inhaled by anyone nearby. So it would be best if we all cover our mouths and noses with cloths or handkerchiefs, and wash our hands thoroughly after handling Mrs Burke.'

'Will she have to stay in hospital?' Violet asked.

Tommy nodded. 'If I'm right, I don't think Mrs Burke will be coming home for many, many months. But we won't tell Sally or her mother yet, just in case I'm wrong.'

Tommy organised all the necessary health precautions. Nikolai helped him carry Mrs Burke and settled her comfortably in the back of the car, with Sally and Tommy beside her. Violet sat in the front beside Nikolai.

They pulled up at the hospital and Tommy arranged for some orderlies to carry Mrs Burke inside. Sally followed along beside her mother, looking strained and pale.

Tommy leaned in through the open car window. 'We'll take good care of her. There's no point us all waiting around, so why don't I telephone you at home, Violet, when we have a definite diagnosis?'

'Tommy, I don't know what we would have done without you,' Violet said.

'I suspect you would have thought of something pretty quickly,' Tommy teased, 'but I am very glad I could help.'

As Nikolai drove off, Violet realised that she enjoyed the feeling of riding in the front — it seemed far more exhilarating. Nikolai drove back the way they had come, past the same rows of shops, chaotic traffic and colourful sights. One sign in particular caught Violet's eye for the second time that day:

Miss Annette Lester. Hairdresser and Wigmaker.
Toupets, Transformations and Wigs.
Lovely Switchings (best hair only).
Hair Dying – All Colours a Specialty.

Underneath was a smaller sign that read, 'Good money paid for quality hair.'

'Nikolai, could you pull over, please?' Violet asked. 'There's something I need to do.'

Nikolai obediently parked the car in a narrow space between a horse-drawn dray and a vegetable cart.

'Are you sure?' Nikolai asked. 'Wouldn't you rather I took you back to Hawthorn to shop?'

Violet swallowed nervously. 'No, I shouldn't be too long. Would you mind waiting for me?'

The hairdresser's shop was small, with a long mirror on one wall. A narrow counter with an arrangement of glass bottles and a stack of magazines ran below it. Three reclining chairs were positioned at equal intervals in front of the mirror; pendant lights dangled from the ceiling. On the opposite wall was a display of wigs, braids, artificial buns and ornate hair pieces.

Violet felt sick with anxiety as she walked in. An imposing-looking woman with impossibly blonde hair piled in a tumble of artful curls stood beside a sink in the centre of the room. The hairdresser cast a glance over

Violet, taking in her clothes, her hat and, of course, her long plaited braid hanging over one shoulder.

'Are you Miss Lester?' asked Violet.

'Yes, can I help you, miss?' the woman asked. 'Here to have your hair styled?'

'No,' Violet said. She swallowed her nerves. 'How much will you pay me for my hair?'

Miss Lester looked momentarily surprised, then a sly look crossed her face. 'You do have beautiful hair, but auburn is not awfully fashionable at the moment.' She pretended to think. 'I shouldn't, but I suppose we could give you a few pennies.'

Violet felt bitter disappointment rise in her throat. She glanced at the wigs on the opposite wall. She remembered seeing catalogues for expensive hair pieces from one of Melbourne's top hairdressers. Surely her hair was worth more than just a few pennies. It occurred to Violet that perhaps Miss Lester was not being entirely honest with her, and she decided to test her theory.

Violet shrugged nonchalantly. 'Never mind. Mr Theiler in Chapel Street offered far more money than that, and he is a rather *exclusive* wigmaker, so I'll go and see him.'

Miss Lester hesitated. 'Let me take a closer look at your hair.'

Violet took off her hat and undid her plait. Miss Lester ran her fingers through it, feeling the weight, length and quality of her hair. 'Now that I've taken a proper look, I can see your hair is of particularly fine quality, so I can match any price Mr Theiler would give you, and I'll style your remaining hair free of charge.'

The two bartered back and forth until Violet was happy

with the pile of shillings and copper pennies she received in exchange for her waist-length, red-gold hair. Violet took her courage in both hands and sat down in one of the black reclining chairs. Her stomach was knotted with nerves as Miss Lester combed the hair thoroughly.

'How long would you like it to be?' asked the hairdresser.

Violet stared at her reflection in the mirror. She looked pale and wan. It wasn't too late to change her mind. With the side of her hand, Violet indicated the length that Audrey had first suggested a few days ago, level with her cheek.

'Just there,' said Violet confidently, as though she meant it.

Miss Lester pulled the hair into a loose ponytail at the nape of Violet's neck with an elastic band, then bound the hair at the end with another. She took the scissors and began to snip above the elastic band, taking the weight of the hair in her other hand.

Violet closed her eyes and held her breath. *Snip. Snip. Snip.* She could feel the metal scissors, cold against the back of her neck. Her head began to throb.

It was done. The long ponytail was laid on the counter, coiled like a copper snake. The scissors continued to snip, shaping the remaining hair into a curly bob with a long fringe sweeping off her face.

Miss Lester stopped and fetched a *Motion Picture* magazine from the counter. She flicked through until she found the photograph she was looking for: a black-and-white portrait of a teenage girl with curly bobbed hair.

'You remind me a little of this American girl called Clara Bow,' said Miss Lester, showing Violet the photograph.

'She won the Fame and Fortune competition last year when she was only sixteen, and is a rising actress in the moving pictures. She has curly red hair like you — an unusual, athletic beauty. Apparently in her latest film, they dressed her up as a boy.'

Violet gazed at the photograph, then at her reflection in the mirror. She could hardly recognise herself. Miss Lester had styled her hair to look like the young American actress. The bob framed her face and made her features seem more delicate, her head lighter. Violet didn't know whether to burst into tears or laugh out loud.

She took one last look at the copper snake on the counter, lifted her chin high and stood up. 'It does look very modern. Thank you.'

Violet picked up her hat and bag and, with her head bare, walked back out to the car where Nikolai was waiting, patiently reading his book. As she approached he jumped up to open the rear door. His tawny eyes widened when he noticed her short hair, but he didn't say anything.

'I might sit in the front again, Nikolai, if that's all right with you,' she said.

'Of course, Miss Violet.' He moved around to open the front passenger door.

'What do you think, Nikolai?' Violet asked in a small voice. 'I've chopped off all my hair.'

Nikolai smiled at her. 'It suits you. You look *très chic.*'

'I sold my hair so I could give the money to Sally,' Violet explained. 'She's going to need all the help she can get with her mother in hospital. I hate to think what Dad will say about it.'

'He'll get used to it,' Nikolai said. 'And he should be proud of you for trying to help a family in trouble.'

Violet wasn't convinced as she played with the hat in her lap. 'Nikolai, have you ever wished that you could change the world?' she asked suddenly. 'Well, perhaps not the whole world — but, I mean, fix things that are unfair, do something to make things better for people?'

Nikolai looked over at Violet, his eyes serious. 'Yes, definitely. It's important to stand up for what you believe in. As the English philosopher Edmund Burke once said, "The only thing necessary for the triumph of evil is that good men do nothing."'

Violet nodded her head thoughtfully. 'When I see life in these streets, people living in such poverty, it just seems so wrong. But the problem seems so big. Far too big for any one person to make a difference.'

'One person can definitely make a difference,' Nikolai said. 'And think about the massive change that might happen if hundreds of people all made little changes together.'

Violet sat in silence, digesting Nikolai's words, before continuing. 'My father's business associate, Mr Ramsay, says that there have always been a few people who are very rich and many people who are very poor — that's the natural order of the world.' Violet paused. 'But I can't actually agree. My grandfather was a poor crofter from Scotland; he was evicted from his home as a child and watched as it burned to the ground. His family had lived there for hundreds of years, but the laird wanted the land for sheep.'

Nikolai turned to her, his eyes filled with compassion. 'That must have been dreadful.'

'Yes. Like so many others, his family migrated to Australia hoping to find gold and a new life. As a teenager, my grandfather Lachlan trudged around the goldfields selling tools and boots and shirts. It was he who started Hamilton's Gloves.' Violet patted the handbag and gloves in her lap. 'My grandfather always said he pulled himself up by his bootstraps, and that he was living proof that with hard work and determination, anyone could make a good life for themselves in Australia.'

Nikolai looked puzzled. 'What does "pull yourself up by your bootstraps" mean?'

Violet laughed. 'It's a funny saying, isn't it? It means to pull yourself to greater heights by the impossible task of dragging yourself up by your shoelaces. To make your fortune through hard work.'

Nikolai chuckled at the image. 'English is definitely a very strange language. But that's what I hope to do in Australia. I'm going to pull myself back up, by my bootstraps.'

'Not back up, just up,' Violet corrected. 'And I'm sure you will, Nikolai. Look how well you're doing already. You're awfully young to be a chauffeur. It's a very responsible position.'

'Thank you, miss,' said Nikolai, looking straight ahead through the windscreen.

'Where did you learn to drive?' Violet asked. 'Was it here in Australia, or in England before you came over?'

Nikolai chuckled and shot Violet a mischievous look. 'It was actually in Russia before the Great War.'

'Before the Great War? That's impossible. You were only a tiny child then!' Violet exclaimed, incredulously.

'I know, but it's true,' Nikolai insisted. 'You see, my cous—, I mean, the son of my father's employer, was given his own small car for his ninth birthday. It was a Peugeot Bébé — a real motor car but made a lot smaller. I was the same age as him, and we often played together, so I learned to drive it too.'

'That's ridiculous! What sort of parents would buy their nine-year-old child a motor car?' Violet huffed.

Nikolai laughed. 'Very wealthy aristocrats who adore their children. Poor Alexei wasn't very well and couldn't do lots of normal, active boy things, so his parents spoiled him. They had a whole fleet of motor cars and several chauffeurs, so the Head Chauffeur taught us both to drive.

'Later on, after the Revolution, when we were in Paris, we stayed in the house of a Russian benefactor, Countess Orlova. When the countess found out I could drive, I became her chauffeur.'

Violet was fascinated. It was the first time Nikolai had opened up with details about his past working for Russian countesses and spoiled princelings.

'I would like to learn to drive a motor car,' Violet said. 'I used to drive the buggy all the time, and I miss it now that the horses are gone.'

'It's easy to drive with a bit of practice,' Nikolai said. 'Perhaps I could give you a lesson one day on a very quiet street.'

'Would you, Nikolai? That would be marvellous.'

'It would be a pleasure. Speaking of driving, would you like me to take you home now?'

She shook her head and laughed. 'I might as well be hung for a sheep as a lamb.'

'Sorry, Miss Violet?' Nikolai asked, looking puzzled.

'I want to go and take some photographs around the streets,' Violet explained, pulling the Kodak Brownie from her new handbag. 'Would you like to come for a walk with me?'

'Absolutely,' Nikolai said. 'It would be good to get some exercise.'

The two walked together, chatting and pointing out interesting things to photograph.

'What about the Chinese market gardener?' Nikolai suggested, indicating a man zigzagging through the crowd with baskets of greens balanced at each end of a long pole over his shoulder.

The market gardener pattered past, wearing traditional Chinese garb — wide blue trousers, heel-less slippers and a long black pigtail hanging below his hat. He stopped, calling out his wares to passers-by. He saw Violet with her camera and stopped to pose, looking very serious. She waved her appreciation and carefully set the shutter speed, framed up the man and clicked the button. She took some of the photographs she had planned earlier — the newsboy selling his newspapers, and an overcrowded tram rattling past, with workers hanging off the back.

The iceman — whose shirt and trousers were soaked with water — pulled up in his horse-drawn cart, yelling, 'Ice. *Ice*. Ice.' His horse stood patiently still by the kerb while he ran into each of the cottages with a huge block of ice wrapped in sacking and balanced on his shoulder. The ice would be put inside the iceboxes to keep food cold.

A crowd of children gathered around the cart, begging and pleading. The iceman teased the kids but then relented, chipping off splinters of ice, which the children sucked with delight. Violet snapped a photograph of the scene, focusing on a boy in the foreground, eyes closed and face beaming as he crunched the unexpected treat.

Suddenly Nikolai noticed the time. 'We'd better get back, miss. I need to get you home so I can pick up Mr Hamilton. He's playing golf this afternoon, and he'll be annoyed if I'm late.'

Violet suddenly felt disappointed — she had been enjoying their laughter and conversation. She packed the camera away in its case.

'Of course,' Violet said. 'I'd hate Dad to be cross with you. He's going to be furious enough when he sees my hair.'

12

In Trouble

Albert Hamilton usually came home in a good mood after playing golf, especially if he'd played well. He arrived just in time to change into his evening clothes for dinner.

Violet had changed into her only good dinner dress — a blue silk, which was getting a little short, with white silk stockings and Mary Janes. She came downstairs and took a seat in the drawing room to wait for dinner. Saunders was standing nearby, ready to serve the pre-dinner drinks. Imogen had already seen Violet's hair, so she made sure she came down early for once, to give her sister moral support.

Violet could hear her father's footsteps on the stairs, right before he strode into the drawing room. She felt a flicker of hope — he seemed to be in a jovial mood.

'Good evening, girls. Did you have a good day?' he asked.

'Delightful,' said Imogen hurriedly. 'How was your golf game?'

Then Mr Hamilton caught a closer look at Violet. For a moment he looked confused, then he looked thunderous.

'Violet, what on earth have you done to your hair?' he demanded, his voice rising. 'Please don't tell me you've cut it.'

'Dad, yes . . . I . . . decided to cut my hair today,' Violet confessed, looking down at the toes of her Mary Janes.

Her father's face flushed. 'What were you thinking?' he shouted. 'How *dare* you cut your hair? No daughter of mine will be seen in public looking like that. It's just not . . . seemly.'

'Daddy, lots of girls cut their hair these days,' Imogen interjected, trying to restore the peace.

'I sold my hair,' Violet explained. 'I gave the money to Sally for her family. Her mother will be in hospital for months with tuberculosis, and I don't know what they are going to do to get by.'

Albert's face crumpled, as though he would break down in tears. 'But why didn't you just ask me for some money? I would have given them something.'

'But I tried last night, Dad,' Violet objected. 'We talked about it and Mr Ramsay said it was just a story to bamboozle me. You were so angry that I'd been to Sally's house that I didn't dare ask you to help them.'

Mr Hamilton came over to Violet. She braced herself for more scolding, but he simply ran his hands through her short curly hair.

'It was your mother's hair,' he said softly. 'Red-gold, like copper. It was always her greatest beauty.'

Violet felt as though she had been slapped. She had not heard her father mention her mother for four long years. It had been as though she'd never existed. Or her brothers. Their names and memories were sealed away, just like the locked tower rooms.

Imogen stood up and clutched his arm. 'Daddy, it's all right. It'll grow back.'

Mr Hamilton turned away abruptly, shaking off Imogen's hold. He looked at the two girls coldly. 'Saunders, please give my apologies to Monsieur Dufour. I have just realised that I have another engagement, so I won't be here for dinner. Can you please send for Khakovsky? Tell him he's to drive me into the city and wait until I'm finished. It could be late.'

'Of course, sir,' Saunders replied. 'May I fetch anything for you, sir?'

'No, Saunders,' Mr Hamilton said heavily. 'Tell Harry he needn't wait up for me.'

'Yes, sir,' replied Saunders, and he turned to go.

'On second thought, Saunders, bring me a whisky in the billiard room,' Mr Hamilton added. 'And call me when Khakovsky's ready to go.'

Mr Hamilton left the girls in the drawing room and crossed over the hall. Imogen and Violet looked at each other as the billiard room door banged shut.

'Well, that wasn't so bad?' Imogen said.

'I guess he could have locked me in my room and thrown away the key,' Violet replied darkly.

Imogen laughed. 'Oh, don't be so glum. Let's play some music. When Daddy's gone, we're going to practise your dance steps. We have the Russian Ball coming up in a few weeks, and I can't have you disgracing me by treading on all the boys' toes.'

A few minutes later, they heard Saunders open the front door and their father stride out without a word to them.

Violet shrugged, her stomach heavy with disappointment. Imogen jumped up, went to the wooden gramophone with the shiny brass horn and cranked the handle. She pulled a record out of its brown paper sleeve and put it on the turntable, carefully dropping the needle onto the track.

'Cheer up, Violet,' Imogen said. 'This is my favourite foxtrot, "Angel Child" by Al Jolson.' The jaunty song blared from the horn. Imogen dragged Violet up from her chair. 'I'll be the boy.'

'Do we have to?' Violet complained. 'I don't particularly feel like it.'

Imogen ignored her and, grabbing her hand, began to dance. Violet laughed despite herself as Imogen crooned along to the music.

The two girls swept around the drawing room, avoiding the furniture, then moved out into the hall where there were fewer obstructions.

'Not quite so upright. Lean into me a little,' Imogen instructed. 'Not so heavy on your heels. Put your weight more on your tippy-toes — and glide gracefully.'

Violet obeyed, concentrating on the rhythm. She went to dance classes every week at the Town Hall, but the Russian Ball would be her first large ball, and she was keen to dance well.

Imogen directed her into a spin.

Saunders came into the hall from the passage that led to the kitchen. He stood by, watching the girls until the music ended. His normally impassive demeanour slipped, and Violet thought she detected a look of affection.

'Dinner is served, Miss Imogen,' Saunders announced. 'Mrs Darling thought you might like something simpler tonight, as Mr Hamilton is out.'

'Thank you, Saunders,' said Imogen, dropping Violet's hand. 'That would be heavenly.'

Saunders hesitated for a moment. 'Don't be too upset by your father, Miss Violet. Mr Hamilton means well, but he just doesn't know how else to deal with his sorrow.'

'Sometimes I think that Dad doesn't care much about us anymore,' Violet confessed, looking at the carpet.

'No, don't say that,' said Imogen, horrified. 'You know Daddy loves us. He just has lots on his mind these days.'

'I've worked for your father for twenty-five years — ten years as head footman and fifteen years as the butler,' said Saunders. 'He was always such a kind and funny man, but all that changed when your brothers ran away to war. Then, when the telegram came and your mother . . . Well, it was just too much for one man to bear. It was too much for any of us to bear.'

Violet blinked back her tears. She felt comforted by this unexpected support from Saunders, the perfect butler who was usually so discreet. 'It *was* too much to bear — you're right, Saunders.'

'Now we don't want to raise the ire of Monsieur Dufour by ruining his meal,' Saunders reminded them with a wry smile.

The girls trailed into the dining room. The huge table had two lonely places set, with all the silver, crystal and candelabra in place. Saunders served a simple meal of roast beef with asparagus and baked potatoes, followed by a green salad. Imogen and Violet chatted about the Russian Ball and all the ideas that Violet had come up with so far.

Saunders cleared the plates. 'Would you like me to serve the pudding, Miss Imogen?'

Imogen exchanged a quick glance with Violet, who shook her head. 'Thank you, Saunders, but we're finished.'

After dinner, Imogen demanded that Violet continue to practise her dancing, but this time she asked Harry to move the gramophone into the ballroom.

'I've selected a lovely set of records, and there's plenty of room in the ballroom,' Imogen explained as she threw open the door and flicked on the light.

The ballroom was a huge open space across the back of the house, overlooking the lawns towards the river. It was painted a pale Wedgwood blue, with the ceiling and plaster mouldings in white, and a waxed timber parquet floor. In the old days, the French doors would all be opened onto the terrace so guests could mingle in the fresh evening air.

The room had very little furniture other than a glossy grand piano, which was rarely played anymore, a few velvet banquettes along the wall and two side tables. Gilt mirrors hung along the inside wall to reflect the light from the chandeliers and the wall-mounted candelabra. Harry set the gramophone up on one of the cedar side tables.

'Will that be all, miss?' asked Harry.

'Yes, Harry,' Imogen replied, and the footman left, closing the white panelled door behind him.

Violet practised her foxtrot steps by herself, gliding around the floor, arms held wide, while Imogen rifled through the records.

'Do you remember that very wet Easter, when it rained for days on end?' Violet asked. 'And Nanny made us play in the ballroom?'

A shadow passed over Imogen's face and she put the records down on the table. The girls usually avoided sharing childhood memories. Imogen nodded stiffly. Violet stopped mid-twirl.

'Do you remember Archie and Lawrie had been playing the most dreadful pranks on everyone?' Violet continued. Their names felt unfamiliar on her tongue. 'Salt in the sugar bowls at breakfast. Buckets of water balanced on the tops of the doors in the servants' wing. And we dressed up as ghosts, in the bedsheets, and haunted the maids' sitting room.'

Imogen laughed at the memory. 'And we used the fire pokers as swords and battled up and down the stairs,' Imogen's eyes grew misty, 'pretending to be the Knights of the Round Table.'

'Archie thought we girls should sit on the top step and be Queen Guinevere and her lady, and cheer the knights on,' Violet said. 'But we soon grew bored with that and attacked them with our own swords.' She mimed stabbing Imogen in the stomach.

'Then, when Nanny banished us to the ballroom, Archie crept upstairs and stole all the chamber pots,' Violet reminded her. 'And we had a battle where we slid the chamber pots across the waxed floor to see whose would go the furthest.'

Imogen giggled helplessly. 'And Nanny was furious because we smashed three of them.'

'Luckily they were empty,' said Violet, trying to keep a straight face.

Imogen laughed even harder. 'That was hilarious, but when Daddy came home, instead of getting cross with us, he just laughed out loud and promised to take us to the cinema.'

Violet's throat closed tight as tears welled up. 'I miss them, Immy.'

Imogen hugged her close. 'I miss them too, Vivi.'

'We never talk about them,' Violet said. 'It's like they never existed.'

Imogen nodded. 'It's for Daddy. He used to get so upset if we ever mentioned their names, so it was easier just to pretend it never happened.'

Violet scrubbed her face with her handkerchief and sniffed. 'I miss the old Dad, too. He always had time to play with us, take us swimming or boating or riding.'

'Do you remember when we were young, and Daddy used to play that game of hide-and-seek with us?' asked Imogen. 'And Romeo would have to track us down?'

Violet nodded. 'We'd run and hide in the gardens or the stables, and Romeo would always find us.'

'He always had an excellent hunting nose,' Imogen said.

Violet hesitated. 'And Mamma? Sometimes I think I catch a hint of her perfume.'

Imogen smiled. 'Sometimes I feel I can sense her presence, as though she's just left the room, or she's watching us.'

'Me too — maybe she is still watching over us.'

Imogen walked to the door and pulled the lever for the servants' bell. Harry appeared a moment later. He looked like he had hurriedly left his own meal.

'Harry, I wonder if you could please bring us some hot chocolate?' Imogen asked. 'And perhaps some of that delicious raspberry cake that was left over from tea? We're going to have a little picnic in the ballroom.'

Harry did his best not to look too surprised by this request.

'Do finish your own dinner first though, Harry,' Violet suggested.

'I'll fetch it straightaway, miss,' said Harry in a tone of mild reproof. 'It will only take a few minutes.'

The girls sat on a rug in the middle of the floor and enjoyed their picnic of hot chocolate and cake. They laughed and chatted and shared memories from their childhood. Violet liked to imagine that the ghosts of her brothers might be sitting on the rug with them, enjoying the stories and thinking up more mischievous pranks.

It hurt to talk about the boys and Mamma, but it somehow also felt good, like a wound that was slowly beginning to heal.

13

Break In

Riversleigh, modern day

Marli parked her bike against the stone wall and went upstairs to knock on the door of Luca's flat. The last few days it had been raining, so the two had spent hours researching old newspapers on the internet and exploring various websites that had revealed grainy photographs of Riversleigh and Hamilton's Glove factory, snippets from social pages and gossip columns, and news reports of the house being given away. The local historical societies had websites with interviews from old residents who had worked at the glove factory and Ramsay's tannery.

Luca and Marli had caught a tram to Victoria Street in Richmond to see the old red-brick building that had once been the glove factory and was now the slick offices of an advertising agency. They had made copious notes about the Hamilton family from what Didi had told them, their internet research and the material they had found in the scrapbook. They had also made popcorn, watched old movies and played endless card games. It had been fun.

Today was sunny again, so the two planned another adventure into the Riversleigh gardens. Marli had borrowed her dad's camera again, but she hadn't told him what for. She felt it should be a secret — a secret between Luca and her.

Luca came out and the two headed for the old blue double doors in the wall that led into the garden. Both of them looked around surreptitiously to make sure that no-one was watching before they pulled open the door and slid through. Marli locked the crossbar behind them. It was dark in the garage. Luca used the torch on his phone to light their way, stumbling through the piles of junk. Marli pulled an old hammer off the wall.

They stepped through the double doors at the other end of the garage and out into the rampant beauty of the sun-filled garden. White butterflies danced above the rose garden. The fairy wren swooped and flitted through the golden air, chasing his tiny brown mate. Hidden bellbirds tinkled their chimes from the shrubbery.

'It's so beautiful, but it looks so unloved,' Marli said with a sigh.

Marli pulled out her dad's camera from her backpack and shot off some photographs of the house, the garden and the garage.

'My grandfather would be horrified,' Luca said. 'I was thinking that we could do some tidying up in the garden. I might be able to borrow Nonno's brush-cutter and mow through the long grass. Then we won't have to worry about snakes.'

Marli imagined what the gardens could be like with some care. 'That's a brilliant idea. And we could get rid of some weeds — I feel sorry for those beautiful roses all choked up.'

Luca nodded. 'It could be a project to do while we research the family.'

Marli looked towards the old house, with its boarded-up windows and peeling paint. 'What do you think?' she asked, swinging the hammer in her hand. 'Shall we explore? Maybe we can find a way inside the house.'

Luca looked at the hammer in dismay. 'You mean break in? What if someone hears us? What if they call the police?'

Around her neck, Marli was wearing the old-fashioned key on its threadbare velvet ribbon that she'd found in Violet's hatbox. She held it up by its ornate bow. 'No, we shouldn't need to break in. I've got the key, and I'm sure it must open one of the doors.'

The first door they tried was the huge, arched front door. Luca used the hammer to carefully prise away the plywood hoarding, revealing a cracked cedar door with a huge iron lion's head knocker. It had clear glass in the middle panels and ruby glass in the sidelights and fanlight above. Marli's hands were trembling with excitement as she tried the large iron key in the lock. The key slid in, but when Marli tried to turn it, the lock wouldn't budge.

'It doesn't work,' Marli complained.

'Let me try,' Luca offered. 'Maybe it's just stiff.' But Luca couldn't unlock the door either.

'We'll try the side door and the French doors on the terrace,' Marli suggested. They carefully removed the hoarding one by one from these doors as well, but the key didn't open any of them.

'It's no use,' Luca said. 'The key could be for anything.'

'I felt so sure that it would open a door at Riversleigh,' Marli said.

The two prowled around the house, checking every potential opening. They peeled away the corners of several boards, but all the windows on the ground floor were locked and there was no way to reach the second-storey windows. At last they came to the back service door, which opened onto the old stable courtyard on the southern side.

'It's the last door,' Marli said hopefully.

'Let's give it a go.'

Luca used the hammer to pull back each corner of the plywood board where it was nailed into the doorframe. The top left-hand side was difficult to loosen, and he had to tug extra hard. The board came away suddenly, smashing down on him. The unexpected weight proved too much and he dropped the board. It clattered loudly onto the stone paving beside him, followed by the hammer.

'*Ow*,' Luca yelled, pulling a pained face.

'Shhh,' Marli reproved. 'Someone might hear you.'

'*Sor-ry*.' Luca checked his arm. There was a long, red graze oozing blood.

Marli was contrite. 'Are you okay?'

'Just try the key,' Luca snapped, rubbing his arm.

Marli took a deep breath and slid the key into the lock. It wouldn't budge.

'It's not the right key,' Marli cried, slumping down onto the brick step. 'It doesn't open *anything*.'

Luca leaned against the wall, then he noticed a small wooden hatch at waist height, near the servants' entrance. He pulled the knob and the hatch opened to reveal a cavity with a matching door further inside. He leaned through and pushed, and the door swung open.

Luca turned to Marli. 'It's an old service hatch. We have one in our apartment. Nonno says deliverymen used it to leave milk or groceries. Do you think you could squeeze through? There's no way I'd fit.'

It was a very narrow gap.

Marli hesitated, feeling uncertain now that there really was a chance to get inside. She tucked the key on its ribbon back inside her shirt. 'I'll give it a go. Let's hope I don't get stuck halfway like Winnie the Pooh.'

Marli took a deep breath and exhaled, then squirmed her way in headfirst. For a moment she felt claustrophobic and had visions of getting jammed. But she kept wriggling through until she tumbled onto the hard floor.

It was dark inside, with the only light coming through the open hatch. The house seemed to creak and groan around her. Something scuttled across her leg. Marli screamed in fright. She pulled out her phone to use as a torch and scanned around, searching for the creature. Her eyes strained to see into the shadows, but there was nothing. Marli shuddered with disgust.

'Are you all right?' Luca peered through the hatch.

'Yes. Something crawled on me. I think it was a rat.' Marli stood up, her throat dry with nerves, and stroked the bangle on her wrist for reassurance. She wiped her dirty hands on the back of her jeans. 'I'll see if I can find a way for you to get in.'

Using the phone's torch, Marli groped around, looking for a bolt or a latch that she could undo, one that might open the door from the inside. The lock remained firmly fastened. She scanned around, checking for scuttling creatures, hoping for inspiration. Then she saw it. There was a hook on the wall with an iron key hanging from it.

Please be the key to the back door. Marli's fingers were slick with sweat as the key stuck for a moment and then turned, grating noisily in the lock. Marli crumpled with relief as she threw open the back door and let Luca in. Lovely light poured in, chasing away the shadows.

They gazed around with anticipation. They were in a narrow corridor, painted a drab grey. Off the corridor were a number of small rooms with empty shelves and battered benchtops, which appeared to be pantries, the scullery and laundry, and a large empty room with windows looking out on the old kitchen garden. Luca flicked a light switch but nothing happened.

'This must have been the servants' sitting room,' Marli suggested.

The dust made Luca cough violently. They moved into the large kitchen, with its stone floor, wide stove and laminate counters covered in grime. The kitchen door on the far side was protected by thick green felt that was stained and torn. The door creaked open as Marli pushed it.

On the other side, everything was different — grander, more spacious. The ceilings were higher with ornate cornices, the floorboards wider and the rooms large with marble fireplaces.

Yet the signs of neglect were everywhere — damp black stains, thick layers of dust, peeling paint, spiders' webs and cracked plaster. Ugly fluorescent bar lights had replaced the original crystal chandeliers. The fireplaces were blocked with painted plywood. One of the front rooms had been partitioned into two with flimsy fibreboard. Marli snapped photographs of the rooms, taking close-ups of architectural details, such as the plaster cornices, old servants' bell levers, mantelpieces and arched windows.

At the very back of the house was a huge room with parquet floors. Light filtered in through the French doors where the hoarding had been pulled away. A massive chandelier, veiled in cobwebs, hung in the centre of the room.

'The ballroom,' said Marli, twirling away across the floor. 'There must have been some wonderful parties in here.'

'This room is nearly as big as our whole apartment,' Luca observed.

The pair crept up the carpeted main staircase. On the landing was a locked panelled door.

'That must lead to the tower,' Marli suggested. 'What a shame we can't open it.'

'It must have an amazing view from the top,' Luca said.

They kept going, exploring the various empty bedrooms on the second floor — the five large family bedrooms with graceful arched windows overlooking the gardens, and their associated dressing rooms and bathrooms. A dead bird lay in the grate of one of the fireplaces. A colonnaded verandah ran across the front of the house, thick with dead leaves.

Towards the far end of this level, a low door led through to the maids' quarters, with three cramped bedrooms.

From here, a narrow and very steep set of servants' stairs went down towards the kitchen.

Marli led the way down the dark stairs by the dim light of her phone, clinging onto the banister with one hand as the steps creaked and groaned beneath her. She put her weight onto a tread and realised too late that the timber was rotten. Her boot crashed through the splintered wood. Luca grabbed her arm and hauled her back up. Marli's heart thudded with fright.

'That was close,' Luca said. He shone his own phone-torch down the stairwell. 'We'd better go back the other way. A few of those steps look nasty.'

Marli hobbled to the main grand staircase and stood on the landing looking down.

'This house is incredible,' she said. 'It has such a mysterious feeling about it.'

'There are so many secrets about the place,' Luca added. 'Why do you think Violet's father gave the house away? What happened to her mother? And why is the tower door locked?'

Marli unconsciously fiddled with the old key hanging around her neck. Suddenly she had a brainwave and swung around, excited. 'The tower. The key.' She pulled the ribbon over her head. 'I bet this key opens the tower.'

The two ran to the locked tower door. With trembling fingers, Marli inserted the key into the lock. For a moment, the key stuck fast, then it turned with a loud click. Marli pushed the door open.

It was like stepping into a different time. The square room was furnished with a white painted desk and chair, photographs in silver frames, a faded blue velvet armchair, a bookcase and a side table piled with tattered old books. To the right a narrow spiral staircase led up to the tower room above.

Marli picked up a photograph from the desk and blew on it, sending dust motes billowing into the air. Luca coughed.

'Sorry,' Marli said, patting him on the back. 'Look. These must be Violet's two brothers — the ones who died in the war. They look so young. Just teenagers, like us.'

Luca recovered his breath. 'It must have been tough for the family. I can't believe that this room has been locked all these years. Maybe the tower is haunted, and that's why it's kept locked up!'

Marli looked around and shivered. 'Well, if it is haunted, it can't be a very nasty ghost. The room's too pretty.'

Luca laughed, which made him cough again.

The two climbed the stairs to the upper room. It was clearly an old artist's studio. Dried-up oil paints and pots of brushes sat on a small table. Paintings were stacked against the walls. An easel, displaying an unfinished painting of flowers, stood in the middle of the room. The dirt-streaked windows on all four sides overlooked the river and gardens.

A ladder led up to a trapdoor, which opened to give access to a rooftop terrace. Luca was right — the view was breathtaking. They could see Luca's place next door, Nonno's vegetable garden, the green-brown snake of the Yarra River, Marli's dad's apartment building in Richmond on the other side, all the way to the silver skyscrapers of Melbourne. A trio of yellow-tailed black cockatoos flapped past, cawing raucously to each other.

Marli's phone beeped. She quickly checked the screen, realising that she had stopped obsessively checking her phone for messages from her friends back home. She had been too busy herself to worry about what they were doing.

But the text wasn't from any of her friends. It was from Dad.

Hi Marli. Sorry. Catastrophe at work so will be late tonight. Order takeaway. Will be home asap. Love Dad xxx

Marli scowled at the text.

'Anything wrong?' asked Luca.

'Dad's going to be late again.' She smiled at Luca, trying to lift her mood. 'He's had dramas at work so he's been working really long hours, but he did say he was going to try to get home early tonight.'

'Why don't you come to my place for dinner?' Luca suggested. 'Mum won't mind.'

Marli felt a rush of relief. 'Really? That would be great. Dad left me some money to order takeaway, but I don't feel like going back to the apartment all by myself.'

'I'll send Mum a text and ask. I'm sure she'd be happy,' Luca assured her. 'Mum loves feeding our friends — she thinks the more the merrier.'

'She sounds lovely,' said Marli. She twisted her bangle, thinking of her own mother so far away.

The two went downstairs again, carefully locking the tower door and the back door. Marli threaded the back-door key onto her velvet ribbon with the tower key.

It was too nice a day to be inside after days of rain, so they sat for a while in the sun on the steps. Then they walked around the rose garden, planning how they could research more information about Riversleigh and the people who'd lived there. As he had done earlier, Luca leaned down and tugged out a fistful of long grass from between the rose bushes. Marli did the same.

At first Marli only intended to make a small start weeding, but she found she enjoyed the work and kept going. It reminded her of helping Mum in their tropical garden at home. The warm climate of Brisbane meant that it was a constant battle to keep their small garden under control.

Luca went home to borrow Nonno's brush-cutter, safety goggles and gumboots from the shed and used it to cut large swathes from the overgrown grass around the rear garden. Luckily his grandparents were out, so there were no awkward questions. Using tools from the old garage, Marli raked up the cuttings and trundled them in a wheelbarrow to a compost heap they made behind the old kitchen garden.

It was hot work in the afternoon sunshine, but Marli found it deeply satisfying as the compost heap grew and the shape of the old garden gradually appeared. The labour made Luca cough, and he had to stop for short breaks to recover.

Marli took photographs to record the transformation.

After a couple of hours, Marli and Luca had a longer rest, sitting on one of the marble benches overlooking the rose garden. Marli wiped her sweaty brow with her hand, leaving a muddy streak across her face. She had grass in her hair, dirt under her fingernails and her skin was pricked with thorn scratches.

'Doesn't that look better?' she asked, gesturing at the rose blooms nodding their heads in the breeze. The air was sweet with perfume. 'You can actually see the roses instead of a jungle of gigantic weeds.'

'Definitely,' Luca agreed. 'Now the plants have some space to breathe.'

'I'm feeling whacked, though.' Marli stretched out her back. 'It's hard work.'

'Let's clean up, then we can go home,' Luca suggested. 'You can have a shower at my place and borrow some clothes from my sister.'

'Great idea. And I'd like to pick some roses for your mother as a present for having me.'

After packing up the tools and wheelbarrow, Marli used an old pair of secateurs to cut an armful of roses in pinks, pale yellow and cream.

They crept back through the double doors at the back of the garage, hoping no-one would see them. Luca put the brush-cutter and goggles away in the shed. As they headed towards the side entrance into the flats, Nonno came around the back of the building, carrying a wicker basket filled with herbs, lettuce, cucumbers, spinach and beans.

'*Ciao*, Luca *caro*,' he said. 'Looks like you two have been having fun.' Luca introduced Marli to his grandfather.

'Could you take this up to your mother for dinner tonight?' asked Nonno. 'And tell her that Nonna is making *pitticelle di zucchine* to bring along.'

'Yum. My favourite.' Luca turned to Marli. 'Nonna makes the best fritters with Nonno's homegrown zucchinis. You'll love them.'

'Mmmm,' said Marli. 'I'm starving.'

Luca took the basket and they went inside.

The Art Deco building that Luca lived in was a block of four apartments with two upstairs and two downstairs. Luca's family lived in the upstairs apartment at the back, overlooking the river, while his grandparents lived in the flat underneath them.

Marli followed Luca upstairs and into his apartment. It was a bright, two-bedroom unit with quaint, old-fashioned features, such as picture windows, ornate ceilings and polished timber floors. Luca's three sisters shared one room, and his parents had the other. Luca slept in the narrow sunroom off the living room, which overlooked the gardens and the river.

Luca's mum, Dani, was in the kitchen chopping egg-plants, while his younger sisters — Lia, Caterina and Siena — were in their school uniforms, doing homework at the dining table. Luca introduced them all. Marli imme-diately felt comfortable as she was enveloped in the warm family atmosphere. It was so much noisier than her own home. Delicious smells came from the pots bubbling on the stove.

'Welcome, Marli,' said Dani. 'It's lovely to meet you. Luca's enjoyed you coming around this week.'

'Thanks for having me.' Marli handed Dani the armful of roses. 'I brought you these.'

'Aren't they divine?' said Dani, burying her nose in the blooms.

By the time Marli had showered, brushed her hair and changed into one of Lia's floral sundresses, the table had been transformed. The homework had been packed up and the table set with candles, colourful painted crockery and two vases of roses. Nonno and Nonna had arrived, as well as Luca's father, Mark, home from work. Lia, Caterina and Siena helped their mother make salad and bruschetta while Luca showered.

'Oh, don't you look lovely, Marli,' said Dani. 'Please take a seat there. Just move Chiara.'

Chiara was a fat, grey cat curled up on Marli's chair. Marli lifted the cat onto her lap and sat stroking her, making Chiara purr. Soon the whole family were sitting around the table, laughing, chatting and joking as Dani passed around platters heaped with antipasti — one with Nonna's zucchini fritters and the other with tomato-and-herb bruschetta on toasted garlic bread.

'*Buon appetito,*' Dani called out. Everyone clinked glasses and replied, '*Buon appetito!*'

The food was delicious and plentiful. The antipasti was followed by homemade pasta with a ragù of eggplant, tomato and olives with shaved parmesan, then the main course of chicken parmigiana and salad greens from the garden tossed with lemon and olive oil.

The girls chattered about their day at school. Dani and Marc talked over the plans for the week ahead. When everyone had finished, the children cleared the table and then Dani served the dessert that Nonna had made. It was an Italian specialty called *cannoli* — pastry tubes filled with vanilla ricotta, shaved chocolate and homegrown strawberries.

'It's nice to see Luca eating again,' said Nonna, kissing him on the cheek. 'He's hardly eaten a thing since he's had that nasty cough. He was fading away to nothing!'

Luca looked appreciatively at his piled-up bowl. 'How could I resist your cooking, Nonna? It's *bellissimo*.'

'So what did you and Marli get up to today?' Dani asked. 'It was too lovely to watch movies again all day.'

Luca and Marli exchanged glances. They had agreed to keep the garden and their research as a secret for the time being.

'Not much,' Luca replied. 'Hanging out, a bit of a walk . . .'

'Exploring the neighbourhood,' Marli added. 'There are some pretty gardens around.'

'You must come and see Nonno's garden,' said Nonna. 'He can grow anything.'

'I learned gardening from my father, Giuseppe,' Nonno explained, putting his spoon down. 'He worked in the gardens next door for many years, when it was a private house, and then later when it became a soldiers' convalescent home. Now *that* was a special garden.'

'Did he tell you anything about the history of the house?' asked Marli, trying not to sound too eager. 'Do you know anything about the family who lived there?'

Nonno gazed dreamily out the window towards the high wall of Riversleigh. 'He was a good storyteller, my father, and he loved to tell stories of the old days, before the Second World War. He said that many sad things happened to the Hamilton family. He thought that perhaps someone had cursed them with the *malocchio* . . .'

Luca glanced at Marli meaningfully. 'Cursed with the evil eye?'

Nonno nodded. 'Giuseppe and his cousin were impoverished peasant farmers from Veneto, in the north near

Venice. Like many Italians of their generation, they were very superstitious and believed that bad luck could be caused by someone cursing you. My father always wore this charm.'

Nonno pulled out a small silver charm that he wore on a chain around his neck. 'A *cornicello*,' he explained. 'It's a horn, which is supposed to ward off bad luck. I don't believe in curses and amulets, so I don't believe the Hamiltons were cursed, but I like to wear the charm to remind me of my father.'

'The Hamiltons did experience a lot of tragedy,' Marli said. 'My grandfather told me that both brothers, Lawrence and Archie, died in the final months of the First World War, which must have been devastating. And then their mother, Margaret, died soon after, but we don't know how.'

Nonno turned to Marli, his face serious. 'I know what happened to Mrs Hamilton. The servants knew all the family secrets, of course. It was very sad. Would you like me to tell you?'

'Oh, yes please,' Marli begged. 'Luca and I have been wondering.'

'Mrs Hamilton died of grief,' Nonno began. 'She just faded away, hardly eating, hardly sleeping, her face to the wall, refusing to see her daughters or her husband.'

Marli felt a shiver up her spine — how devastating for Violet and Imogen, and their father. Violet must have felt that her mother had abandoned her, that she didn't love her enough to have something to live for.

'She couldn't cope after her boys died,' Nonno said. 'Everyone thought she should just buck up and get on with things, but she went into a deep depression and couldn't get out of bed for weeks. When she died, Albert locked up her tower studio and never mentioned her name again.'

Everyone was silent for a moment, trying to imagine the terrible sorrow that Albert must have felt.

'Can you tell us any other stories about Riversleigh and the Hamiltons, Nonno?' Luca asked.

Nonno's eyes lit up with memories. He settled back in his chair. 'Oh, yes. I certainly can . . .'

14

Nikolai's Family

Riversleigh, 22 November 1922

On Wednesday morning, when Violet came down to breakfast, Imogen was already seated at the table. Romeo bounded over to greet her.

'Good morning, Romeo! Yes, I missed you too,' Violet said, rubbing his ears. When she took a seat, Romeo plonked beside her with his head on her knee.

'Hello, sleepyhead,' Imogen said, putting down the newspaper.

'You're up early this morning.' Violet poured herself a cup of tea. 'That's most unlike you.'

'It's a glorious day and I'm off on an adventure,' Imogen replied, indicating her loose-fitting, white blouse, navy skirt and sturdy boots.

'Sounds like fun. What kind of adventure?'

'I'm going hiking up in the mountains with Audrey.'

Imogen averted her eyes as she buttered her toast. 'She's picking me up any minute.'

'And anyone else going?' Violet asked.

Imogen took a bite of her toast and marmalade, delaying her answer. 'Actually, Tommy O'Byrne and Jim Fitzgerald,' she replied nonchalantly. 'Tommy has the day off.'

'Sounds fun,' said Violet, a twinkle in her eye. 'Don't fall down the mountain! But I guess if you do break an ankle, it'll be handy to have a medical student close by.'

Imogen rolled her eyes. 'Very funny. What are you going to do today?'

'I thought I'd start sketching decoration ideas for the Russian Ball,' Violet replied. 'I've been meaning to do it for days, but I don't know where the week has gone.'

Saunders appeared in the doorway. 'Miss Williams and Mr O'Byrne have arrived to pick you up, Miss Hamilton.'

'Thank you, Saunders. I'm coming.' Imogen stood, dropping her napkin on the table.

'Where's Dad?' Violet asked. 'He's usually down by now.'

'He left early for golf. There's a competition or something on.' Imogen picked up her wide-brimmed hat from the sideboard and checked her reflection in the mirror as she pinned it on her head. She pulled on her gloves and picked up her bag.

'I'll come with you for a moment,' said Violet. 'I want to ask Tommy about Mrs Burke. He might have some news.'

The girls went out the front door and down the front steps, Romeo bounding ahead. Saunders followed. Audrey was sitting at the wheel of her green-and-silver tourer. Audrey and Tommy both jumped out to say hello.

Violet stared at Audrey's outfit in surprise. Audrey was wearing a loose white shirt and a tight-fitting green cloche hat with tan gauntlet gloves, driving coat, knee-high boots and breeches.

'Hello,' Tommy called, sweeping off his tweed flat cap. 'What a beautiful morning.' He was dressed in baggy knickerbockers, an open-necked white shirt, vest and hiking boots.

'Love your hair, Violet,' Audrey cried. 'It looks adorable.'

'Thank you,' Violet replied, self-consciously brushing back a curl.

'What on earth are you wearing, Audrey?' asked Imogen, putting her hand to her brow, pretending to be horrified.

'Don't scoff,' Audrey retorted, handing Imogen a bag. 'I've brought you a pair of breeches too. You can't possibly walk in the mountains wearing a skirt.'

'*Breeches?*' Imogen laughed and exchanged a guilty look with Violet. 'Whatever you do, don't tell Daddy! I'd be disinherited.'

'Why ever not?' Violet said, raising her eyebrows. 'It would be heavenly to have you in terrible trouble for once instead of me.'

Imogen poked out her tongue. 'I'll race upstairs and get changed. See you in a moment.'

Violet turned to Tommy. 'I was wondering if you've heard any news about Sally's mother.'

He smiled reassuringly. 'Mrs Burke has been moved to the tuberculosis ward at Austin Hospital for Incurables.

Luckily, Dr Trumble believes we picked it up early, which increases her chance of survival. But even if the treatment is effective, she'll still need to be in hospital for months.'

Violet wasn't sure whether to be relieved or worried. 'Thanks, Tommy. I'll let Sally know.'

A moment later, Imogen hurried out again, wearing baggy breeches instead of her skirt, a long coat over her arm. She stood on the top step and struck a theatrical pose. 'Tada!'

'Very daring,' Audrey assured her.

'But I brought a long overcoat, so I won't shock Daddy when I get home,' Imogen explained. 'He hasn't recovered from Violet chopping off all her hair.'

Violet pulled a rueful face.

'Well, I think you both look utterly charming,' Tommy said, offering Imogen his arm. 'Shall we go fetch Jim?'

Saunders opened the rear car door for Imogen to get in.

Violet stood at the bottom of the front steps with Romeo as the hiking party drove off. Audrey gaily tooted the horn in farewell and rounded the carriage driveway.

Violet and Romeo headed back inside. The house seemed dark and quiet with Imogen gone. Upstairs, Violet could hear the murmur of voices and faint thumping as the housemaids tidied and dusted the bedrooms.

Violet sat at the table in the morning room, doodling scenes of children ice-skating in her sketchbook, but the drawings seemed lifeless.

Feeling restless and bored, she pulled over the newspaper that Imogen had discarded and began reading the headlines. Her eye was drawn to an article titled 'Knight Versus Housemaid' about the upcoming election, where

Sir Robert Best was being opposed in the electorate of Kooyong by a housemaid called Miss Jean Daley. Violet enjoyed the incongruity of the image. A lowly, working-class maid challenging a wealthy male politician — maybe the world was changing. Violet hoped that the housemaid might prevail and be the first woman elected to Federal Parliament. But on second thought it seemed completely impossible.

Next she read the letters to the editor, focusing on local issues of the day, such as the Children's Hospital, the spread of noxious weeds and the need for financial support for soldiers who lost limbs in the Great War.

Suddenly an idea came to her — perhaps she could write a letter or an article for the newspaper about the injustice that she saw with the wealthy suburbs and the poverty-stricken slums separated only by the river. Perhaps she could support her article with photographs of the living conditions in Richmond and Sally's family's neighbourhood.

Violet thought about her camera and realised that she now had two rolls of film to develop and print. Then she could write an article to go with them. She decided to ask Nikolai if he was available to take her to the photography shop in Burwood Road.

Rather than ringing the bell to call for the chauffeur, Violet went looking for him. She strolled out through the French doors of the morning room, onto the stone terrace and down to the lawns, Romeo following at her heels.

Hidden away on the southern side of the house were the kitchen gardens, the poultry runs and laundry yard. Coming around the corner, Violet saw Sally with a basket over her arm, collecting fresh herbs from the kitchen garden.

Joseph was helping her. Both of them started when they saw Violet in the service area and quickly sprang to attention, Joseph tugging his cap and Sally bobbing her head.

'I'm just looking for Nikolai to drive me on an errand,' Violet said.

'Would you like me to fetch him, miss?' asked Sally.

'No, no,' replied Violet. 'I can do it.'

Nikolai was in the bluestone cobbled courtyard of the old stables, washing the Daimler, wearing a khaki mechanic's boiler suit. Sudsy water dripped onto the ground as he rubbed the sponge over the car. Romeo gambolled over towards Nikolai, trying to steal the sponge.

'Careful, boy,' Nikolai warned. 'Mrs Darling will have your hide if you gobble my sponge.'

'Oh, you're busy,' said Violet with a twinge of disappointment. 'I was hoping you might be able to run me up to Burwood Road and then perhaps to Glenferrie Road so I can look at some material for the decorations.'

Nikolai straightened up, dropping the sponge back into one of the buckets. 'I'm nearly finished. Would it be all right if I took you in about ten minutes?'

'Perfect,' replied Violet, feeling relieved. 'I'll just get my bag and hat.'

Nikolai wrung out a chamois cloth and began to polish the paintwork intently. 'Miss Violet, I had an idea about your Russian Ball. I thought perhaps my sisters might be able to help you with some of the decorations and the entertainment.'

Violet felt a flash of excitement. 'Truly? Could they?'

Nikolai nodded as he continued to polish. 'I mentioned it to my sisters when I was visiting on my half day off, and we'd all like to contribute. We, of all people, want to help the starving Russians back home.'

'Of course you do,' Violet replied. 'Well, that would be marvellous.'

Nikolai rubbed hard at a smear on the duco. 'My three sisters are all excellent seamstresses, so they could sew the costumes,' he explained. 'And they can dance the old Russian dances. Plus, we know lots of people in the Russian community, so we can ask them to help too.'

The dry, lifeless list that Violet had written suddenly seemed alive with possibilities.

'Oh, bless you, Nikolai. I've been thinking and thinking about how to get everything done and make the ball as authentic as possible. This is a perfect solution.'

Nikolai grinned, his toffee-coloured eyes sparkling. 'Well, perhaps if you wrote down a list of what you'd like, I could take it to the girls and see what they can help you with?'

'Or better still, perhaps you could take me to meet them and we could talk about it,' Violet suggested. 'That would be much more efficient.'

Nikolai nodded. 'They should be home this afternoon, but they don't have a telephone, so I'll send a note around to check. Would you like me to take you over for tea?'

Violet did a little hop. 'That would be perfect.'

Violet went upstairs to fetch her hat, gloves and new chocolate bag, together with the camera and the exposed films. She collected up her drawings and notes for the ball and folded them away.

After Violet had dropped off the film, Nikolai drove her across the river to Richmond and down Swan Street.

He parked the car in a narrow stone laneway behind the shopping strip.

'My family lives above one of the shops,' Nikolai said, pointing up to the second storey. 'Are you sure you want to come up and meet them?'

Violet craned her head to look. The area behind the shops was stacked with crates, boxes and garbage bins. The strong stench of rotting rubbish and rancid cooking oil came through the open shop window. Nikolai looked embarrassed. 'They'll understand if you'd rather not.'

'Of course I'm coming,' replied Violet. 'I'm looking forward to meeting your family.'

They climbed up the rickety wooden stairs at the back of the building. At the top was a small landing with a blue front door and an old wash tub planted with flaming orange poppies and blue forget-me-nots. A collection of old buckets were planted with lush green herbs – chives, parsley, dill, chervil and tarragon.

Nikolai knocked on the door and it was opened by a blonde-haired girl with very pale skin and brown eyes. She looked to be about the same age as Violet.

'Nicky!' the girl cried with delight.

'Anoushka-myshka,' Nikolai replied with equal enthusiasm. He turned to Violet and gestured. 'Miss Violet Hamilton, this is my sister, Anastacia Petrovna Khakovska.'

The two girls shook hands and exchanged greetings. Violet noted that Anastacia also spoke excellent English with a soft Russian accent.

'Khakovska?' Violet asked. 'I thought your surname was Khakovsky.'

Anastacia and Nikolai laughed.

'In Russian, the ending of the name changes depending on whether you are a female or a male, so the feminine version of a name usually ends in "a",' Nikolai explained. 'Russians always have three names. Their first name is followed by a patronymic name, which indicates who your father was, and lastly your family name.'

'That sounds confusing,' said Violet, wrinkling her nose.

Anastacia led the way into the apartment through a short hallway. At the back, overlooking the laneway, were two small bedrooms and a bathroom. Violet glimpsed beds covered in colourful patchwork quilts of scarlet and indigo as she passed.

The rest of the family was gathered in the living room overlooking the street at the front, working on their embroidery. The other two sisters rose from their chairs and nodded their heads in greeting. Violet was immediately struck by their appearance: they were all tall, fair-haired and slender with brown eyes. They seemed unusually graceful, like a corps of prima ballerinas, and were dressed stylishly in flowing day dresses, white stockings and low-heeled strap shoes.

'Mamma, may I present my employer's daughter, Miss Violet Hamilton,' said Nikolai formally. 'My mother, Elizaveta Ivanovna Khakovska. And my sisters, Miss Tatiana Petrovna and Miss Ekaterina Petrovna.'

These sisters looked to be about sixteen and seventeen.

'How do you do, Miss Hamilton?' Mrs Khakovska asked. 'Please take a seat. Can we offer you some tea?'

'Delighted to meet you,' Violet replied, shaking her hand. 'Tea would be lovely, thanks.'

Nikolai's mother was slightly shorter than her daughters and looked careworn, but like her daughters, she was smartly dressed and stood with her spine straight and chin high. Violet suddenly felt underdressed as she sat down in the velvet armchair offered to her.

She glanced around the living room in surprise — it was beautifully but simply furnished with armchairs grouped around the fireplace, a writing desk near the window, and a timber table and dining chairs at the far end. A faded Persian rug covered the floor. The furnishings were of good quality but somewhat worn. Attempts had been made to hide the worst of the wear with well-placed cushions and throws in warm tones of crimson and rose, contrasted with forest-green velvet. Framed watercolours hung on the walls, vases of flowers brightened the room, and a number of old photographs stood on the mantelpiece in silver frames. The room was far more like what one would expect in a genteel but impoverished country house than an apartment above a busy shop.

Nikolai pulled over a dining chair to sit beside his mother while Anastacia left to fetch the tea things from the kitchen, which was hidden behind a painted folding screen.

'I hope you don't mind if we continue with our needle-work,' said Tatiana, who looked to be the eldest girl. 'We are working on some frocks for a client and need to get them finished by Monday.'

Violet looked at the silk evening dresses that the three girls were embroidering by hand. Each dress was very different — one in vibrant watermelon, one emerald-green and one in silver — but all were decorated with ornate beading and embroidery. Violet bent closer to Tatiana's emerald frock with its delicate gold detailing.

'How exquisite,' exclaimed Violet. 'These are some of the most stunning evening dresses I've ever seen.'

'I'm glad you like them,' Tatiana replied. 'Katya designed them based on the latest looks from Paris. We sew them for Madame Collette's in Collins Street, and we hope to find a few private clients of our own.'

'We're starting our own label,' Katya said as she sewed tiny silver beads onto the sheer chiffon. 'We're thinking of calling it Mademoiselle Perrot.'

Violet noted that Katya's French accent, like Nikolai's, was perfect.

'We think it will appeal to the ladies of Melbourne more than Miss Khakovska,' joked Tatiana.

'I love the name Perrot,' said Violet. 'It sounds very stylish.'

'Perrot means "little Peter",' explained Tatiana. 'And our patronymic name is Petrovna, which means "daughter of Peter", so we thought it was apt.'

'Or we could just call ourselves something English, like Peters,' suggested Nikolai, joining in the conversation. 'Australians don't like foreign-sounding names, as we've discovered. French is very appropriate for a fashion house, but a Russian name arouses instant suspicion.'

'Truly?' Violet asked, but then she thought back to Sally's suspicions that Nikolai might be a Bolshevik revolutionary. 'I suppose many people are wary of foreigners.'

'We just need to start building up a clientele of our own,' Katya said. 'Eventually we'd like to acquire some beautiful rooms on Collins Street, modelled on the great couturiers of Paris. Tatiana and I worked for Madame Chanel when we were living in Paris.'

'Coco Chanel?' asked Violet, surprised. The famous designer had taken the fashion world by storm with her understated elegance. Before the war, women used to wear fussy clothes and tight corsets, but Coco's designs were much more comfortable. 'That must have been an extra-ordinary experience.'

Tatiana nodded as she snipped the gold silk thread with a fine pair of scissors. 'Madame Chanel was a compassionate supporter of the Russian exiles in Paris, and she was very kind, teaching us about *haute couture* – or high fashion. We worked on the beading and embroidery finishes, and modelled the clothes for special events.'

'Her fashion house – her *maison de couture* – at Rue Cambon sold everything an aristocratic lady would need,' Katya added. 'From exquisite ball gowns, to sporting attire, hats, bags, fans – even jewellery and perfume. So one day we hope Mademoiselle Perrot will have a *maison* like that, dressing all the most fashionable women in Melbourne.'

Tatiana sighed, putting down the frock she was beading. 'But that dream is rather a long way off for now.'

Nikolai's family was charming, and he seemed different around them. *Nikolai is more relaxed*, Violet thought, *less like a servant. Not that he's ever really behaved like a typical servant . . . Perhaps he's just less guarded.*

'Well, let me know when you do open, because I'll be your first client. And I'll drag all my friends along as well,' Violet promised. 'I would love an elegant gown like one of these for our Russian Ball.'

'We'd be delighted!' Katya said. 'I can see you in a filmy green-and-silver silk chiffon, to bring out the colour of your extraordinary eyes.'

Violet was thrilled by the compliment. 'That sounds heavenly. Do you make tea gowns as well? I think I need a completely new wardrobe.'

'We can make anything you need,' Tatiana replied with a chuckle. 'And I promise that we can do it for a fraction of the price you'd pay in Collins Street.'

'Even better,' Violet agreed. 'Dad will be ecstatic.'

Anastacia returned, carrying a tray with a pretty tea set, mismatched fine bone china cups and a golden-brown cake dusted with icing sugar. Nikolai's mother poured the tea while Anastacia passed the cups and saucers. Katya served the cake. Violet took a forkful. The cake was moist, airy and not too sweet, with tiny flecks of soft green apple baked through it.

'It's a Russian Sharlotka cake,' explained Nikolai's mother. 'Anastacia made it. Just like the ones we used to have back home.'

'Anastacia has become quite a chef since we moved here,' Katya added, 'which is lucky because the rest of us can't cook. Can we, Mamma?'

The girls chattered on, teasing each other about failed cooking attempts and disastrous dinners. Nikolai's mother fussed over him, insisting that he eat more cake and have more tea, as though he was starved at Riversleigh.

Nikolai brought the conversation around to the Ball by fetching Violet an old book that was perched on the mantelpiece. 'I thought you might like to borrow the book of old fairytales that we brought from Russia. Some of the illustrations might give you inspiration for your Russian Relief Fund Ball.'

'It's gorgeous, Nikolai,' said Violet with delight as she leafed through the old book with its mysterious Russian script.

'This is Vasilisa the Beautiful, who has a little wooden doll that was given to her by her dying mother,' Nikolai explained, indicating an illustration of a fair-haired girl in a blue smock. 'After a time, her grief-stricken father remarries and travels abroad on business, leaving Vasilisa with the cruel stepmother and two foolish stepsisters, who starve her and make Vasilisa work day and night, but the little doll magically helps her.'

'It sounds something like our Cinderella tale,' said Violet. Her eye was caught by a picture of an ugly old woman flying through the forest. 'Who's this?'

'Baba Yaga — a terrifying witch who flies on a mortar and pestle and eats people,' Nikolai continued, using a scary voice. 'The wicked stepmother sends Vasilisa to Baba Yaga's hut to fetch a light, hoping she'll be gobbled. The girl is terrified, but with the help of her mother's blessing — the little wooden doll — Vasilisa outwits the witch and carries home a human skull filled with coals. The stepmother and stepsisters are burned to ashes by the skull, and eventually the brave Vasilisa marries the *very* handsome Tsar.'

Violet laughed. 'Of course she does, lucky girl.'

Next, Nikolai showed her an illustration of twelve dancing princesses. 'This story is called "The Midnight Dance", about twelve lovely princesses who sneak off each night to the accursed Tsar's underground home. They dance all night until their new shoes are ruined.'

Violet examined it closely. 'These illustrations are superb. Perhaps I could paint large canvases of some of these scenes for the ball.'

Nikolai closed the book, looking pleased. 'I hoped you'd like them. Perhaps you could tell the girls about the Russian Ball, and we can think of some other ways we can help.'

Violet outlined the ideas that she had come up with so far, inspired by her discussions with Nikolai.

'We can sew traditional Cossack uniforms for the waiters and costumes for the dancers,' Katya said. 'And we'll ask the local Russian community for help.'

'We can buy the fabric from wholesalers in Flinders Lane so it won't cost very much,' Tatiana assured her. 'We know several Russian suppliers there who will help us.'

Violet beamed around at the Khakovsky family. She felt like she had stepped into another, more exotic world. Despite the slightly shabby furnishings, this apartment felt warm and welcoming, and so very different to her own home.

'Perhaps you might like to come to one of our Russian Club evenings to see some of the dances,' Anastacia suggested. 'Then you can see what we are talking about. We have a social dance every Monday night with chess and music and a Russian supper. Would you like to join us?'

'I'd love to,' Violet agreed. 'I suddenly feel like organising the Ball will be much easier than I'd feared.'

'And in a couple of days I can design you an entire modish wardrobe for your approval,' promised Katya. 'A ball gown, tea gowns, summer frocks — and even an archery outfit if you need one.'

Violet laughed. 'Not so sure if I need an archery dress, but the rest sounds heavenly.'

Before they left, Katya took Violet into one of the bedrooms to take her measurements and pull out some fabric samples. There was a sewing machine on a table by the window. Katya unrolled sheer silk chiffons, thick satins and stiff tulle in a rainbow of colours.

'I love this tea gown in cream lace,' said Katya, showing Violet a sketch from the latest French *Vogue* magazine. 'I think that would look pretty on you, and how about this style for an evening dress in a pale sage green with silver beading?'

'It's heavenly,' Violet agreed. 'I've never owned anything as beautiful as that.'

Katya jotted down her measurements and noted the frocks that Violet liked the best.

'Thanks for being so kind to my brother,' Katya said as they finished. 'It was very hard for him to go into service. He's so lucky to have found a family that treats him well.'

Violet nodded. 'It's our pleasure.'

But there was something about Nikolai's family that didn't quite add up. The girls with the grace of prima ballerinas. Nikolai with his demeanour that was always polite but never servile. And the home that was well-worn but stylish — a far cry from Sally's house on the other side of Richmond.

15

Maison de Mademoiselle Perrot

Imogen was delighted when Violet told her about the talented Russian seamstresses who had promised to make her some dresses. So it was arranged that the sisters would visit Nikolai's home in Richmond a few days later to choose some fabric and order gowns to be made for the Russian Ball. Katya had designed a number of outfits for Violet, and Tatiana had bought some rolls of fabric on approval from a Russian haberdasher in Flinders Lane.

The girls sat at the round dining table while Anastacia made coffee. Mrs Khakovska was at her writing desk by the window, doing the accounts.

Katya had a sheaf of several drawings of outfits she had designed.

'I can't believe you have done all those drawings already,' said Violet, pulling off her gloves and laying them in her lap.

'I do hope you like some of them,' Katya replied. 'I started work on them soon after you left, while your colouring and figure were fresh in my mind.'

Anastacia came back in carrying a tray with a coffee pot and cups, and a plate of biscuits. 'Don't start just yet. I want to see them too.' She poured the coffee into the cups and offered one to each of the girls, along with the milk jug and sugar bowl.

'Thank you,' said Imogen, taking her coffee cup and pouring in the milk.

'And a Russian tea biscuit?' Anastacia offered.

The homemade biscuits were golden pastry scrolls filled with raspberry jam, walnuts and raisins, and dusted with cinnamon sugar. Violet nibbled one. It was flaky and delicious with the coffee.

Katya spread several pastel-colour drawings across the table, each one with suggestions for matching hats, gloves and jewellery. The afternoon dresses flowed softly to mid-calf, with elbow-length sleeves and rounded bateau necklines.

'You said you might want four or five frocks, so I designed a few for you to choose from,' Katya said. 'I designed them all to be loose-fitting, comfortable and easy to move in, but also chic with gorgeous fabrics.' Violet examined the stylised drawings on the table. As a keen artist herself, she recognised the skill in the sketches. 'Firstly, this tea gown is a sheath of cream lace with an ivory silk underdress that would be lovely to wear for summer garden parties or afternoon tea. The cream sash at the waist can be changed to give a very different look. For example, it could be sage green with a creamy silk gardenia worn at the hip, or dusky pink with a trio of roses.'

Tatiana unrolled the lace fabric and placed it over the silk so Violet could see how it would look.

'What divine lace,' said Imogen, stroking the fabric.

Katya pointed to the next drawing. 'This dress has a rose-pink underdress with sheer silk chiffon over the top in mossy green. It's finished with embroidery and satin ribbon detailing in matching rose and green.'

Tatiana displayed the two layers of fabric, while Katya showed a close-up sketch of the embroidery design.

'And the last one is a sheer blue-and-white patterned fabric with a wide, white collar,' Katya continued, showing the final dress sketch. 'Not quite as dressy as the other two, but the fabric drapes beautifully.'

Anastacia held the sheer fabric up against her to show how it swished when she moved.

'All the afternoon dresses would be worn with a long string of beads or pearls and a wide-brimmed white straw hat, changing the colour of the band to suit,' said Tatiana.

'All three of them are perfect,' Violet said, slipping the sheer silk through her fingers. 'I don't think I could choose between them.'

Katya smiled widely. 'I'm so pleased you like them. It's always a bit daunting showing the designs the first time.' She dramatically spread out another fan of drawings. 'And now for the evening gowns. These dresses are made for *jazzing*.'

Violet leaned forward to view the three drawings. These dresses were sleeveless with square necks and fell to mid-calf. They were worn with long, elbow-length satin gloves and beaded headbands. One dress was midnight blue, one was sage green and another was blush pink.

'It's a little difficult to see the beading on the drawing, so Tatiana and I took the liberty of making one to show you,' Katya said. 'Don't worry, if you don't like it, we can sell it to Madame Collette.'

Tatiana fetched a long, straight dress on a coat hanger. The green silk georgette was embroidered with silver beads, which glittered in the sunlight.

'It's absolutely heavenly,' Violet said.

'Would you like to try it on?' Anastacia asked. 'You can get changed in our bedroom.'

'I can help you,' Imogen offered, and the two girls left the room.

Imogen helped her sister do up the tiny buttons at the back of the bodice, and Violet came out and twirled in the middle of the living room. Anastacia held up a long mirror so she could see her reflection. The silk georgette floated out as she pirouetted.

'You look simply gorgeous,' Imogen said.

'It's not quite finished,' Katya explained, tweaking the dress. 'I need to take it in a little here, and the embroidery is not done on the back, but it gives you the idea.'

'We thought that if you like it, we can try to finish it so that you can wear it to the Russian Club on Monday night.'

'Oh yes, please,' Violet replied. 'You'll come with us to the Russian Club, won't you, Immy? Dad wouldn't let me go otherwise.'

'It sounds like fun, especially with a new gown to wear. Could you make one for me too?' asked Imogen.

Katya shook her head reluctantly. 'I'm sorry, Miss Hamilton, but it will be difficult enough to get this one finished in time for Miss Violet. But we could make you both gowns for your Russian Ball — we still have a few weeks before that.'

'I would adore that, thanks. But how on earth to choose!' said Imogen.

Tatiana and Katya exchanged glances.

'Speaking of the Russian Ball, there is one more design to show you,' Katya said, pulling out the last page. 'We decided our Mademoiselle Perrot label would feature peacocks. Peacocks symbolise beauty, confidence and nobility — all the things we want our label to represent. And so we created this for you . . . .'

The drawing showed an ankle-length gown in a pale seafoam-green, with a square neckline, a draped sash at the low waist and shoestring straps worn with long, cream satin gloves. The bodice of the dress was straight and long, encrusted with turquoise, emerald green and jet beads to create the effect of peacock feathers.

'Oh,' said Violet. 'A peacock gown. It's amazing . . .'

'It certainly is,' Imogen agreed, frowning. 'But it looks rather expensive. We promised we wouldn't send Dad bankrupt!'

Katya beamed. 'Miss Violet Hamilton will be the first customer of Mademoiselle Perrot, and she will look so stunning that all her friends will demand to know where she had her dress made. We'll be famous!'

The three sisters exchanged glances.

'We are determined to make our business work,' Anastacia confided. 'We have to make a new life for ourselves here in Australia, and our own *couture* label makes the best of our combined talents. If it takes off, then we can help Nikolai to —'

Tatiana picked up a list from the table and presented it to Violet, cutting Anastacia short.

'I've made a list with the cost of each dress,' Tatiana explained. 'And if you order a number of dresses, we'll give you a discounted price — especially if Miss Hamilton orders a ball gown as well.'

Violet and Imogen scanned the list together. The prices were indeed very reasonable, so Imogen suggested that she order four dresses, plus the peacock ball gown, with the bill to be sent to Mr Hamilton. Violet dithered over the drawings.

'It's impossible to decide,' she insisted.

'Make a decision or I'll do it for you,' Imogen threatened. 'Then I'll take the very best ones for myself!'

'You wouldn't dare!' Violet retorted playfully. 'All right then — I choose the cream lace and the rose-pink tea gowns, the green georgette evening gown and the . . . the blue-and-white afternoon dress.'

Katya gathered the selected sketches into a separate pile. 'Perfect.'

'And do you think you could make me the midnight-blue gown with the jet beads?' Imogen asked, stroking the soft fabric.

While Imogen was being measured for her dress, Violet began to doodle on some loose sheets of paper. A *maison de couture* would need labels, packaging and hatboxes.

She drew peacocks, flowers and ferns in delicate swirls. She chose coloured pencils from Katya's jar on the table and coloured the swirls in muted tones of turquoise, green and lavender. Finally, she scrawled an elaborate label in black ink.

And so the fashion house of Mademoiselle Perrot was born.

16

Sailing

On the weekend, Theodore Ramsay had invited a small group to go out sailing on his father's yacht, including the Hamilton sisters, Audrey, Jim Fitzgerald and Tommy O'Byrne. He had clearly chosen the party to please Imogen. Theodore arrived at Riversleigh to pick up the two girls in his red two-seater Bentley sports tourer, its black canvas roof folded down.

'It'll be a bit of a squash,' said Theodore. 'Miss Hamilton, you sit in the middle, and your sister can sit with your bag at her feet on the side.'

Theodore drove fast, hitting the horn impatiently and overtaking other vehicles that slowed him down. Violet had to hold on to her hat to stop it escaping its hatpins. Theodore pulled up next to the St Kilda Yacht Club and parked carelessly on an angle.

'I say, I didn't scare you, did I?' Theodore asked as he came around to open Violet's door.

Violet felt a thrill of anticipation as she slid out of the car and breathed in the strong scent of saltwater and briny seaweed drifting from the bay. 'Not at all — it was quite a ride. I think today might be rather an adventure.'

The girls followed Theodore past the two-storey club-house and onto the pier, where majestic wooden yachts of all sizes bobbed and swayed. Halfway along the pier was a sleek timber ketch with two masts. Two crewmen in smart navy-blue uniforms were loading crates onto the yacht and stowing them down below.

'Can't go sailing without oysters and champagne,' Theodore joked. 'Welcome aboard the *Mariette*.'

He took Imogen's hand to solicitously help her across the gangway and on board. Violet decided not to wait for Theodore's help and leaped across the gap between pier and boat, landing lightly on her feet. The deck rolled and pitched gently with the waves.

'Take a seat aft,' Theodore suggested, waving towards the back of the yacht. 'You ladies will be safely out of the way in the cockpit.'

Violet gazed around, taking in the neatly coiled ropes, fluttering pennants, glossy varnished woodwork and fresh white paint.

'Thank you, Theodore,' Imogen said. 'She's definitely a beauty.'

'Then she's a fit setting for such delightful company,' flattered Theodore.

Violet caught Imogen's gaze and lifted her eyebrow. Imogen stifled a giggle.

There were two bench seats scattered with red cushions running on either side of the cockpit. Violet and Imogen took a seat, and Audrey, Tommy and Jim joined them.

White with the odd stripe of navy were the colours of the day, with the three girls wearing white linen dresses, white stockings, wide-brimmed hats and low-heeled shoes. The men wore white shirts and flannel trousers, straw boaters and blue blazers. Theodore had a debonair cravat knotted at his throat, and his hair was slicked back.

One of the crew members presented himself and saluted to Theodore. 'All set, Cap'n.'

'Fine. Fire the engine and cast off,' Theodore ordered.

'Aye, aye, Cap'n,' the crew replied, running to do his bidding.

The engine rumbled to life and Theodore stood at the timber steering wheel, reversing the ketch out into the vast indigo bay. Sunlight danced on the lapping water. Seagulls swooped and shrieked over the beach. A flock of ungainly pelicans flew in formation, descending to land with unlikely grace on the bay. Violet sighed with pleasure.

The crew hauled on ropes, hoisted sails and tightened trim. In moments, the ketch was flying across the water, heeling to starboard. As their speed picked up, the wind ruffled Violet's hair, loosening it from its bobby pins. She closed her eyes and turned her face to the sun and the wind, listening to the slap of water on the hull and the whoosh of wind over the white sails.

As the yacht was skimming south, the guests began to chat and tell stories. One of the crew members came up with glasses of champagne on a silver tray.

Violet shook her head. 'No, thanks. Would you have any water, please?'

'Very good, miss,' replied the crewman.

'Me too,' said Tommy. 'I'm working at the hospital tonight.'

'A little glass won't hurt you,' Theodore protested. 'It's French. Nothing but the best on the *Mariette*.'

Tommy shook his head firmly. 'I'd hate to lose a patient because of a fuzzy head.'

'Suit yourself,' Theodore replied. 'Another glass, Jim?'

Port Phillip Bay was a huge body of water, enclosed on all sides, except for the narrow heads leading to the ocean many kilometres to the south. The coastline was ringed with sandy beaches, scrubby vegetation and small villages. Behind them to the north was the city of Melbourne, with its skyline of tall buildings. To the west were the piers, dockyards and huge ships of Williamstown.

The coastline quickly dropped away behind them until it was a shadowy smudge on the horizon and they were sailing out into the open water of the bay. After a couple of hours, Theodore ordered the crew to drop the sails. The ketch lost speed and came upright, gradually coming to a stop, where it bobbed up and down on the small waves.

Violet looked around, shading her eyes with her hand. As far as she could see was a vast expanse of navy-blue water under a cerulean sky, the thin ribbon of land barely visible. It was as though they were the only people in the whole world. It made her feel very insignificant.

'Time for a swim, then we'll have lunch,' Theodore announced. 'Why don't you ladies go down below and get changed?'

One of the crew members dropped a rope ladder off the stern while the other fetched a pile of fluffy towels. After several minutes, Violet, Imogen and Audrey emerged from the cabin in their swimming costumes.

Violet was up first, loping to the stern. She stared down into the sparkling water, wondering what was down there — hopefully not any sharks. She took a deep breath and dived cleanly into the deep. The icy water shocked her, making her feel invigorated and alive. Violet struck out, swimming strongly away from the safety of the hull. Moments later she was joined by the others — squealing, laughing and splashing. Tommy grabbed Imogen and threw her overboard, then plunged in after her. Jim did a huge bomb off the stern, spraying everyone.

Theodore challenged them all to a swimming race around the yacht, then pretended not to care when Jim won.

Afterwards, they lazed on the deck, letting the saltwater dry on their skins.

The crewmen served platters of sandwich triangles — egg and lettuce, chicken and tarragon, ham and mustard, and finely sliced cucumber — along with oysters in their half-shells, strawberries and a creamy wedge of camembert cheese with crackers. The sunshine and salty air gave them all a good appetite, but there was more food than they could possibly eat.

'The fish will have a fine feast tonight,' Theodore said after slurping the last oyster out of its shell. 'Throw the scraps overboard.'

The crewmen made to throw the remnants of the picnic over the side.

'No!' said Violet. 'Don't.' Everyone looked at her. 'I mean, it was all so delicious — it would be a shame to waste it. Surely we could pack it up and perhaps your servants might —'

Theodore guffawed. 'Our servants get plenty to eat. We're not living in the Middle Ages.'

'Violet,' Imogen admonished, looking embarrassed. 'Not now.'

Violet flushed but pressed on doggedly. 'I just thought perhaps the servants could deliver the food to poor families who might need it, like our maid Sally's family in Richmond.'

Imogen shot Violet a warning look.

Theodore chuckled, shooting a glance at Imogen. 'Is she always like this?'

Violet flushed, mortified. She supposed it wasn't ladylike to talk about poor people at a boating party. Tommy leaned forward, as though to shield her.

'Perhaps we should think about turning back,' he suggested to Theodore, changing the subject. 'I'm working tonight, and it's a long sail to port, especially now that we're heading into the wind.'

Theodore grumbled but gave the order to prepare the sails. Everyone took it in turns to get dressed down below. Theodore grabbed the wheel gallantly and began chatting to Imogen, flattering her with compliments.

'Look, dolphins off the bow,' Tommy called. 'Violet, do you want to come and take a closer look?'

'Absolutely.' She and Tommy scrambled forward to the bow. It was a little difficult, as the boat was tilting at a steep angle, beating into the wind. The wind was chilly on Violet's face, tangling her hair and whipping her skirts.

The two of them stood at the bowsprit, watching the pod of grey dolphins racing alongside the yacht, surfing the bow's wake. A dolphin leapt right out of the water, so close that Violet could almost reach out and stroke its slippery back. She gasped with exhilaration. The dolphin dived back deep underwater with a splash. Violet laughed as droplets flung up, wetting the hem of her skirt.

'Aren't they beautiful?' she exclaimed, hanging onto the forward stay as she leaned over to get a closer look. 'That one looked as though he was just as curious about us as we were about him.'

'They say that dolphins are some of the most intelligent animals on earth,' Tommy said. 'Certainly a lot smarter than some humans I know.'

Violet laughed. 'Me too!'

Tommy looked back to the south and frowned. All around them the sky and sea were a vast, glassy blue, but down on the horizon, at the mouth of the bay, black clouds were boiling.

'I don't like the look of that,' Tommy confessed. 'Looks like we might have a southerly buster on its way.'

'Wouldn't like to get caught out here in a storm,' Violet agreed.

'Come on,' Tommy said. 'We'd better warn the others.'

The merry mood on the yacht evaporated as the black clouds raced towards them. The crew pulled on the sheets to gain as much speed as possible, but it was impossible to outrun the storm behind them. One moment the breeze blew from the north, then the next the southerly change slammed into the yacht. The sails flapped violently. The sea transformed from glassy blue to choppy grey. Waves smashed over the rails. Stinging rain lashed the boat.

Unprepared for the sudden change in wind direction and his reflexes slowed by the champagne, Theodore slipped and let go of the wheel. The sudden loss of steering made the boom swing wildly, slamming into Jim and knocking him to the deck. He screamed in pain, clutching his arm. The yacht rocked violently from side to side.

'Watch your heads!' shouted Tommy as he jumped forward to grab the spinning steering wheel. He regained control and steered the yacht to stop the rocking.

Violet was sitting closest to Tommy. 'Take the wheel please, Violet, and keep the bow facing exactly where it is now,' he asked.

Violet did as she was told, concentrating hard to fight against the pull of the wheel.

Tommy raced forward to where Jim was writhing in agony on the deck. He checked him over quickly. Audrey crawled over to help him.

Theodore struggled to his feet and pushed Violet out of the way, seizing the wheel. 'I'll take over now – you girls, get down below. And close the hatch. We're going to turn the yacht into the wind and reef the sails.'

'Just give me a moment to stabilise Jim,' Tommy pleaded. 'He's in a lot of pain.'

'So am I,' grumbled Theodore, 'but you don't see me making such a fuss.'

'He's fractured a bone, possibly two,' insisted Tommy. 'I need to get him into the cabin and stabilise the arm. I just need a minute.'

Imogen and Violet gathered up cushions and picnic cups, plates and silverware. Violet climbed down the steps, carrying a load of towels in one arm, until a sudden lurch sent her hurtling into the cabin, sprawled on the floor. She staggered to her feet, rubbing her bruised thigh ruefully.

A moment later Audrey came down, followed by Tommy supporting Jim's weight. The yacht listed to the port side. Jim was pale and trembling with pain.

'Are you all right, Jim?' Audrey asked, moving to help Tommy.

'I think I'll live,' he joked weakly.

'He appears to have fractured both bones in his forearm — his radius and ulna,' Tommy explained. 'A sling will keep it as still as possible until we get back to shore.'

Audrey helped Tommy fashion a sling from a towel and knotted it firmly behind Jim's neck. Imogen helped to make him comfortable with cushions behind his back.

'That's better,' said Jim with a grimace. 'It's almost worth the pain to be fussed over like this.'

'That's all we can do for now,' Tommy said. 'I'll go up and help Theodore.'

Violet perched on the edge of a bunk, one arm up, bracing herself against the bulkhead. Waves crashed over the deck, making it difficult to see out the windows. It was stuffy and hot in the cabin, and the pitching motion made her feel ill. She longed to breathe fresh air on deck.

'I'm going up,' Violet announced, jumping to her feet. 'There might be something I can do to help.'

'No, Violet,' cried Imogen. 'It's not safe. Theodore told us to stay below.'

'I can't stand it in here anymore.' Violet opened the hatch, pushing hard against the wind, then slammed it shut behind her.

She gulped in mouthfuls of cold, fresh air. The rain stung her cheeks as it lashed against her, soaking her dress in moments. Tommy was back at the steering wheel, holding the yacht's bow into the wind, while Theodore and the two crew members worked to pull down and stow the foresail.

Violet clambered over to Tommy. 'I thought I was going to be sick down there.'

Tommy nodded, his eyes scanning the storm-swept horizon to the south. 'It's better up here in the open.'

Violet recovered almost immediately. She should have been frightened as the storm raged around them, tossing the yacht on the waves, yet, strangely, she felt calm.

'Is there something I can do?' Violet asked.

'Actually, could you steer for a moment and hold this bearing? I'll help Theodore reef the mainsail.'

Violet nodded confidently and took the wheel. 'Of course.'

Tommy showed her the compass and told her to keep the yacht pointing due south. It was harder than it sounded as the wind and waves sought to force the yacht around. With Tommy's help it was easier for the four men to pull the mainsail partly down and lash it securely. With a smaller sail area, the wind wouldn't buffet the boat as much.

Theodore returned to take the steering wheel. The crew eased the boom to starboard, the shortened mainsail bellied out, the bow swung around, and the *Mariette* began racing north before the wind.

At once the motion became smoother. For a moment, Violet felt reassured, but then she caught sight of Tommy's face and realised they were not out of danger yet. It wasn't until an hour later, when they safely moored the yacht at St Kilda, that the tension eased.

Violet shivered on the deck as she gathered up her belongings. She was soaked, aching and exhausted, but euphoric with relief. It had indeed been quite an adventure.

Theodore turned to Tommy. 'Good of you to help out there, old chap. I didn't realise you were such an experienced sailor.'

'No trouble,' replied Tommy, shaking Theodore's hand. 'My great-grandfather was a fisherman at Killybegs on the west coast of Ireland; he migrated to Australia during the potato famine. My grandfather and father were dockers at Williamstown, so we always had boats growing up.'

'A docker?' Theodore sneered. 'So how did the son of an Irish-Catholic dockworker end up studying medicine?'

Tommy looked embarrassed by Theodore's patronising tone. 'Very hard-working parents and the gift of a scholarship,' he replied, lifting his chin.

'And I'm sure you'll make a wonderful doctor,' Violet added with a warm smile.

17

Tea with Tommy

The next day, Imogen spent the afternoon having a picnic at the beach with Audrey, Tommy and Jim, whose arm was in plaster. She returned with pink cheeks and a sparkle in her eyes. Violet was in the morning room, sketching more rough ideas for Russian scenes.

'Was it fun?' asked Violet, putting down her pencil.

'It was heavenly,' Imogen said and hurried towards the stairs. 'But let me just get changed. Could you be an angel and let Mrs Darling know that Tommy will be joining us for tea?'

Violet rang the bell and gave the instructions to the housekeeper, then went upstairs to tidy her hair and change her dress. When she came down, Imogen was already sitting in the drawing room, wearing her best tea gown, her hair up in a low chignon.

A few minutes later, Saunders showed Tommy in. He

had also changed from his sporting clothes into a smart three-piece suit; his blond hair was slicked back neatly.

Sally brought the tea tray and set it on a side table. Imogen poured three cups, leaving one aside for her father. The three chatted about their day as they sipped tea and ate raspberry sponge cake with dainty silver forks. Imogen and Tommy kept smiling at each other, as if they had a tantalising secret.

Mr Hamilton came in from the hall and looked momentarily surprised when he saw they had a visitor. Tommy stood up and stepped forward.

'O'Byrne, old chap,' said Mr Hamilton. 'Nice of you to drop by.'

The two men shook hands.

'Yes, sir.' Tommy looked slightly embarrassed. 'Actually, I was hoping I might be able to have a private word with you while I'm here.'

Violet looked up at Tommy, then at Imogen, who flushed a deep rose and dropped her eyes to her lap.

'Oh indeed?' asked Mr Hamilton, frowning. 'Well, I suppose you had better come into the library; we can talk there.'

The two men left the room and walked across the hall. Violet heard the library door close behind them.

'What's going on?' Violet asked. 'Tommy seems a little fidgety this afternoon.'

Imogen jumped to her feet and went to the door, trying to make out the murmuring voices in the library. Violet put her tea cup down and followed her.

'What are you doing?' Violet demanded. 'You're being very mysterious.'

Imogen clutched her sister's arm tightly. 'I think . . .' Imogen began, flushing even deeper. 'I think Tommy has gone to ask Daddy for my hand . . . in marriage.'

Violet hugged her sister, her heart thumping with exhilaration. '*Truly?* Are you sure?'

'Yes — Tommy proposed today at the beach, when we went for a walk. He says he loves me desperately and wants to get engaged.'

'Oh, Imogen, that is simply marvellous news. I thought you two have been getting on well. So when will you get married?'

Imogen giggled, her whole face alive with happiness. 'Not yet. Probably not for a couple of years. I'm only seventeen and Tommy has to finish his medical degree, so it will take a while before he can support me properly, but he wants to make it official.'

Violet had a sudden vision of her sister in a white satin dress and veil, her hair wreathed in flowers. 'You'll make the most beautiful bride, Immy darling. I can't wait for the wedding — are you sure you have to wait two years?'

Imogen nodded. 'Yes, but I thought you might like to be my bridesmaid when the time comes. You do like Tommy, don't you, Vivi?'

'Of course, you silly. He's absolutely lovely. You'll make a perfect couple.'

The two sisters sank side by side onto the sofa, their tea forgotten, and they chattered about dreams for the future.

'I'm so glad you like him, Violet,' Imogen said. 'Tommy is the kindest, funniest man I've ever met.'

Just then the library door opened again and Imogen jumped to her feet. Tommy hurried into the drawing room, his face dark.

'Tommy?' cried Imogen. 'Whatever is the matter?'

'My apologies, Miss Hamilton and Miss Violet,' Tommy said, his voice strained. 'I cannot stay to finish my tea after all.'

Mr Hamilton followed on his heels. 'I've just rung for Saunders to show you out, Mr O'Byrne.'

Saunders appeared with Tommy's hat, and a moment later he was gone, giving one last agonised glance back at Imogen.

Mr Hamilton waited for Saunders to close the door and return to the kitchen before he spoke. 'Did you know about this ridiculous nonsense, Imogen?'

'What . . . what do you mean *nonsense*?' Imogen stammered.

'That young pup had the nerve to ask me if he could marry you,' Mr Hamilton thundered. 'Damned impertinence.'

Violet looked from her father to her sister. She wrung a handkerchief between her fingers, as though she might burst into tears any moment.

'But Dad,' began Violet. 'Tommy's —'

'Tom O'Byrne is a nobody,' Mr Hamilton interjected. 'He's a Catholic nobody. It's inconceivable that he should marry my daughter.'

Violet and Imogen exchanged shocked glances.

'You can't mean that, Daddy,' Imogen said. 'Tommy's studying to be a doctor. He's very clever and works terribly hard . . .'

Mr Hamilton strode up and down the crimson-and-blue Chinese carpet, his hands behind his back. 'His father is an Irish docker and his mother was a shopgirl. Besides, I won't tolerate a Catholic marriage. It's absolutely impossible. I won't hear of it.'

'Tommy loves me,' Imogen wailed. 'He wants to start his own practice. He wants to build a life together.'

Mr Hamilton stopped pacing and stared at his two daughters. 'Imogen. Enough,' he shouted. 'You are not yet twenty-one and you cannot marry Tom O'Byrne. I forbid him to come to my house again.'

Imogen looked crestfallen and stared at the floor.

Violet felt a wave of fury welling up. 'Dad — you can't be so cruel.'

Mr Hamilton turned on his heel and stalked towards the door.

'Not another word,' Mr Hamilton ordered. 'Tomorrow night we will have the Ramsays for dinner. Imogen, you will instruct Mrs Darling that I would like a particularly fine meal. Theodore is fond of salmon, I believe.'

Mr Hamilton stormed out of the room, leaving Imogen sobbing on the sofa and Violet standing on the rug, her fists clutched tightly. She suddenly wondered how her father knew that Tommy's father was a docker. She remembered the conversation between Tommy and Theodore on the deck of the *Mariette*. Could Theodore have told her father about Tommy's background just to make trouble?

Violet turned to Imogen and sat down beside her, taking her hand. 'Dad will come around,' she whispered. 'He just needs time to get used to the idea.'

Imogen shook her head. 'He's made up his mind. There's nothing I can do about it.'

Violet gazed into Imogen's eyes. 'Do you love Tommy?'

Imogen scrubbed her eyes with the handkerchief. 'Of course I love him. I've loved him almost since the first time I met him.'

'Then you have to fight for him, Immy,' Violet insisted. 'Does it matter that he comes from a Catholic family? Does it matter what his father does? Tommy is a good person — you know that.'

Imogen took a deep breath while she thought. She shook her head. 'I can't disobey Daddy. It would break his heart, and I can't do that to him again.'

'So you'd break Tommy's heart and your own instead?' demanded Violet, her voice harsh with frustration.

Imogen stood up and dabbed at her eyes, checking her reflection in the mirror. 'We'll see what happens when Tommy has finished studying and I turn twenty-one.' Imogen put her handkerchief away in her pocket. 'The important thing is not to upset Daddy. He's been through so much already.'

'And haven't we?' Violet said bitterly.

18

Argument

Richmond, modern day

It was late when Marli's father, looking pale and tired, finally arrived to pick her up from Luca's home. He was very apologetic, murmuring an excuse about an argument with a contractor who was behind schedule.

When they arrived home, the apartment seemed cold and quiet after the noisy warmth of the Costas' dinner. Dani had packed up some leftovers for Dad, which he warmed up in the microwave.

Marli felt a wave of anger: her father had promised not to work late. Her mother had almost always made sure she was there when Marli came home from school, even if it meant having to work late at night, after Marli had gone to bed.

'Did you have a lovely day, myshka?' Dad asked, sitting at the kitchen bench with his bowl of pasta.

'It was all right,' Marli replied grumpily, playing with her bangle.

'A funny coincidence that your friend Luca's family lives right next door to Riversleigh,' he continued. 'They seem like kind people.'

'They *are* kind people,' Marli growled.

'Did I tell you that I spoke to the lawyers today about the handover of the Riversleigh estate?' Dad asked. 'They're drawing up the paperwork now; we should get the keys in a few days.'

Marli pricked up her ears. Riversleigh and its mysteries would soon no longer be a fascinating secret for her to share with Luca. It would belong to Didi.

'I spoke to council to see what the planning regulations are,' Dad continued. 'Fortunately it's not heritage listed. With that size block of land we'd be able to build thirty low-rise apartments, with a mixture of one-, two- and three-bedroom floor plans.'

'You can't,' said Marli, her voice rising. 'Didi would be devastated if you knocked down the house.'

Dad rubbed his forehead. 'The land's worth a fortune, myshka, and the house is a disaster. Didi could never live there, not now.'

Marli felt a rush of pent-up anger with her father for always working late. For leaving her and her mother. For wanting to destroy Riversleigh.

'You don't care what Didi wants,' Marli shouted. 'You don't care what I want. You never listen. You're never there for me.'

Dad sat there staring at her, looking shocked and wounded. Marli ran into her room and slammed the door.

This isn't my room — this is Dad's office, filled with his work, his drawings. She thought of her own cozy cottage at home and Luca's crowded, wonderfully chaotic, family-filled home. This apartment wasn't a home — it was a sleek, stylish, soulless hotel suite. And Dad wanted to pull down Riversleigh and build more just like it.

Marli fought back her tears. There was a knock at the door and Dad came in. He sat on the edge of the sofa bed and Marli turned to face the wall.

'I'm sorry I was late, Marli,' said Dad, putting his hand on Marli's arm. 'I wanted so much for us to spend some time together.' He paused, waiting for her to respond. Marli stayed stubbornly silent. 'I didn't want to worry you with it, but we've had some problems at work. The project has gone way over budget and my boss is putting pressure on everyone to cut costs. I've been going through the figures with the accountant, trying to work a way out of this mess. Sometimes I wonder if it's all worth it.'

Marli felt her resolve melting, but then she steeled herself. Figures, budget blowouts and accountants seemed so foreign to her.

'Well,' Dad said, 'goodnight. I want you to know that I'm so happy you've come to stay, and I promise we'll still have a great Christmas and do our amazing road trip in January.'

He kissed the back of her head, turned off the light and closed the door behind him.

Marli lay awake for hours. Gradually the anger and the problems of the present ebbed. Her mind filled with the stories that Didi had told her and that Nonno had shared around the dinner table. Her imagination began to flicker with images of Riversleigh and the Hamilton family and all their servants — Violet and Imogen, their father Albert, Saunders, Mrs Darling, Sally, Guiseppe, Monsieur Dufour, Alf and Nikolai Khakovsky . . .

19

Nikolai's Story

Riversleigh, 1 December 1922

On Friday morning, Violet finished a painting of Vasilisa the Beautiful and the witch Baba Yaga, inspired by the illustrations from Nikolai's book of Russian fairytales. *Vasilisa is a little bit like me*, Violet thought. *Her mother is dead, just like mine, and her father stays away because of his grief. At least I don't have a wicked stepmother and stepsisters to deal with. At least I have Imogen.*

Violet looked closely at the other illustrations. Through the story, Vasilisa was transformed from an innocent, subservient young girl, protected from harm by her dead mother's blessing, into a strong, independent young woman, who triumphed over both Baba Yaga and her stepmother to become a talented weaver and win the heart of the tsar. Violet smiled to herself. *Fairytales seem to be the same the world over.*

She set the painting to dry and sat at the morning room table to write. She worked on her newspaper article about the problems faced by the poor families in the Richmond slums — high rents, low income, dilapidated housing, unsanitary living conditions, disease and inadequate education.

She planned it out, wrote a rough draft, then edited and polished it until she was sure it was as good as she could make it. Finally, she wrote it out three times in her best handwriting. She could imagine the article being printed together with her own photographs of everyday people living in the slums.

Actually *seeing* what real life was like for people living in poverty must educate the rest of society and change people's minds about what was fair and just. Probably nothing would change the mindset of people like the Ramsays and the Marchants, but it might make a difference, even if just a little one. Surely if people knew what was happening, they too would be outraged and demand change. Perhaps she might even be paid for her article, and she could give the money to Sally for her family and help the other Richmond children she had met.

Finally, Violet wrote three covering letters to the editors of the three major Melbourne newspapers, asking them to publish her article and offering to send her own photographs to support the story.

The postman brought notes from Violet's ill school friends — Hen, Bea and Cecily — who were feeling much better but still in quarantine in the boarding house and moaning about how bored they were. Violet wrote them a return note, trying to make it as funny and newsy as possible. Sitting at her desk, she realised that school and her friends seemed such a long time ago. So much seemed to have happened since then.

It was a beautiful summer's day with a deep blue sky. Violet decided to walk Romeo up to the shops to post the articles and letters and collect the photographs that had been printed. Romeo zigzagged along on the lead, sniffing the ground and barking at birds. It was a twenty-minute walk up to Burwood Road. Violet felt nervous and excited as she bought stamps and posted her article to the newspapers. Then she headed into the camera shop, Romeo at her heels.

'Good morning,' Violet said to the shop assistant. 'I've come to collect my photographs.'

'Good morning, Miss Hamilton.' He rummaged under the wooden counter and pulled out a small package with her name on it. 'Here you are. I must say, they turned out rather well for a beginner.'

'Have they? I thought I might have mucked it up.' She opened the package nervously and fanned the prints out on the counter.

'A couple are a little blurred, so just be careful with your focusing,' the assistant advised, pointing to a shot of a newsboy. The assistant rifled through the prints then selected a photograph of the children playing cricket outside Sally's house. 'But this one's awfully good.'

Violet felt a rush of exhilaration as she scanned the photographs. Then she saw one photograph that she hadn't taken. It was a photograph taken four years ago on her brother Lawrence's eighteenth birthday, just a few days before the boys had run away to war.

It was the whole Hamilton family having afternoon tea in the summerhouse. Dad was beaming with love and pride. Mamma looked elegant and happy in a long white dress with ruffled sleeves. The two girls wore their best dresses and ribbons in their hair, while the two boys stood tall and proud in their stiff suits, gazing at the camera. It was a snapshot of the perfect family. Violet closed her eyes, fighting back the tears.

She slid the prints back inside the brown paper packaging and pulled out her purse. 'Lovely,' she said, too brightly. 'Could I buy two more packets of film, please?'

Her errands done, Violet began walking home again, but she remembered how quiet and lonely the house had been when she'd left. Nikolai had driven Mr Hamilton to a business meeting, and Imogen had been invited to have morning tea with Mrs Ramsay. Violet felt too melancholy after seeing the old photograph to go back alone.

Violet decided she needed a brisk walk in the sunshine to dispel her mood, so she headed to St James Park. The park was an oasis of rolling lawns, meandering gravel paths and majestic English oak and elm trees in grand avenues. Once through the gate, Violet unclipped Romeo's lead so he could run free.

Romeo bounded around Violet in wide circles, his tail wagging madly. Suddenly he caught a whiff of an enticing scent and dashed off, nose to the ground. Violet followed, glad he was having a good run.

Romeo followed the scent trail for a few moments then raced straight towards a young man sprawled on a rug in the sunshine, a wicker picnic basket beside him.

'Romeo,' Violet called. 'Romeo. Come!'

The dog ignored her, intent on his quarry. Violet hurried after him, calling again. Violet's fears were realised when Romeo barrelled straight into the young man and began licking him all over his face. Violet flushed with embarrassment and ran. 'Romeo, come here at once.'

The young man pushed Romeo away and sat up, his book discarded beside him. Violet recognised him with a start. It was Nikolai.

He jumped to his feet at once and smiled at Violet. His dark hair was somewhat dishevelled after the rumble with Romeo, and it made him look more relaxed than his usual slicked-back formality. Violet liked it.

'Good morning, Miss Violet,' Nikolai said. 'I can see that Romeo is taking you for a good run.'

'I'm so sorry, Nikolai. I wondered why Romeo was so intent on following that scent — he knew it was you.'

Nikolai bent down to rub Romeo on the belly. 'It doesn't matter. It's rather nice to be adored for a change.' Romeo whined with happiness.

'When we were children we used to play hide-and-seek with Romeo all the time,' Violet said. 'No matter where we hid, he'd always track us down. He has the most extraordinary nose.'

'He's a good dog,' Nikolai said. 'I miss our dogs. We had to leave them behind when we left Russia.'

'What sort of dogs did you have?' Violet asked. She suddenly remembered the picnic basket and hesitated.

'I'm sorry — I didn't mean to disturb you. You're probably meeting someone.'

Nikolai smiled. 'Not at all. I'm waiting for your father, so I thought it was better to read out in the sunshine than sit in the car. Mrs Darling kindly packed me a picnic lunch.'

Romeo had run off again and returned dragging a stick, which he dropped at Nikolai's feet, looking at him adoringly.

'Fickle dog,' Violet complained. 'I thought you loved me best.'

'Romeo often comes to visit me in the garage when I'm waiting for your father.' Nikolai picked up the stick and threw it, and the dog gave chase. 'It's nice to have the company. There're only so many times I can polish the headlights.'

'Of course,' Violet said awkwardly. 'I should probably go and leave you to your book.'

Nikolai looked momentarily disappointed. 'Your father won't be finished with his meeting for a couple of hours, and it seemed too nice a day to go back and dawdle at the house. Monsieur Dufour hates me in the kitchen, and Mrs Darling doesn't want me under her feet either.'

It suddenly occurred to Violet that Nikolai, a foreigner living away from home and family, might get lonely. Romeo ran back and dropped the stick at Violet's feet. Violet threw it as far as she could.

'Do you mind if I join you for a little while?' she asked. 'Romeo needs a good run, and I haven't walked him for ages.'

'Please do,' Nikolai replied. 'Romeo reminds me of our old Russian hunting hounds, who also hunted by scent, although our dogs had much thicker coats to keep them warm in those freezing winters. I had a Siberian Laika called Max, who followed me everywhere.'

Romeo bounded around in a circle, shaking the stick back and forth in his mouth, as though it were alive. Violet and Nikolai ambled along under the trees.

'What's a Siberian Laika?' asked Violet.

Nikolai wrestled with the stick in Romeo's mouth, pretending to steal it.

'They look very much like wolves.' Nikolai's eyes lit up at the memory. 'Big dogs with shaggy grey coats, a curled-up tail and almond-shaped eyes. They're loyal till death.' Then a wave of sadness crossed Nikolai's face. 'He was a brave friend.'

'It must have been awful leaving Max behind,' said Violet.

'We had to leave, but you're right — leaving the people and animals behind was harder than anything else.'

Violet took a deep breath. 'Nikolai, your family weren't servants in Russia, were they?'

Nikolai looked at her in surprise. He threw the stick for Romeo again, playing for time. 'What do you mean?'

Violet shrugged. 'I could tell when I visited your family. You all speak French and English perfectly. You're well-educated with the manners of a gentleman. You try but you don't behave like a servant.'

Nikolai flushed and looked at the ground. 'I'm sorry, miss. I'll endeavour to do better.'

'No — it wasn't a criticism,' Violet assured him. 'I just wondered, that's all.'

Nikolai laughed, then he clicked his heels together and

bowed formally. 'Count Nikolai Petrovich Khakovsky at your service.'

'*Count?*' Violet cried. 'You're a *count.*'

Nikolai shook his head ruefully. 'A former count, actually. My father was Count Petrov Alesandrovich Khakovsky and my mother is Countess Khakovska,' Nikolai confessed. 'Before the revolution we lived in a pink-and-white palace in St Petersburg on the Fontanka River and had several estates in southern Russia.'

'I knew there was a mystery about you,' Violet crowed. 'You lived in a *palace.*'

They reached the edge of the park and turned around, walking back towards the rug.

'I know it sounds grand, but my father believed in a very strict military upbringing for all of us,' Nikolai continued. 'Camp beds in the nursery, up at 6 am, daily walks in all weather and ice-cold baths for the children. We had an English nanny, a French governess and a German tutor, so we spoke English with the nanny, French with our parents, Russian with the servants and German on Monday and Tuesday – at least before the war. Then we never spoke German again.'

Violet turned to Nikolai in surprise. 'Didn't you go to school?'

Nikolai looked nostalgic. 'No school at all – we had a *very* happy childhood. Of course, we studied with our tutors, but we also did fencing, horseriding, shooting and dancing lessons, as well as ice-skating and playing with the other children of the court.'

Mention of the 'children of the court' reminded Violet of something. 'Who was Alexei, who you said was the son of your father's employer? The one who was given a motor car for his ninth birthday?'

'Alexei was the son of Tsar Nicholas II, the last emperor of Russia, and Tsarina Alexandra,' Nikolai admitted. 'He was my second cousin.'

Nikolai hesitated then took a deep breath. 'Alexei, his parents, his four sisters and their servants were murdered by the Bolsheviks in July 1918. Alexei was not yet fourteen years old. His sisters — Anastacia, Maria, Tatiana and Olga — were between seventeen and twenty-three. They were lovely girls and great friends of my sisters.'

Violet felt a wave of anguish. 'I'm so sorry, Nikolai.'

Nikolai picked a leaf from a tree and began to shred it between his fingers. 'Like many of his friends, my father believed that the tsar was incompetent and weak,' he explained. 'He urged him to make economic and social reforms before it was too late. Tsar Nicholas refused to accept that the world was changing. He insisted it was his divine right to rule as he saw fit.'

'It was a costly mistake,' Violet said.

Nikolai nodded. 'I remember them as a kind and gentle family. No matter his faults, they didn't deserve to die like that.'

'No, of course not. So what happened to your family when the revolution began?'

Nikolai rubbed his hand through his hair, mussing it further. 'When the bread riots began in February 1917, my father was away fighting the Germans. Our family always spent the winter in St Petersburg, so we were at Khakovsky Palace when the tsar was forced to abdicate.'

Nikolai's voice cracked with emotion. He paused for a moment before continuing. 'It was a terrible time — fighting in the streets, strikes, violent uprisings against the aristocracy. Many aristocrats were murdered just going about their business. One of my friends was killed when he was caught up in a riot on his way home from school. We all wondered if we would be next.'

Violet shivered despite the warm summer sunshine. She couldn't imagine what it would be like to live in fear for your life.

'Things only became worse when the Bolsheviks seized control in October that year.' Nikolai huffed. 'Mamma heard from our estate manager that our *dacha* — our hunting lodge in the south — had been burned to the ground and all the cattle and livestock seized by the peasants. Then in March 1918 the Bolsheviks signed a treaty with the Germans and my father returned home wounded.'

They reached the rug and Nikolai stopped, his agitation evident.

Violet touched his arm. 'You don't need to tell me if it's too painful.'

'Yes, it is painful,' Nikolai confided, 'but I haven't spoken to anyone about the civil war since it happened. Somehow now it feels like a release to finally share my story with someone who wasn't there.'

'I know what you mean,' Violet said, thinking of her own family history. She hoped that Nikolai would keep talking. She found the insight into his former life fascinating.

The two began to walk along another of the sun-dappled gravel paths bordered with crimson roses and shady trees. Romeo trotted beside them.

Nikolai glanced at Violet. 'All the servants left. There was no money and little food — just mouldy bread. Mamma had sold some of our heirlooms on the black market to buy the bread, despite my father forbidding it. He thought the trouble would blow over in a few months, but the violence went from bad to worse — people were being executed every day.

'Then of course the tsar and his family were murdered, but still my father refused to leave. He said it was our duty to stand by Russia in her time of need.' Nikolai shook his head in exasperation.

'So what changed your mind?' Violet asked.

'One night in October 1918, a gang of armed men broke in,' Nikolai answered, his voice hardening. 'They ransacked the palace, looking for jewels and food, and used the portraits of our ancestors as target practice. My father tried to stop them. Of course, he was shot and died in my mother's arms. The gang just laughed and busied themselves with dragging away sacks of family treasures, leaving us to our grief.'

A lump rose in Violet's throat. 'How very dreadful, Nikolai.'

'Mamma was like a lioness, protecting her cubs,' Nikolai continued, speaking quickly, as though rushing to get the story out. 'She refused to stay and let her children be killed too.

'She implemented a plan at once, which made us think that she must have been scheming for months. Mamma had hidden a stash of her jewels in an old teddy bear in the nursery. There were diamonds, emeralds, pearls and rubies, all set in necklaces, bracelets, earrings and tiaras.

Most precious of all was the famous Khakovsky sapphire ring, which was given to my mother by Tsarina Alexandra as a wedding gift.

'My mother and sisters worked all night to sew the jewels into the hems of their petticoats and my waist-coat. Mamma had old clothes and shawls stockpiled in the servants' quarters, and we disguised ourselves as peasants, with dirt smudged on our faces so no-one would look too closely at us.

'We crept out before dawn, taking nothing but the ragged clothes we wore, the hidden jewels, some of Mamma's favourite photographs sewn into the lining of my coat, a bag with oddments of food and the book of fairytales that I lent you. We trudged to the railway station through the snow, keeping to the shadows. When the train finally came, there was a stampede to get on. People climbed onto the roof and hung from the doors. It was total chaos.'

Nikolai stopped walking and turned to Violet. 'You have to understand that we had no identification papers or travel documents, so if we were questioned we would have been arrested or shot. It was a terrible risk, but we fought our way onto the train.'

Violet nodded, her heart thumping as she imagined the scene. They turned and strolled back towards the rug and picnic basket.

'The train was so crowded that it was impossible to sit down, but it turned out to be a blessing because the guards couldn't get through to check our papers,' Nikolai continued. 'It took nine days to get to the south, a journey of about a thousand miles. We ran out of food, and when I jumped off the train at a station to try to buy some,

I couldn't get back on. Mamma and the girls had to pull me in through the broken window. Twice we had to bribe our way through, using diamonds from Mamma's tiara.

'Later we learned that the next train south after ours had been attacked by Bolsheviks and everyone on board was shot. We were so lucky.'

Romeo sensed Nikolai's tension and nuzzled against his leg. Nikolai fondled the dog's ears as he talked. 'The last part of our journey was made on foot, sleeping in barns and haysheds. When we finally arrived at Yalta in the Crimea, our feet were blistered and bloody. There was a large population of Russian royals and aristocrats — many who'd been there since the beginning of the revolution — so we sheltered there for the winter. We had no passports, no visas, but in the spring of 1919 we bribed our way onto a leaky fishing boat across the Black Sea to Constantinople.

'It was a bitter sight to sail away from the shores of our homeland, not knowing if we'd ever see Russia again. We stayed in Constantinople for several weeks, sleeping on the stone floor of a monastery, hoping that the anti-communist White Army would overthrow the Bolsheviks and we could return home. Finally, we applied for travel visas for France and arrived in Paris in late summer. There was a strong community of Russian émigrés there, and we stayed for two years with the help of friends, studying at school and finding work wherever we could.'

'That's when you became a chauffeur,' said Violet. 'And your sisters worked with Coco Chanel.'

'Yes, but at last we realised we didn't want to stay in Paris. There were so many émigrés living there, clinging to the old ways, their bags packed, waiting for the chance to go home. Then, as time went on, more and more Russian refugees arrived and it was harder for them all to find work. So we sold some jewels, moved to London and, finally, here we are.'

Violet felt emotionally drained by Nikolai's story of escape and survival. 'Yes, here we are, Count Khakovsky.'

Nikolai frowned. 'I'm not Count Khakovsky anymore. We left all that behind when we left Paris. Please don't tell your father. In fact, I think we should change our name to something more English. It's not safe to be a Russian aristocrat — even here on the other side of the world.'

20

The Russian Club

On Monday evening, Nikolai parked outside a small church hall in Fitzroy. A full moon was rising in the east, bathing the bluestone building in its silvery light. From inside the hall, Violet could hear shouts of laughter and a babble of voices. Nikolai opened the rear door of the car for Violet and Imogen to alight. Violet was wearing her new green-and-silver evening dress that had been delivered by Nikolai that afternoon. She felt very glamorous as she swept into the hall.

About thirty people of all ages, from young children to the elderly, crowded the room. A group of tall men stood in a corner, drinking vodka and sharing jokes, shouting with laughter. Nikolai's mother, Countess Khakovska, was holding court in another corner surrounded by several regal-looking women, sitting with spines ramrod straight and gossiping as they sipped their tea. Other groups were playing chess or cards, while a group of women set up the supper table with a bubbling samovar and platters of food.

The room itself was a typical church hall, with a battered old piano and a dusty stage, but it had been transformed into something far more exotic. On the wall hung a red banner with the double-headed eagle of the Russian Imperial coat of arms. Beside it was a formal photograph of the Romanov family — the girls in long white dresses and Alexei in a sailor suit. The supper table was covered in a colourful gypsy cloth, decorated with bunches of vibrant flowers and dozens of candles. In the far corner was a shrine bedecked with flowers, lamps and a collection of religious icons.

Katya and Tatiana came over to welcome them.

'I love my new dress,' said Violet. She suddenly felt shy, realising that the Russian girls were actually countesses. Should she call them by their titles, or treat them as she always had?

Katya beamed with pride. 'It looks gorgeous on you.'

'Come and say hello to Mamma, then take a seat over here with us,' Tatiana said. 'We all enjoy our evenings gathering together.'

Violet and Imogen chatted to Nikolai's mother for a few minutes. Violet noticed that Countess Khakovska was wearing a stunning pearl necklace, a diamond bracelet and a huge sapphire ring on her finger. The sapphire glittered and sparkled in the candlelight. This must be the famous Khakovsky Sapphire — the wedding present from the tsarina. Violet wondered how she could ever have imagined that Nikolai's mother was a humble seamstress.

The girls withdrew and sat on some folding chairs near the stage.

'So everyone here fled Russia after the revolution?' Violet asked, looking around with fascination.

'Yes, most of them fled east on the Trans-Siberian Railway to Manchuria in northern China, and then came by ship to Australia,' Tatiana explained.

'That young lady over there is a ballet dancer, Olga Lopokova, who used to perform with the Imperial Russian Ballet,' Katya continued. 'She is talking to Tamara Belinskaya, who was a prima donna singer at the Mariinsky Theatre in St Petersburg. She might sing for us later.'

'We thought they might be willing to perform at your ball,' Anastacia added.

The two women were dressed in shabby clothes that had been neatly patched and mended, but they carried themselves with grace and confidence, as though they were on a stage, playing a part.

'Over there is the Petschenko family,' said Tatiana, indicating an older couple with two daughters aged in their twenties. The parents looked rather sad and out of place. 'The father was a general in the White Army, and his family were imprisoned by the Bolsheviks and treated very badly.'

'Both their sons were executed,' Anastacia added, 'but the mother and daughters escaped and were reunited with the general in Manchuria. The family arrived in Australia just a few weeks ago with literally nothing but the clothes on their backs and their *balaikas*.'

'What are *balaikas*?' asked Violet.

'Traditional three-stringed musical instruments that look something like a guitar but have triangular bodies,' Katya explained. 'The daughters are very talented musicians, but they're working as cleaners at one of the local schools.'

Anastacia glanced at three broad-shouldered young men who were laughing and joking together. They all wore loose-fitting shirts with their trousers tucked into high boots.

'And those three — Aleksandr, Stepan and Ivan — are Cossack officers who came here via Shanghai. They fought with the White Army until the bitter end. If we're lucky, they'll have a few vodkas and give us an impromptu display of Cossack dancing,' Anastacia said. 'They said the Russian émigrés in Shanghai are literally starving, so they were lucky to get on a ship to Australia. They work as labourers now.'

A dark-haired man with round glasses and a clipped beard was playing chess in the corner against a taller man with a military moustache. They both looked very serious. Tatiana indicated the shorter man. 'Dr Davidoff is an academic from Moscow University. They say he and his wife keep their bags always packed, certain that news will come through that the Red Army has been defeated and they can go home.'

Violet looked around in wonder. So many stories of escape and courage. So many stories of lives and loves left behind.

Nikolai arrived, having changed out of his chauffeur's uniform and into a suit, and began chatting with a number of acquaintances. Violet thought he looked very handsome in everyday clothes.

'The band is just about to start,' said Nikolai. 'I've asked Madame Belinskaya if she'll sing for our guests.'

A group of players was setting up instruments on the

stage. The two Petschenka sisters had their *balaikas*. One young man was playing an accordion, while another was tuning a particularly large *balaika* that looked almost like a double bass.

The music, when they began to play, was slow and melancholy, but the tempo gradually increased until it was lively and impossibly fast. It made Violet think of gypsies dancing around a fire in a ring of caravans, like a scene in a film she had seen last year.

After several melodies, Madame Belinskaya sang a number of gypsy folk songs, her voice strong and clear. She curtseyed, acknowledging the enthusiastic applause.

Imogen leaned over towards Nikolai. 'She's marvellous. Do you think we could convince her to sing at the ball?'

'I can almost guarantee it,' Nikolai agreed with a smile. 'She hasn't performed to a decent audience since she fled St Petersburg.'

Aleksandr, Stepan and Ivan performed an energetic Cossack dance, kicking up their feet and squatting down on their haunches, arms crossed. Violet cheered and clapped along with the rest of the crowd.

Supper was served while the musicians took a break. The women had all brought various dishes to share. Everyone took a plate, piled it with whatever took their fancy, and ate it where they could — sitting or standing. The table was laden with bowls of creamy potato salad and a dish with tangy tomato, cucumber, onion and dill. There were beef dumplings, golden pastries and stuffed cabbage leaves, slices of black rye bread, pickled cucumbers and onions, and delicately spiced oval meatballs. Everything was served with huge dollops of sour cream.

Violet wasn't sure if she would like the food — it all looked so foreign to her — but she bravely took a few spoonfuls, along with a tiny taste of sour cream.

'You have to try the *pelmeni* and the *pirozhki*,' Anastacia insisted, offering her a platter of steamed dumplings and another of flaky baked pastries. 'They are absolutely mouth-watering.'

Katya leaned over with another plate. 'My favourites are the *katleti* — pork meatballs — made by our very own Anastacia. But you need more sour cream than that.'

'Don't let the girls bully you,' Nikolai cautioned. 'You don't have to eat anything.'

'You're just saying that so there's more for you,' teased Anastacia.

Nikolai pretended to be shocked. 'Never.'

Violet obediently took some of each. The girls were right — they were delicious.

After supper, the band began playing dance tunes. People of all ages paired up and danced the waltz and foxtrot. Violet and Imogen took it in turns to dance with the three Cossacks. Then an unfamiliar, lively tune began.

'A *mazurka*,' Katya explained. 'It's my favourite music because it's so bold and fast.'

Violet and Imogen stood back to watch as the younger dancers took their positions, bowing and curtseying to their partners. This dance was energetic, with lots of gliding steps, stamping, heel clicks and side-hops. Violet enjoyed watching the partners spin and twirl, skirts and coat-tails flying. Nikolai danced with graceful Madame Lopokova, then Madame Petschenka, while his sisters danced with the cheerful Cossacks, who stomped and shouted with glee.

At the end of the second dance, Nikolai came over to Violet. 'They're about to start another *mazurka*,' he explained. 'Would you care to dance?'

'I don't know how,' Violet admitted.

'I can teach you,' Nikolai offered. 'It's actually quite simple because the dancers are supposed to improvise. We can try it over to the side so we don't get in anyone's way.'

Violet smiled. 'Then I'd be delighted.'

While they waited for the music to start, Nikolai explained some of the steps: 'It's originally a Polish folk dance, which they say was inspired by the beauty and power of horses galloping across the steppes. The dancers must be strong, spirited, graceful and swift. So we take hands and gallop sideways left with a heel click — one, two, three, four steps. Now to the right — one, two, three, four steps.'

Nikolai talked her through the circling dance movements, stamping his feet and swinging her in his arms. Then Nikolai went down on one knee and Violet danced around him. It took a couple of practices to memorise the steps, but the joyful energy of the dance filled Violet with exhilaration.

She was feeling flushed and breathless as Nikolai led her back to his sisters. Violet glanced around the room. Everyone was laughing, joking, singing, dancing, chatting and enjoying their food. Violet felt as though she had been transported to another world, another age. *This is the feeling we want to create with our Russian Ball,* thought Violet, *not the stiff, grand formality of the Imperial balls, but the wild exuberance of this gathering.*

21

Theodore's Proposition

The next morning, Violet, Imogen, Edie and Audrey were drinking tea on the northern terrace, seated on green wicker chairs at a round wicker table overlooking the croquet lawn. A fairy wren, with its iridescent blue markings, flitted back and forth above their heads.

The garden was golden in the sunshine, the beds bursting with late spring flowers in shades of mauve, blue, pink and white. Romeo was chasing his own shadow around the lawn, and Juliet was washing her paw on the top step, pretending not to notice the birds.

The four girls were having a progress meeting to discuss the Russian Ball. Edie and Imogen had updated them on delivery of the invitations, advertising and ticket sales.

Afterwards, Violet explained her ideas for the decorations and entertainment. The others listened, making suggestions and asking questions where necessary. Lastly, she showed the sketches she had drawn for the costumes and sets.

Audrey placed her teacup into its saucer. 'I must say that you've done a splendid job, Violet. These drawings are marvellous — and I love the idea of the *mazurka* dance and the gypsy songs. It will make the whole event far more remarkable than your run-of-the-mill charity ball.'

Saunders came out through the French doors, carrying a silver salver. There were a number of envelopes on the tray with a bone-handled letter opener.

'Mr Theodore Ramsay has called to see you, Miss Hamilton,' Saunders announced. 'Shall I tell him that you are otherwise engaged?'

'No need, Saunders,' Imogen replied. 'Please show him in and ask Mrs Darling to send another pot of tea.'

'Very good, Miss Hamilton,' said Saunders.

Audrey pulled on her gloves. 'I think we've covered everything for now. We'll leave you to see Mr Ramsay.'

Everyone rose to their feet to say their farewells. Imogen quickly checked her hair.

Saunders offered the salver to Violet. 'Two letters for you in the post today, Miss Violet.'

Violet felt her heart pound with excitement as she took the envelopes and the letter opener. A quick glance at the back of each revealed that they were from two of the newspapers where she had sent her article. Her hands were trembling so much that she had trouble slitting the envelope.

But good manners meant that she could not read her

mail until she had said goodbye to Audrey and Edie, and exchanged pleasantries with Theodore Ramsay. Sally arrived with the fresh pot of tea, and Imogen and Violet resumed their seats.

Theodore was shown in and stood at the edge of the terrace, looking out at the garden. Violet took the opportunity to peek at her letters while Theodore and Imogen exchanged news. The first letter was a disappointment: the editor of the paper with the biggest circulation in Melbourne regretted that he would not publish her article, but he wished her good luck with her future writing. Violet quickly pulled out the second letter, feeling hopeful, but this one was worse. The editor's secretary had sent a short form letter, saying that her submission could not be accepted. Two out of the three newspapers had said no. All that work for nothing.

'Are you quite well, Violet?' Imogen asked quietly. 'You look rather pale.'

Violet pulled herself together, hiding the letters in her lap. 'No, it's nothing. Could I have another cup of tea please?'

'So have you had a pleasant morning?' Theodore asked, taking a seat as Imogen poured the tea.

'Yes, we've been planning the Russian Ball,' replied Imogen. 'We've sold nearly half our tickets, so we've almost covered our costs. If we sell the remaining tickets, we'll make a tidy sum for the Russian Relief Fund.'

Theodore took a sip of tea. 'Well then, I suppose it doesn't matter whether you get any more people, so long as you've covered your costs. It will be a jolly evening, I'm sure. A bit of fun for you girls.'

Violet bristled — Theodore always seemed to irritate her. Romeo barked under the table. The dog apparently didn't like Theodore either.

'Not just fun,' Imogen corrected him. 'We do hope to make nearly two hundred pounds. The Russian Relief Fund says that every pound will save a child's life.'

Theodore put his hand in his breast pocket and pulled out a cheque book. 'Well, in that case, I'd better buy my ticket. Will twenty pounds cover it?'

Imogen's eyes widened. 'The tickets are twelve shillings six pence . . .'

Theodore wrote out the cheque, signed it with a flourishing hand and presented it to Imogen. 'And the rest is a donation to your ball fund — I am assured it will be a huge success.'

'That's kind of you,' Violet said.

Theodore turned to face Imogen. 'Now, I was wondering if I might be able to have a private word with you?'

Imogen glanced at Violet in alarm, laughing nervously. 'I'm . . . I'm sure we can talk in front of Violet.'

'There's no impropriety,' Theodore assured her. 'I have already spoken with your father at the factory this morning, and I have his approval to speak with you.'

Imogen looked to Violet in mute appeal.

Violet paused for a moment, then gathered up the letters from her lap and pushed back her chair. 'I'll just work on my scrapbook in the morning room. Call me if you need me, Immy.'

Romeo stalked after her, clearly ignoring the interloper.

The morning room had French doors leading onto the terrace. Violet sat at the round table and began laying out her mementoes — the invitation to the Russian Ball, photographs she had taken around Riversleigh and in Richmond, cinema tickets, the drawings she had kept of Katya's, swatches from her new dresses, her own sketches.

Violet wasn't exactly eavesdropping, but Theodore's booming voice carried easily through the open doors: 'My dear Imogen, would you do me the honour of becoming my wife?'

Violet put down the gluepot. *Theodore to marry Imogen?*

'It's beautiful but . . . I'm not —' Imogen began before Theodore interrupted.

'I know you're only seventeen, but I think we'll make a good match. Our fathers are already business associates, so it makes sense to align the companies more closely. And now that your father has no sons, he assures me that if we marry you will inherit the house and half the assets.'

'But it's —' Imogen's voice quavered.

'Mother thinks we should be married at Scots Church next spring, after your eighteenth birthday, then we can have the wedding reception here at Riversleigh,' Theodore continued. 'You don't have your own mother to help you, so Mother said not to worry — she'll make all the arrangements to ensure it's the wedding of the year. Then we can travel to Europe for six months for our honeymoon.'

'I don't . . .' Imogen tried to respond but sounded dazed.

'Of course it's a lot for you to take in, Imogen dear,' Theodore soothed. 'I imagine you are feeling rather overwhelmed, but you needn't — I'll take care of everything for you.'

'Daddy knows you're asking me to marry you?' Imogen asked, her voice desperate now.

Violet felt sick with dread. She longed to rush in and stop this nonsense altogether, but it would be terribly bad manners to interfere in her sister's wedding proposal. She had to sit with gritted teeth and wait until Theodore left.

'He's absolutely delighted,' Theodore assured her. 'Oh, I nearly forgot . . . I have a little present to match the engagement ring, something for you to wear to your Russian Ball.'

There was a scraping sound as Theodore rose from his chair.

'It's stunning, Theodore, but I can't take it,' Imogen said. 'I need time to think.'

'Nonsense, Imogen,' Theodore insisted. 'You know I'm mad about you, and we'll make a very handsome couple — I won't take no for an answer. We'll be very happy. Now I'd better be getting on.'

Imogen made some indecipherable reply.

'Don't worry about calling for the butler; I can show myself out. And Mother says she'll telephone you to organise a little dinner to celebrate at our house and a visit to Madame Collette's to buy the clothes for your bridal trousseau. She said to tell you it's such a triumph for you to be engaged so early in your first season and not to worry — she'll send the announcement to the newspapers today.'

Theodore took himself back inside through the side corridor and was gone.

Violet jumped up and went out to Imogen, who was staring at the pearl ring on her finger. Around her throat was a long double strand of perfect, creamy pearls.

'Immy, are you all right?' Violet asked.

'I . . . Daddy wants me to marry Theodore . . .' Imogen looked utterly miserable.

Violet gave her a hug. 'You can't marry Theodore. You love Tommy.'

Imogen burst into tears. 'But what's the *right* thing to do?' She twisted the ring on her finger. 'I don't know. I just don't know.'

Violet handed her a handkerchief. 'The *right* thing to do is to return Theodore's ring and tell him that you can't get engaged until you are sure,' she insisted. 'You know that's what Mamma would tell you if she was here.'

'But Mamma's not here, is she?' Imogen retorted. 'She left us. And Daddy hates Tommy because he's poor and Catholic, and he approves of Theodore because he's rich and Anglican and they're in business together.'

'But it's about who *you* love.'

Imogen wiped her eyes and sat up tall. 'Girls like us are supposed to marry wealthy, respectable men. I can't let everyone down. I can't let Daddy down.'

Violet shook Imogen by the shoulder. 'You can't spend the rest of your life with someone you don't love — you'd be miserable. And if Dad truly loves you, he can't want you to have a miserable life.'

22

The Riot

Imogen slept in late on Saturday morning and Mr Hamilton was at his usual golf game, so Violet breakfasted alone. Saunders brought in the freshly ironed newspaper and the post on a silver salver.

'A letter for you, Miss Violet,' said Saunders. Violet took the envelope and letter opener from the salver. She felt nervous, certain it was a rejection from the third newspaper editor, Mr Gibson.

'I hope you don't mind my asking, but I was wondering if Miss Imogen was quite well?' asked Saunders, looking concerned. 'She seemed very pale last night.'

Violet knew perfectly well that the servants must know about the marriage proposals from both Tommy and Theodore. It was impossible to keep secrets in a household full of staff. 'It's kind of you to ask, Saunders. Imogen's still sleeping, and I hope she'll feel better soon.'

'Very good, Miss Violet.' Saunders placed the newspaper

on the table. 'Please let me or Mrs Darling know if there is anything at all we can do to help either of you.'

Violet felt comforted by his concern. 'We do appreciate it, Saunders.' When Saunders withdrew, Violet finally opened the letter and read it.

Friday, 8 December 1922
Dear Miss Hamilton,
I acknowledge receipt of your letter, dated 1 December 1922, and the article you submitted on the slums of Richmond. I would be interested in publishing your article but would request that you provide a wide selection of photographs to illustrate it. I look forward to your response at your earliest convenience.
Yours Truly,
Edward Gibson

He's going to publish my article, Violet thought, hugging the letter to her chest. *My article will be published in one of Melbourne's top newspapers.* Violet was so excited that she decided to go at once on an expedition to Richmond to take more photographs.

She set off walking, camera case over her shoulder, towards Hawthorn Bridge. She stopped in the middle of the bridge and looked down at the green-brown Yarra River, flowing fast below her. Its swirling eddies refracted the reflections of weeping willows and majestic gums. To her right were the spacious estates and hilly parklands of wealthy Hawthorn, with their elms, oaks and pines. To her left was the dilapidated, flat Richmond slums.

A tram rattled past across the bridge, filled with workers on their way home for Saturday lunch. Violet jumped and swung around as it rang its bell. She took a deep breath and set off, crossing to the other side of the bridge. Once again, the energy felt quite different as soon as she crossed the river, moving from quiet gentility to working-class bustle. She felt brave and daring to be walking on her own among the crowds. She hated to think what her father would say — nothing good, she was certain about that!

Violet pulled her camera from its case and slung the strap around her neck. As she walked up Bridge Road, past the tram sheds, she heard a commotion from one of the side streets. For a moment she thought about turning back and heading home, but curiosity enticed her and she turned down River Street towards the clamour.

On the river side of the road were a number of large factories with smokestacks, surrounded by smaller sheds. One of these sheds had Ramsay's Tannery painted in large letters on the wall. *This must be Theodore's family business, which supplies Dad with his leather*, thought Violet.

Gathered outside the tannery was a large group of men, who were yelling and catcalling, but the mood of the crowd seemed festive rather than angry. Violet took a photograph of the men and stood back watching. Suddenly, she recognised a young boy in an oversized flat cap, standing on the edge of the throng. It was Sally's brother Frank. She strolled towards him.

'Hello, Frank,' called Violet. 'What's going on?'

Frank's face was alive with excitement at the novelty of the situation. 'We've gone on strike, Miss Hamilton.

The bosses say they want the workers to take a pay cut to increase profits. But we won't put up with that.'

'That doesn't seem fair,' Violet agreed.

'They're not good bosses here, not like at some of the other factories,' confided Frank. 'They don't care about their workers.'

'You mean Mr Ramsay and his son?'

'Yeah. We call the son Lord Muck, because he comes in wearing his film-star clothes, swans around for a few minutes givin' orders with his nose wrinkled up from the smell, then drives off in his fancy Bentley.'

Violet laughed at the perfect description of Theodore. 'So are you enjoying working here, despite Lord Muck?' she asked.

'I don't mind it,' said Frank. 'The other boys are fun, an' I'm even gettin' used to the smell.'

Violet chatted to Frank for a few minutes about his job. It sounded like dirty, dangerous work.

'One of the blokes lost his fingers on an unhairing machine last week,' Frank said. 'They gave him some money, but he'll find it hard to get another job.'

'That's dreadful,' replied Violet. 'That poor man . . .'

'It happens quite a lot,' Frank said. 'But don't worry, I'm careful.'

Violet noticed a gang of young men swaggering down the road towards the mob, dressed in flashy suits with fedora hats. They had an air of bravado that seemed threatening. She snapped a quick photograph of them.

'Look, there's Mr Ramsay's car now,' Frank said as Theodore's familiar red Bentley zoomed down the road and swerved to a stop near the gate that led into the tannery yard, close to where Violet and Frank were standing. Violet hoped Theodore wouldn't notice her, but he seemed focused on the striking workers.

'What's going on here?' boomed Theodore. 'Any man who goes on strike can expect the sack.'

'That's 'im — Lord Muck and his fancy car,' yelled one of the workers.

'Boo! Down with the bosses!'

'Bloated capitalist! Fat on the sweat and blood of 'is workers.'

Violet noticed that the group of swaggering young men had joined the mob of workers and seemed to be stirring up antagonism. There was shouting and fist-shaking as the workers surged forward. Theodore soon disappeared, lost in the crowd.

'The crowd's getting worked up,' Violet said nervously. 'Perhaps we should go. I think there might be trouble.'

'Those lads who came down don't work at Ramsay's,' said Frank. 'They're larrikins from a local push. The gang entertain themselves by getting into fights, smashing shop windows and streetlights, and scaring old ladies.'

One of the gang members wrenched some timber palings off a nearby fence, snapped them in half and handed them out as weapons. Violet could feel the aggression ripple through the air, sharp as an unsheathed knife.

'I'm going to fetch the police,' Violet decided, feeling anxious for Theodore.

Frank pulled back on her arm. 'No. They'll only cause trouble.'

Violet could never be sure what happened next, but one moment she and Frank were standing apart from the crowd and the next it had surged forward, surrounding her and Frank. Fear gripped Violet's throat.

'Miss Violet,' cried a familiar voice. 'Violet, over here.' She wrenched her head around — it was Nikolai, his face pale and anxious. He was wearing a tweed suit and flat cap instead of his chauffeur's uniform. Violet almost didn't recognise him. He struggled through the jostling bodies towards her.

'We need to get out of here,' he warned. 'This crowd is turning nasty.'

'How did you find me?' asked Violet. 'How did you know where I was?'

Nikolai pulled her forward by the arm, through the angry crowd. Violet grabbed Frank's hand and towed him along, too.

'I was catching a tram home for my half day off,' Nikolai yelled over the hubbub. 'I saw you crossing Hawthorn Bridge and was worried. It's not safe to be walking around the streets of Richmond on your own. So I jumped off the tram and came looking for you.'

'Thank you, Nikolai. I'm grateful,' Violet shouted. 'We were watching from afar, taking some photographs, then suddenly we were swallowed by the crowd.'

Nikolai glanced over his shoulder, scanning the throng, wiping his brow with the back of his hand. 'I've seen mobs like this in Russia. They can turn murderous in moments. We need to get away *fast*.'

The angry mob surged forward, dragging the three of them along with it.

Violet saw a Richmond Push lad pull a glass jar filled with liquid out of his bag. He threw it against the tannery wall, where it smashed, releasing a strong stench of petrol. Violet automatically lifted her camera from around her neck, roughly aimed it and shot off a photograph of the lad tossing another jar towards the factory.

A second push member did the same. Then he flicked a burning match towards the spilled petrol. The effect was instantaneous. Flames roared into the air. The blaze licked the windows, the door, the walls, racing out of control as it took hold of the aged timber soaked with the grease from thousands of animal hides. A shout of excitement went up from the mob.

'Fire,' yelled one of the workers. 'Fire!'

The crowd pulled away from the flames. Violet knew she had to capture the chaotic scene on film. She lifted her camera and shot photos, regardless of keeping steady or framing shots. There simply wasn't time, and Nikolai was dragging her back.

Violet realised that she'd finished her first film and quickly wound it back into its cartridge. She opened the camera and slipped the finished one into her pocket, quickly winding on the second film and snapping the back of the camera closed.

'Come on, Violet,' Nikolai hissed. 'It's not safe. We've got to go.'

Violet shot off another couple of photographs of the men jostling, illuminated from behind by the flames, and the Richmond Push lads attacking Theodore's car with their fence palings, smashing the headlights and denting the duco.

'Look, she 'as a camera!' warned one of the push lads.

Violet heard him and turned to flee. Nikolai put his arm around her protectively, hugging her to his side.

'They've seen you, miss,' warned Frank. 'You'd better get out of here. They won't like you takin' photos.'

Nikolai and Frank started to run, but a big, burly man barrelled into Violet. He clutched her arm, leering in her face, his breath rank with alcohol and raw onion.

'Not so fast, young lady,' he sneered. 'I'll take that.' The ruffian snatched the camera from Violet's hands and flicked the back latch.

'Leave her alone,' Nikolai demanded, battling back through the throng to help her.

'No,' cried Violet. 'You'll ruin the film.'

The man grabbed the film and ripped it out of its cartridge, exposing it to the light. He thrust the camera back in Violet's hands, and she clutched it desperately.

'That's the idea,' he slurred. 'Can't have you takin' incriminatin' photos now, can we? You're lucky I don't smash your camera as well. Better get home where it's safe, missy.'

Violet planned to do exactly that when a loud whistle sounded from up on the main road. A group of policemen came running, their truncheons at the ready. The crowd dispersed and men began running for the side streets and laneways. A man burst between Violet and Nikolai, breaking them apart. Violet felt her hat get knocked off and saw it trampled underfoot.

'It's the coppers,' yelled one of the protesters. 'Get out of here!'

'Come on,' Nikolai urged. 'He's right.'

Running through the throng was like battling a huge wave. Violet and Frank were swept one way. Nikolai was swept another. Truncheon blows fell down on shoulders, heads and backs. Violet saw Nikolai sink under a rain of blows.

'Nikolai!' she screamed.

'Go home!' Nikolai yelled, his arms flailing to protect himself.

Frank was pushed over by the surge. He fell flat on his belly and cried out in agony as dozens of tramping boots stomped over him.

Violet leaned down and dragged Frank, who was whimpering in pain, to his feet. She searched in vain for Nikolai, but he had been swept away. Violet didn't know what to do. She searched the crowd fruitlessly. A block away, men were being arrested and shoved into the back of two police cars.

Frank retched and groaned, holding his side. His face was white as a cloud. Violet decided that her priority was to lead him to safety.

'Come on, Frank,' Violet whispered. 'Let's get you back to Sally.'

'I feel crook,' Frank gasped. 'My ribs feel like they're on fire.'

Violet murmured reassuringly, 'It'll be all right.' She carefully pulled his arm around her shoulder and set off, carrying his weight.

Violet looked back at the top of the road, scanning the crowd. Men were fighting and fleeing, but there was no still sign of Nikolai. Violet bit the inside of her cheek. There was nothing she could do. At last, she turned away. Nikolai had survived Bolshevik soldiers, starvation and violence. She was sure he would be all right.

It was a long walk back to Riversleigh with Frank

injured. Finally, they sneaked around the back of the house and came in through the servants' entrance. Violet sat Frank down in the servants' dining room and searched for Sally.

Sally and Mrs Darling were in the kitchen mending linen. They leapt to their feet as soon as they realised it was Violet.

'Miss Violet, whatever's the matter?' asked Mrs Darling. 'You look terrible.'

Violet forced a smile to reassure her. 'Sally, please don't panic, but your brother Frank is here — he's been injured in a strike riot.'

'Cripes,' said Sally, her face crumpling. 'How bad is he?'

Mrs Darling raced into the dining room to check over Frank and wash his wounds. 'I think the poor lad has broken some ribs,' she said. 'He'd better stay here the night. Sally, you can make him a bed in the men's quarters.'

Mrs Darling and Sally fussed over Frank, strapping him up and feeding him a hearty meal. Violet left them to it and crept up the back servants' stairs. At the top, she opened the door and peeked through to make sure the way was clear, then she crept into the bathroom to wash and change.

When she was respectable again, Violet ran down the main stairs and went through to the kitchen to see if Nikolai had returned. Mrs Darling shook her head. 'He was expected back by now, but he hasn't arrived yet. I hope he's not much later or Mr Saunders will be very unhappy with him.'

'Could you please let me know when Nikolai gets back?' Violet asked, trying to sound calm. 'I just need to check something with him urgently.'

23

The Tower

Hawthorn, modern day

In the morning, Marli woke to find that Dad had gone to work. Under the muesli packet on the kitchen bench was a note:

Good morning, myshka. Sorry, I had to go early — there's been a problem at work. Tell you all about it this afternoon. Love, Dad ☺ xx

Marli felt her anger at her father well up again — even after their argument nothing had changed. She picked up the note, crumpled it into a ball and threw it at the garbage bin. It missed and rolled on the floor.

She had to get out.

Marli grabbed the peacock hatbox, the camera and backpack, and cycled as fast as she could to Riversleigh. This time she went in through the double blue door, through the garage and into the service courtyard. She unlocked the back door, then went through the kitchen and its green baize door, into the front of the house and up the stairs.

It felt eerie being in the empty house by herself, without Luca to give her courage.

Using the large iron key, she unlocked the door to the tower and went inside. Somehow she felt calmer in the small forgotten tower room, with its relics of a bygone age.

Using a wad of tissues from her bag, she dusted off the desk and began laying out all the items from the hatbox — the scrapbook, the Kodak Brownie camera, the key and various loose photographs.

Marli sat at the desk and closed her eyes, fiddling with the engraved silver bangle on her wrist. She thought about everything that had been going on in her life for the last few weeks. Her anger with her mother for going away without her, and now with her father for working so much. Her fascination with the Hamilton family and their secrets. Her friendship with Luca and his family. The discovery of Riversleigh and her determination to ensure that it wasn't destroyed. Learning about her great-grandmother Violet and life in the 1920s.

Didi had said that Violet had been disinherited by her father, and Nonno had said that Violet's mother had died of grief, leaving her daughters behind. Despite her own dramas with her parents, she couldn't imagine having her family torn apart by war and grief.

Marli thought about her mother and realised that she had always put Marli first. The realisation made her feel warm and happy, but also guilty. *I've been punishing Mum for not getting my own way.*

Marli pulled out her phone and hit her mum's number. The phone rang for a few moments before she answered, sounding groggy but panicked. 'Hello, Marli? Is everything all right? Has something happened?'

Marli suddenly realised that it was ten o'clock in the morning in Melbourne, which meant it was eleven o'clock at night in Cambridge. 'Oh, Mum. I'm so sorry to wake you. Yes, everything's all right. I just wanted to talk to you.'

'Are you okay, darling? You sound upset.'

'Yeah, well, it's Dad. He's working all the time. He's hardly ever home.'

There was silence for a moment on the other end of the line. 'That's not like Alex,' Mum said. 'He was so excited about you coming down. He said he'd planned lots of fun things to do with you. I would never have sent you to Melbourne if I'd thought he'd neglect you.'

Mum sounded upset, and it made Marli feel even more guilty. Things weren't as bad as Marli had made them sound.

'He's had some dramas at work,' Marli explained. 'He seems super stressed.'

'I'll ring Aunty Julia now and organise for you to go there until I sort something out,' Mum decided. 'I can get you on a plane this afternoon, right after I speak with your father. Julia can meet you at the airport in Brisbane.'

Marli thought about the offer. *Do I really want to leave Melbourne? Do I want to leave Didi and Dad and Luca? What will happen to Riversleigh if I leave?* She remembered

Didi talking about Violet: 'She would always fight for what she believed in.'

'Thanks, Mum,' replied Marli, 'but I'll be okay. I don't want to leave Melbourne just yet. I just need to talk to Dad. And I've been having fun most of the time.'

'Are you sure?' Mum asked. 'I don't like to think of you being on your own all the time.'

'I haven't been alone all the time,' Marli admitted. 'I've been hanging out with a nice boy called Luca, who lives nearby, watching movies, exploring the area, doing stuff. He has a big Italian family, and they've had me for dinner a couple of times. And I've been visiting Didi, which has been lovely. Dad and I are going out tonight, so I'm fine, really.'

Mum sighed. 'Well, if you're sure. But if you change your mind, let me know and I'll have it all organised in a jiffy.'

'Thanks, Mum. Thanks for everything.'

Marli could almost feel Mum's smile down the line. 'I love you, darling.'

'Love you, Mum.'

'You know, Marli, your dad loves you very much too. He would never want to do anything to upset you.'

Marli felt her pent-up emotion release. 'I know.'

'And I'm so glad you're enjoying Melbourne.' Mum paused. 'I was waiting to see how you found it before I mentioned an idea to you. We've been offered an opportunity that could mean moving down there.'

'Moving? What do you mean?' Marli asked.

'I've been offered a huge promotion, but I turned it down. It was as a senior lecturer at Melbourne University, starting next year.'

'Wow,' Marli exclaimed. A multitude of emotions raced through her brain — pride in her mum, anxiety about the possibility of change, curiosity. 'That's great, but why did you turn it down?'

'I didn't think you'd want to leave your friends, your school, your life in Brisbane. And when I arranged for you to visit Alex, you made such fuss. I realised I was right, so I turned the job down. But they rang me again today with an even better offer. They've given me a few days to decide. So I thought I'd give you the chance to think about it too, and we can make the decision together.'

They chatted for a few minutes about Mum's research and her lectures at Cambridge, then they said goodbye. Marli felt relieved. She was glad she wasn't arguing with her mum any more. And the thought of moving to Melbourne wasn't as terrifying as it might have been a few weeks ago.

Marli began to think about Riversleigh as she flipped through the scrapbook, examining the photographs and invitations. How could she convince Dad that Riversleigh should be saved and restored, not knocked over for soulless flats?

When she reached the back of the scrapbook, there was a pocket on the inside of the black leather cover. It bulged. Something was hidden in there. Marli slipped her fingers inside the flap and drew it out.

Marli spent the rest of the day with Luca. They played soccer on the freshly mown back lawn and had a picnic lunch on the back terrace. At about five o'clock, a text message pinged on her phone. It was from Dad.

Hi sweetie. I'm home. Where are you? See you soon. Love Dad xx

Marli quickly texted a reply: Coming

'Gotta go,' Marli said to Luca. 'See you tomorrow.'

She cycled back to Dad's apartment in Richmond, parked the bike in the garage and caught the lift upstairs.

Dad was sitting at the kitchen bench, looking exhausted. But as soon as Marli walked in his face brightened and he sat up. 'How was your day, myshka?'

Marli told him about playing soccer with Luca and having a picnic, but she didn't mention where. She looked at Dad and noticed that the tense lines around his face had softened while he listened to her stories.

'How about your day, Dad?' Marli asked. 'Looks like it might have been tough.'

Dad looked surprised for a moment and then sighed. 'I didn't want to bother you with it, myshka, but it's been a horror.'

'Tell me about it. I'd like to know.'

'There was an accident at the building site today,' Dad began. 'One of our workers was seriously injured, and it should never have happened. The proper safety regulations weren't being observed.'

Dad gathered his thoughts, before continuing. 'Because the project costs have blown out and we've had to cut costs, our suppliers have switched to poorer quality materials — not the ones I originally specified — and the contractors have been forced to take shortcuts.

'I have spoken to my boss, Tony, several times about my concerns, but he refuses to listen. I was worried something like this would happen. Now a man with three young children is seriously hurt — it's a miracle he wasn't killed. I watched him fall and couldn't do anything to stop it.'

Dad shook his head, as though trying to clear the image of the accident from his mind. 'I had a huge argument with Tony today, and he gave me my marching orders.'

'Marching orders?' Marli asked, feeling anxious.

Dad stroked her cheek to reassure her. 'The company has been cutting costs for a few months; several people have been retrenched. Now I'm the latest one.'

Marli felt sick. She had been so angry and horrible to Dad, and the whole time he was trying to save her from worrying about his problems.

'I'm so sorry, Dad,' Marli said. 'You should have told me things were so serious.'

'I didn't want to spoil your holiday. But I realise I've ruined it anyway — your mum rang me today and was furious that I've been neglecting you. I really wanted to spend lots of time with you, but Tony insisted that everyone work extra-long hours to get the project done. Anyone who didn't would lose their job.'

'That's awful,' said Marli. 'So you've been working six or seven days a week for months, and now you've lost your job anyway?'

Dad shrugged. 'I'll get paid a lump sum of money, but it will be hard to get another job in the construction industry now. So many companies are finding it tough.' He gave

Marli a hug. 'That's why I think we should build apartments at Riversleigh. It would be a way to make money. I could use my payout to fund the building and borrow the balance from the bank, using the land as security. It would be the perfect solution to all our problems.'

Marli felt her heart sink. The future of Riversleigh was looking grimmer than ever.

24

Police Visit

Riversleigh, Saturday, 9 December 1922

Violet walked through into the morning room where Imogen was stretched out on the chaise longue, reading a book. She glanced up as Violet walked in.

'How was your day?' Imogen asked, putting her book aside. Violet noticed that her sister was still wearing Theodore's pearl ring and shivered. Imogen looked concerned. 'Is everything quite all right? You look very pale.'

Violet nodded. 'I just have a little headache, that's all. I went for a walk to try to clear it.'

Romeo was lying in the sun, but he came over to Violet and pushed his nose into her hand. He licked her fingers to comfort her.

Mr Hamilton popped his head around the door. 'Here you are. I've just heard the most dreadful news from Mr Ramsay.'

Imogen sat up. 'What was it?'

Violet stayed silent. She had a terrible feeling she knew what her father was going to say.

'He telephoned to say there's been a riot down at his tannery,' Mr Hamilton explained, wandering into the room. 'The workers went on strike this morning and set fire to the factory. The firefighters are still trying to subdue the flames, but they've lost over two thousand hides. The damage is already estimated to be more than thirty thousand pounds.'

'How dreadful for the Ramsays,' Imogen replied. 'But won't it be insured?'

Mr Hamilton shook his head. 'The insurance won't go anywhere near covering the damage, but the police are investigating. Theodore says they've arrested a Russian Bolshevik. They're questioning him now.'

Violet's mouth went dry and she felt as though she might be sick. *A Russian has been arrested. Could it possibly be Nikolai?*

'What would a Russian be doing setting fire to the tannery?' Imogen asked.

'The young foreigner was sneaking around the factory, where he had no reason to be, inciting violence,' Mr Hamilton continued. 'You know that Bolshevik Zuzenko, who was deported a few weeks ago? Apparently he had been encouraging workers to revolt against their bosses and burn down their places of employment. The police say Zuzenko left a ring of Bolshevik spies behind, and it seems they've finally arrested one.'

There couldn't have been any other Russians near the tannery, Violet thought. *It must be Nikolai. They think he's a spy.*

'Why would the strikers do such a thing?' asked Imogen. 'Surely Ramsay's staff will be worse off if they can't work at all? It doesn't make any sense.'

'Revolutionaries don't necessarily have much sense,' Mr Hamilton retorted. 'But fortunately they've caught this one. Zuzenko had to be deported due to lack of evidence, but after burning down the tannery, this Russian fellow will rot in prison for the rest of his days.'

Violet swayed. This couldn't he happening.

'Are you sure you're all right, Violet?' Imogen asked again. 'You don't look very well.'

'I have a bad migraine,' Violet croaked. 'I'll get a powder from Mrs Darling.'

Her head was spinning with all the information. She needed to find out if it was Nikolai who'd been arrested. If she told her father, he would know that she'd disobeyed his orders by going into the slums. He'd be absolutely furious — and if it wasn't Nikolai, she'd be in trouble for nothing. Maybe it actually was a Bolshevik spy who'd instigated the riot. The newspapers were always full of stories about the Bolshevik threat. Nikolai was probably home with his family, drinking tea, and he'd laugh at Violet's concern that he'd been arrested.

Violet had just convinced herself that she'd let her imagination run away with her when the doorbell rang. Saunders went to answer it. There was a low murmur of voices.

Saunders came to the morning room door. 'Excuse me, sir, but there's a Senior Sergeant Brooks and a Constable Lawson here to see you. They are investigating a fire in Richmond today and believe you may be able to help them with their inquiries about a person of interest.'

Mr Hamilton huffed as he rose to his feet. 'As if I know anything about the fire at Ramsay's!'

'Shall I send them away, sir?' asked Saunders. 'Only they do seem very insistent.'

'Very well,' Mr Hamilton said. 'Show them into the library. I'll come at once.' He turned to the girls. 'Don't worry yourselves about this arson attack. The police will sort it out very quickly.'

'Poor Theodore,' Imogen said. 'What a terrible business.'

'Is he all right?' Violet asked her father. 'Was he hurt?'

'Theodore was there when it happened. He was set on by some of the workers and beaten, his car vandalised, but the police arrived just in time.'

Violet shuddered at the memory. 'That's a relief. I'll just go and get that headache powder.'

'Do you want me to ring for Mrs Darling?' Imogen asked as Violet stumbled to the door.

Violet shook her head. 'I'll just go to my room and lie down for a while.'

But Violet didn't go to her room. She took the key to the locked tower room and went inside, fastening the door behind her. She sat on the floor with her head on her knees. Somehow she felt closer to her mother in the tower, in the rooms that had been her very own.

'What should I do, Mamma?' Violet cried. 'Why did you leave us when we still need you?'

Violet took a deep breath to steady herself. There was no response from her mother, so she'd have to figure it out for herself. Why had the police come to question her father? The only possible reason could be that they had interrogated Nikolai and he had told them he was a chauffeur employed at Riversleigh.

But would the police believe Nikolai, that he wasn't a Bolshevik? How could she prove his innocence?

Violet could almost sense her mother's presence. Her mother had always said she must stand up for what she believed in. That she must do the right thing, no matter what the consequences. And the right thing to do was stand up for her friend. But how? Would her word be enough?

Suddenly she remembered the roll of film she had taken at the riot — the photos of the smartly dressed push lads who had handed out fence palings as weapons and thrown the bottle bombs. Surely that might be evidence.

Violet jumped to her feet and raced back into her bedroom. The roll of film had been in the pocket of the skirt — now soiled and crushed — that she had flung onto the chair in her bedroom. But her skirt and shirt were gone. Sally must have been tidying up. Violet checked her wardrobe and chest of drawers, but the clothes weren't there. Sally must have taken them to the laundry.

Violet ran down the servants' stairs to the laundry, taking the narrow steps two at a time.

'Sally!' she called urgently. 'Sally, where's my skirt?'

Sally stuck her head around the kitchen door. 'It's being washed, miss. Lizzy is boiling up all the darks.'

The film will be ruined if it is boiled, Violet thought. She bolted past the scullery to the laundry. A young maid was standing at the copper kettle filled with scalding water, sleeves rolled to the elbows, her face flushed from the steam. The maid was stirring clothes with a long stick.

'Lizzy?' asked Violet with a sinking heart. 'Have you washed my skirt yet?'

'Yes, miss.' She used her stick to fish out the navy blue skirt. 'Shouldn't I have? Only Sally said it was very dirty and she thought you might need to wear it tomorrow.'

Violet thought she was going to cry. 'No, that's all right, Lizzy. You did the right thing. It's just that I left something precious in the pocket.'

Lizzy looked worried. 'I always check the pockets of everythin', miss, like Mrs Darling taught me, but I didn't find nothin' precious, only a film.' Lizzy gestured with her elbow towards the windowsill. 'I put it up there.'

Violet nearly wept, this time with relief. 'Oh, thank you, Lizzy. That's exactly what I was looking for. You've been a marvellous help.' Violet snatched the film and went through the kitchen towards the front of the house. She paused outside the library. Inside, she could hear low voices.

'You know what these foreign wogs are like,' said one of the policemen. 'Slippery as mud — can't believe a word he says. But we'll pin it on him.'

'So what do you know about this Khakovsky character?' asked the other. 'How long have you employed him as a chauffeur?'

'Not long at all, I'm afraid,' Mr Hamilton replied. 'He's only been here a few weeks. I would never have employed him if I'd known he was a Bolshevik. He just seemed a decent young chap who was hard on his luck. And he had excellent references from his last employer, Countess Orlova in Paris.'

'The letter was probably forged,' the policeman suggested. 'He'd be operating under an alias. The local communists seem highly organised and are committed to sparking a revolution here in Australia.'

'I hope word of this doesn't get out,' Mr Hamilton said. 'The last thing I need is a scandal about us harbouring a Bolshevik spy.'

Violet took a deep breath, finding her courage and holding it tightly. She knocked on the door and ventured inside the library. Her father was sitting at his desk; the two policemen in navy blue uniforms were sitting opposite, their black leather caps on their laps.

'Dad?' said Violet.

'Not now,' her father replied. 'I'm rather busy with the police right now. There's been an unfortunate allegation about our chauffeur, Khakovsky. Looks like he was a bad egg.'

'That's why I'm here, Dad. Nikolai isn't a Bolshevik at all. He wasn't involved in setting fire to Ramsay's tannery, but I know who was.'

Mr Hamilton looked puzzled and turned to the policemen. 'Sorry, you must excuse my daughter Violet. She is rather soft-hearted when it comes to our servants. Violet, this doesn't concern you and you couldn't possibly know anything about Khakovsky or the fire.'

'But you see, Dad, I do,' Violet pleaded. 'I know because I was there at Ramsay's when the fire started.'

'That's impossible,' Mr Hamilton blustered, his face flushed with anger. 'What on earth do you mean?'

Violet turned to the policemen. 'Nikolai isn't a Bolshevik. He's a White Russian, an anti-communist. Actually, he's Count Nikolai Petrovich Khakovsky. And his mother is Countess Khakovska. His family escaped from the revolution after his father was murdered by Bolsheviks.'

The constable was writing copious notes. Senior Sergeant Brooks turned to Violet, his face impassive. 'This is all very romantic, but it doesn't explain what Khakovsky was doing participating in a strike by the workers of one of your father's associates. The only possible explanation is that he was there to cause trouble. We have questioned the young man and he refuses to give a satisfactory explanation other than that he was just passing by on his half day off. Which is highly unlikely.'

Violet shook her head. 'He wasn't just passing by.'

'See?' her father replied. 'It's all a bit fishy to me.'

'The truth is that Nikolai was there because he was worried about me,' Violet said in a small voice. 'I went to Richmond to take photographs of the slums. I wrote an article for a newspaper, and the editor said he would publish it if I could send him some more photographs of slum life to illustrate the story.'

'You went to the slums with Khakovsky, and he let you get caught up in a *riot*?' Mr Hamilton thundered. 'Then he's fired without a reference. He should be flogged.'

'No, Dad,' said Violet. 'I went there by myself. Nikolai just happened to be on a tram going home to visit his family, who live in Richmond. He saw me walking across Hawthorn Bridge and thought I wouldn't be safe.'

Mr Hamilton glared at her. 'Of course you weren't safe.'

Violet ploughed on. 'So he jumped off the tram at the next stop and came looking for me. By the time he found me, the crowd had turned nasty and I was swept up in the riot. Nikolai came in to help get me out, even though he must have been terrified. He's seen violent riots in St Petersburg — riots where people were murdered.'

The constable kept scribbling down notes.

Senior Sergeant Brooks looked sceptical. 'You claim he followed you down to the tannery? That he wouldn't have been there if it wasn't for you?'

'Yes, exactly,' Violet replied. 'He may have even saved my life. We couldn't get out of the crowd. Nikolai came in and dragged us out.'

'We?' asked the policeman. 'I thought you went on your own?'

'I did,' Violet said, 'but I met Frank Burke there. He's the thirteen-year-old brother of our maid Sally. He works for Ramsay's tannery and was there with the strikers. Frank saw what happened — you can ask him. He's sleeping in the men's quarters. He was badly hurt in the riot and may have broken some ribs, but he'll support my story.'

'He's just a kid.' The policeman waved his notebook dismissively. 'Mr Theodore Ramsay said that the violence was initiated by a group of troublemakers who weren't workers at the tannery. He said the Russian Khakovsky was one of them, and Mr Ramsay is determined to press charges against him.'

Violet felt a wave of fury rise up in her chest. 'Theodore Ramsay couldn't have seen Nikolai do anything, because I saw Theodore get pulled down into the crowd before Nikolai even arrived. But I did see two larrikins from the Richmond Push throw jars of petrol at the tannery then flick a match.'

'How do you know they were from the Richmond Push?' Senior Sergeant Brooks interrupted.

'Frank told me — and I took some photographs.' Violet held out her fist and opened it, revealing the film cartridge on her palm.

'You took photographs of the arsonists?' Mr Hamilton demanded. 'If they'd seen you, they might have killed you.'

Violet decided she wouldn't tell her father that she had indeed been caught by one of the gang members. He'd had enough of a shock for one day.

'If you develop the photographs, you'll be able to identify the real arsonists,' Violet insisted. 'Nikolai Khakovsky is innocent.'

The senior sergeant continued to ask the same questions over and over, in slightly different ways. Or he'd deliberately misunderstand her, as if trying to catch her out. Then he pulled Frank out of bed and asked him a lot of questions about the riot. The boy looked frightened but answered the questions truthfully, once Violet had nodded her head to show him he should.

It was much later when Frank was finally allowed to go back to bed. The policemen said good night and took the film away to have it developed at the police laboratory.

Mr Hamilton sat at his desk, slumped back in his chair, hand over his eyes, looking defeated.

'Dad, I'm sorry I went into the slums by myself when you told me not to,' Violet said. 'I know now how reckless that was.'

Mr Hamilton looked up at her. 'Violet, I don't know why you are so rebellious. So determined to flout authority. Why can't you just behave decorously, like a well-bred young lady? I'm trying to do my best to raise you, but it's so hard to know what to do when . . . when you don't have a mother.'

Violet came around next to her father and hugged him around the shoulders. 'Dad, I don't mean to upset you. I'm only trying to do what I think is right.'

'I am determined to ensure that you girls are securely settled,' said Mr Hamilton. 'All I want is to see you both married into respectable families, to take your rightful place among Melbourne society, with no hint of scandal. Otherwise, everything I've striven for will be in vain.'

'The world's changing, Dad,' said Violet. 'The old rules don't matter so much to us anymore.'

Mr Hamilton shook his head despondently. 'I refuse to accept that, Violet. The old rules still matter to me. It's the duty of people like us to uphold the old rules — or society will fall utterly apart.'

25

The Russian Ball

Two days later, Violet was in the summerhouse, making the final touches to her painting of the twelve princesses dancing at the secret ball, when she saw a police car pull up at the front gate. A moment later the gate swung open and Nikolai limped up the driveway.

Violet dropped her paintbrush and flew up the driveway to meet him, her heart thumping. Romeo galloped close behind and gambolled around Nikolai, barking with excitement.

Nikolai was looking pale and haggard, as though he hadn't slept for days. He had a purple bruise on his cheek and multiple grazes. His clothes were torn and grubby. Violet had to resist the urge to hug him.

'Are you all right?' Violet asked, gazing at him anxiously. 'You're hurt.'

Nikolai grinned as he patted Romeo on the head. 'Not badly, it's nothing. What about you?'

Violet felt a rush of relief and happiness. She had been so worried about him — she hadn't been able to think of anything else since he'd been arrested. 'Thank goodness. Yes, I'm fine too, but poor Frank was injured. He was trampled on by the mob and broke a few ribs, but he seems to be on the mend now. I'm trying to convince him to go back to school.'

'I hope he listens to you.'

Violet looked around. They were standing near the marble fountain. A blue-and-brown fairy wren and his mate were splashing in one of its pools. The morning sun shone down, bathing the gardens in golden light. It felt so idyllic that the events of the last few days seemed like an impossible nightmare.

Images of the riot came back to Violet — Frank being trampled, Nikolai disappearing into the flailing mob, the factory burning out of control. She felt desperately guilty about putting him in danger.

'I'm so sorry, Nikolai,' Violet began. She put out her hand and touched his arm. 'I should never have gone near Ramsay's Tannery that day. You wouldn't have been arrested or hurt by the mob if you hadn't come to help me. I've been so worried about you.'

Nikolai raised his eyebrows. 'I'm glad someone has been worried. Here I was, thinking that no-one would even notice that a lowly Russian chauffeur was missing.'

Violet laughed. 'All of us have been feeling anxious. Sally says that even Monsieur Dufour has been asking after you!'

Nikolai suddenly looked vulnerable. 'I wasn't sure if your father would want me to come back . . . after being arrested.'

'Your job here is safe for as long as you want it,' Violet said. 'The police rang Dad to tell him you were innocent, and I told Dad I'd never speak to him again if he didn't let you come back.'

Nikolai smiled at her fierce expression. 'Then I am doubly grateful. Constable Lawson told me that you defended me, and that it was your photographs that identified the men who started the fire. Apparently they had been trying to find evidence against one of them for some time.'

'I'm so pleased,' Violet replied. 'Do you think you'll feel well enough to come along to our Russian Ball on Thursday? It would be such a shame if you missed it after all the help you've given us.' Suddenly Violet felt like all her excitement about the ball would evaporate completely if Nikolai didn't go.

'I wouldn't miss it for the world,' said Nikolai with a grin. 'I'm looking forward to dancing a *mazurka* or two.'

Violet was so exhilarated that she felt like dancing right there in the carriageway. 'Perfect — but you must be exhausted. We should go in.'

They walked together up the drive, then Nikolai veered left to go to the service entrance and Violet continued straight towards the front door.

The next three days were a flurry of organisation. Nikolai's sisters were making costumes late into the night. Audrey, Imogen and Violet were finishing the decorations. The ball had been fully subscribed, and more than 600 people were expected to attend, raising nearly two hundred pounds for the Russian Relief Fund.

Everyone who Violet had met at the Russian Club had agreed to attend, and Katya had helped Violet plan a list of entertainment. Two days before the ball, Imogen's dress was delivered, but Violet's was not yet finished. She worried that Katya had set them an almost impossible task to have it finished in time.

At last the day of the ball arrived. The girls spent all day with the committee at Town Hall, directing florists and delivery men. Finally, everything was done.

In the late afternoon, Sally came into the drawing room where Violet and Imogen were sitting, reading over their checklist. Sally was carrying a large oval box tied with turquoise ribbon.

'A delivery has just arrived for you, miss,' Sally explained, her face alive with curiosity.

The box was printed with an intricate design of peacocks, ferns and flowers in turquoise, cobalt blue, emerald green and lavender. Printed on a plaque on the side was a curlicue script that read: *Maison de Mademoiselle Perrot.*

'They used my peacock design for the hatbox,' Violet said with delight.

'Of course they did, Violet,' replied Imogen. 'It's gorgeous.'

Violet felt a thrill of pride to see her drawing printed as professional packaging. 'It must be my new dress,' she said, unknotting the satin ribbon. 'It's finally arrived. I was certain it wouldn't come in time.'

Inside the box, wrapped in tissue paper, was the seafoam-green ball gown with its intricate peacock detailing. Violet pulled it out and held it up to look at it. 'Oh, Imogen, isn't it divine?'

'Yes, but there's more,' said Imogen, looking inside the box.

Violet drew out the other items one by one — a cream velvet clutch bag, long cream satin gloves and a sumptuous cream velvet evening wrap.

'Goodness,' Violet cried. 'They've made all the accessories to go with it.'

Imogen stroked the thick silk velvet wrap. 'It's utterly gorgeous.'

'There's a note,' Violet said, pulling out the folded notepaper.

Dear Miss Hamilton,
Thank you for everything you have done for our family. You have made us feel truly welcome in a strange new land. May you feel like a Russian princess tonight.
Yours truly,
Katya Khakovska

Sally gathered up the items in the hatbox. 'I'll take the clothing upstairs and hang it all up, miss, so it's ready for you when you get dressed.'

'Lovely, Sally,' Violet said. 'I'm coming up now to bathe. It's time to get ready.'

After Violet had towelled off, dressed in her underwear and done her make-up, she sat in front of the mirror, wrapped in her colourful silk kimono. Sally stood behind her, arranging her copper hair into sleek finger waves with the curling iron.

'How is your mother?' Violet asked.

'We all went to see Ma in hospital on the weekend. She's allowed visitors now, an' looks so much better, though the doctor says she must stay in bed for weeks.'

'I'm so glad.' Violet dabbed on some perfume. 'I was wondering, Sally, do you like your job here?'

'Yes, miss, of course,' Sally replied, looking flustered. 'Why do you ask? Have I done somethin' wrong?'

'No, you're not in trouble,' Violet assured her. 'I just wondered if this is what you truly want to do?'

Sally put down the curling iron and thought for a moment. 'This is a good job for a girl like me, from Richmond. I get paid so I can help my family, an' I get food an' board. One day I'll work my way up to head housemaid, an' then a proper lady's maid. One day I might even be a housekeeper like Mrs Darling, or become a cook, or perhaps find a sweetheart and get married.'

'Was there ever anything else you thought you'd like to do?' asked Violet. 'It's hard work being a housemaid.'

Sally pushed a diamante slide into Violet's hair to help the finger waves hold.

'It's hard work being anythin' when you've left school at twelve,' Sally replied. 'When I was fourteen an' started workin' here, it was the first time I'd had a full belly, the first time I'd slept in a bed by myself, and the first time I'd had boots an' clothes that weren't patched an' hand-me-down. It seemed like fair luxury to me.'

Sally went to the wardrobe and took out the seafoam-green peacock gown. Violet stood up so Sally could drop the gown over her head and fasten the multitude of tiny buttons running up the back.

'I see what you mean,' Violet continued. 'Have you ever wished that you'd stayed on at school?'

Sally shrugged. 'I couldn't say, miss. There wasn't any choice — I had to leave school to help Ma with the cleanin' and washin'. But Nikolai has lent me some books to read, and he's helped me with my learnin'. He said I'm quick with the lessons, although mostly I'm too tired to do much at the end of the day.'

Violet felt uncomfortable when she thought of Nikolai teaching Sally. Surely she wasn't jealous that Nikolai was kind enough to help Sally with her lessons. 'I have lots of books you could borrow if you want to read them.'

Sally put the cream satin dancing shoes down for Violet to slip her feet into and buckled up the straps.

'That's kind, miss,' Sally replied. 'Nikolai's very clever. He says one day, when he's saved enough money, he's going to university to study law.'

'Nikolai would be capable of anything he turned his mind to,' Violet replied warmly. *So that explains the textbooks.*

Violet pulled on her long satin gloves and Sally did up the tiny buttons. Then Sally passed her the cream velvet wrap and bag. She was ready.

Violet descended the stairs, the silk skirt billowing around her ankles in contrast to the stiffly beaded straight bodice. She walked past the locked tower door and imagined her mother watching from the doorway with loving approval.

A glimpse in the gilt-framed hall mirror confirmed that she looked as elegant as she felt.

Mr Hamilton was in the drawing room, dressed to go to his club. Imogen was already down, looking bewitching in her midnight-blue ball gown, complete with the double strand of pearls and her engagement ring worn over her long black evening gloves.

'Are you sure you won't come with us, Daddy?' Imogen asked.

'Thank you, girls, but my ball days are over,' Mr Hamilton replied. 'I'm sure it will be a brilliant success.'

Nikolai drove them to the Hawthorn Town Hall, with its soaring sandstone clock tower. He would drop Mr Hamilton to his club in Collins Street before returning. The girls jumped from the car and hurried up the steps to the ornamented portico. The inside foyer had been transformed into a garden with potted palm trees, foliage twisted around pillars and urns filled with masses of hot-pink and orange roses.

Violet's Russian fairytale paintings, inspired by Nikolai's book, had been hung on the walls. One showed twelve princesses dancing at the secret ball until their shoes fell apart. Another showed the witch Baba Yaga being outwitted by Vasilisa the Beautiful. She had also painted Father Frost in a snowy forest, a shaggy grey wolf and the flaming Firebird soaring through the sky.

The girls passed through into the vast green-and-cream ballroom, admiring its polished parquet floor, elaborate chandeliers and arched mirrors. Trailing green foliage was draped from the galleries and stage. Banks of potted palms lined the corners, along with urns overflowing with creamy roses. Violet felt a thrill of excitement to see how her concepts and sketches had turned into a beautiful reality. Her first real ball would be a night to remember forever.

Audrey, Dodo and Edie were directing some workmen who were putting the finishing touches to the floral arrangements. Audrey had booked one of the best jazz orchestras in Melbourne, and they were setting up on stage.

'There you are, *cheries*,' called Audrey. 'You both look adorable.'

'Thank you,' Violet replied. 'So do you.'

'Violet, I do love your dress,' said Edie. 'Wherever did you get it?'

Violet twirled, making the skirt billow. 'From a new designer called Maison de Mademoiselle Perrot,' she said airily. 'They made Imogen's dress too. It was so hard to choose — they have such gorgeous gowns.'

Edie and Dodo took a closer look at Imogen's dress.

'I must look them up. Could you give me the address tomorrow?' Edie asked.

'Of course,' Violet replied, lowering her voice. 'But only if you promise not to tell anyone. It is rather a secret find.'

Dodo immediately looked intrigued. 'Could you give me the details too, Violet? I promise not to tell anyone. I'm going to Sorrento for Christmas and I'll need a whole new wardrobe.'

'They are rather busy,' Imogen added. 'But perhaps if you mentioned that you are special friends of ours, they might be able to fit you in.'

Audrey waved her hand. 'I have a feeling that Mademoiselle Perrot will be the talk of the ball with you two as her celebrity models.'

Edie and Dodo went to wait in the foyer for the first guests to arrive, while the others examined the supper rooms.

Several smaller rooms were filled with dozens of round tables set with starched white tablecloths and napkins, glittering silver and crystal glasses. Each table had a centrepiece of golden candles and sweet-scented roses in blood red and snow white. At the far end of the main supper room, set on a table, was a massive ice sculpture inspired by the onion domes of Russian churches. It was surrounded with delicate pastries, fruit and petits fours.

'Doesn't the ice sculpture look wonderful?' Violet asked.

'All the decorations are marvellous, Vivi,' said Imogen. 'I just *knew* you'd do a brilliant job.'

'We're very much obliged to both of you,' said Audrey. 'We couldn't have done it without you. Tonight will be a huge success, I just know it. But now we'd better join the reception line to welcome our guests.'

A long queue of motor cars had pulled up at the steps of the Town Hall, dropping off guests. The men were dressed in white ties and tailcoats, the women in long ball gowns in a rainbow of jewelled colours. In the foyer, uniformed waiters took the guests' coats and top hats. Each lady wore a dance card on a string, with a small pencil attached, so she could write down the name of the gentleman to whom she was promised for each dance.

At 8.30 pm the orchestra began playing a Viennese waltz. Immediately the dance floor was filled with dozens of couples of all ages, swirling around the room. Other guests watched from the side and the galleries above. Violet's dance card was quickly filled, and she twirled and jazzed nonstop with a succession of amiable young men.

At ten o'clock, Madame Belinskaya took the stage

to perform a number of passionate gypsy songs to huge applause, followed by Madame Lopokova, who danced an exquisite ballet solo.

Aleksandr, Stepan and Ivan ran onto the stage dressed in baggy black trousers, black caps, white shirts, red sashes and swords. The three Cossacks performed the acrobatic *hopak* dance — leaping, twirling, sword-fighting and shouting with joy. The finale was their fast and furious display of high kicks from a squatting position, which had the audience cheering and clapping. This was followed by a *balaika* performance. Violet applauded harder than anyone, beaming with pride. The Russian entertainment had been an outstanding success.

The orchestra struck up the opening chords of the *mazurka*. Seven Russian couples promenaded out onto the ballroom floor. The men, including Stepan, Ivan and Aleksandr, wore white tie and tails, while the women, including Tatiana, Katya and Anastacia, wore vibrant evening gowns in cerise, orange, cobalt, cyclamen and raspberry with matching long satin gloves.

The crowd pressed back against the ballroom walls to give the dancers space.

Nikolai appeared from somewhere in the throng, now changed into a white tie, tailcoat and vest. He bowed low in front of Violet and extended his hand.

'May I have the pleasure of this dance?' he asked with a mischievous smile.

'But Nikolai . . . I can't dance the *mazurka* properly. I'll spoil it.'

'You'll spoil it if you *don't* dance. You know it looks better with eight couples.'

Violet glanced around, looking for a way to escape. 'But —'

'I dare you,' Nikolai challenged.

Violet finally relented, taking Nikolai's outstretched hand, and together they promenaded out onto the ballroom floor to join the others.

The dancers formed two circles of four couples each, bowing and curtseying to the partner on either side. Then the joyful dance began. Hand in hand, everyone galloped clockwise. With a lively clicking of heels and stamping of feet, they changed direction to counter-clockwise. The colourful skirts flounced and swirled. Nikolai guided Violet through the dance so that her steps were sure, even when she thought she'd forgotten what came next. Violet felt light and graceful as she floated in his arms.

Nikolai went down on one knee and Violet danced around him. Too soon, the music slowed and the partners bowed and curtseyed to signify the end of the performance. The audience clapped, then the orchestra swung straight into a popular foxtrot.

The audience surged into the middle of the ballroom. Violet moved to leave the dance floor, but Nikolai took her hand. 'Just one more?' he asked, and then whisked her away.

The male singer began to sing the familiar words to 'Angel Child'.

As they wove through the crowd, Violet glanced over Nikolai's shoulder and saw Imogen dancing with Tommy. Imogen threw her head back and laughed at something he'd said. The joy on her face was infectious.

Violet smiled up at Nikolai. 'I'm so very glad you came to Riversleigh.'

Nikolai looked serious as he thought for a moment. 'You know what, myshka? I'm very glad too. The old world and the old ways are dying. I think the new world and the new ways are filled with endless possibilities.'

Nikolai spun Violet around in a pirouette. The ballroom revolved around her in a golden glow of candles, chandeliers, roses and shimmering gowns. The singer crooned: 'Do you love me too?'

Violet laughed — who knew what joys and troubles the future might hold? Whatever else happened, she felt sure that her life would always be full of adventures. And Nikolai would hopefully be by her side through them all.

26

The Ballroom

Riversleigh, modern day

The sun beat down from a clear, blue sky. Lorikeets squabbled over the bottlebrush in the shrubbery. The fairy wren and his brown mate were building a dome-shaped nest of grass, threaded through with spider web, almost hidden by the undergrowth.

Marli and Luca were working in the gardens at the rear of Riversleigh. Luca was trimming the box hedge, wrestling it back into shape. Marli was weeding the stone urns along the western terrace, thinking about the dilemma swirling around in her head: Dad had lost his job and wanted to bulldoze the old house and build apartments.

The phone in her pocket rang, interrupting her reverie. Marli checked the screen. It was her friend Evie, calling from Brisbane. She answered the phone, walking down the path towards the river, away from Luca's noisy brush-cutter.

'Hi, Evie,' said Marli warmly.

'I haven't heard from you for a while, so I thought I'd give you a call,' Evie said.

'How's it going up there?' Marli asked. 'Have you been having a great time?'

Evie snorted. 'I wish! It's been deadly boring and stinking hot for the last few days. I don't feel like doing anything much but lying on the couch in the air-conditioning and watching TV.'

'How's Tess? Have you been to the beach?'

'Okay, I guess,' said Evie, sounding annoyed. 'We went to the beach last week, but we had a bit of a fight so she's been hanging with Ruby. They just walk around the mall all day.'

Marli stood on the shady bank of the Yarra River, a cooling breeze ruffling her hair. Down below, two rowers in a narrow skiff shot across the water, leaving ripples in their wake. From here, Richmond on the opposite bank was completely hidden by a grove of thick trees. Marli felt a long way from her old life.

'That's not much fun,' Marli said sympathetically. 'Maybe you should just give her a call?'

'What about you?' Evie asked, not sounding particularly interested. 'Are you still having an awful time with your dad?'

'No, it's been great, actually.' Marli thought for a moment. 'I told you about the boy I met, Luca. We've been having an awesome time exploring the old house and finding out about the family who lived here. And Dad and I are getting on much better now.'

'Oh,' said Evie. 'That's good.' There was another pause.

'Anyway, I better go. Charlie's coming over to watch a movie soon. I'll catch you later.'

'Bye, Evie. Say hi to the others for me.'

Marli put the phone in her pocket and walked back up the path towards Riversleigh. Evie's call made her see things differently. *Nothing much seems to have changed back home. I thought they'd all be having an amazing time, but Evie sounds bored and annoyed.*

She walked across the lawn towards the terrace. Luca finished trimming the hedge and turned off the brush-cutter. He wandered towards her and gazed out over the sunken rose garden, breathing in deeply.

'Did you fertilise the roses?' asked Luca, wrinkling his nose.

'Nope,' Marli replied, turning to check.

'Well, someone has tipped bags of cow manure around the rose garden. And if it's not you, then I'm guessing Nonno might have had something to do with it.'

'Mmmm.' Marli pushed her silver bangle up her arm. 'So then, was it you who planted the seedlings in the kitchen garden?'

Luca shook his head and laughed. 'Wasn't me. I suspect Nonno just couldn't help himself. He must have discovered the side door unlocked.'

Marli liked Luca's grandfather very much and didn't mind him discovering their secret. She felt sure that he would be an ally in their scheme to bring Riversleigh back to its former glory.

'Dad is taking Didi for a meeting with the lawyers today to sign the papers and pick up the keys,' Marli said, perching on a marble bench. 'He asked me if I wanted to go with them, but I said you and I had already made plans.'

'That's exciting,' Luca replied and sprawled beside her. 'Then I guess we won't officially be trespassers anymore.'

Marli frowned at him. 'But Dad has lost his job and plans to bulldoze the house and build apartments to make money — I wish I could change his mind somehow.'

Luca thought for a while. 'Perhaps you have to convince him that there are other ways to make money,' he suggested. 'Like restoring the house and running it as some kind of business.'

Marli mulled over this for a few moments. She thought about some of the beautiful historic houses she had stayed in when she was travelling in Ireland with her mum. Some were run as guesthouses, restaurants, conference centres and beautiful wedding venues. She and Mum had been to a gorgeous wedding for one of Mum's colleagues, which was held in a castle in the Connemara. Her mind started to buzz with possibilities.

'Riversleigh could be a beautiful guesthouse, or a wedding venue, or a tea house, or anything! But how can I convince Dad?'

She thought of the house the way she liked to imagine it in the old days — full of light and love and beauty. Not cursed and forgotten.

'I have an idea, Luca,' Marli said, her voice pitched high with excitement. 'Why don't we have a party to celebrate the house returning to the family? We could invite Dad and Didi, and your grandparents, and your family. All of us have a link to Riversleigh.'

Luca looked at Marli in confusion. 'What did you have in mind?'

'We'll have to work hard, but we have a few hours.' Marli began outlining her plan.

Just before they began, Marli texted her mother: Say yes to job, Mum. Let's move to Melbourne! ☺

The sun still shone warmly in the early evening. Marli waited out the front of the wrought-iron gates of Riversleigh. Beside her on the footpath was a calico bag, and inside the bag was the fragile peacock hatbox that held Violet's treasures. Marli swayed impatiently from foot to foot.

Dad and Didi were running late. Her muscles ached and she was tired, but it was a good tiredness. The day had been spent shopping, cleaning, moving furniture and scheming with Luca. They had taken Didi and Nonno partly into their confidence to help pull off the great surprise.

Now she was freshly showered and changed into her best summer dress. For once she wore her hair out long and wavy, gleaming copper and gold in the sunlight. She saw Dad parking his car on the roadway and ran forward to meet them.

'Hello, Dad, hello, Didi,' she cried as they climbed out of the car, giving them both a hug and a kiss.

'Hello, Marli-myshka,' Dad said. 'You're all dressed up. What's the occasion?'

Marli exchanged a complicit glance with Didi. He, like Dad, was wearing a dark lounge suit and tie from their meeting with the lawyers.

'I thought tonight should be a celebration,' Marli said. 'To celebrate getting the keys to our very own, long-lost, abandoned and possibly cursed mansion.'

Dad turned serious at the mention of a curse. 'We found out something very surprising about that today, but we'll tell you later. Perhaps we can go out for dinner after we've looked over the place?'

Marli laughed. 'We'll see.'

'I brought my toolkit,' Dad said, getting it out of the back of the car. 'Apparently the house is all boarded up and there's no electricity or running water. I brought a torch as well.'

The three walked up to the gate, with its stone-topped pillars and nameplate. Marli carried the peacock hatbox.

Dad flourished a big set of keys. 'Well, here goes.' He unlocked the padlock that fastened the chain around the metal barricade and dragged it away. Then, using another key, he removed the padlock on the tall wrought-iron gates.

Dad gestured to Didi. 'Perhaps you should have the honour?'

'Let's do it together,' Didi suggested.

The three of them pushed against the huge gate. It screeched in protest, the rusty hinges moving for the first time in a decade. They slipped through the opening and into the front garden of Riversleigh. Dad closed the gate behind them, stopping to gaze at the house, in all its faded grandeur.

'Come on,' urged Marli, taking them both by the hand. 'Come and explore Riversleigh. Look how beautiful it is.'

They climbed up the front steps and onto the colonnaded verandah. Dad frowned when he saw the graffiti scrawled on the front of the house and the timber hoarding prised away from the arched front door. 'It looks like vandals have been here. I hope they haven't caused too much damage.'

'Would you like to open the front door, Marli?' Didi asked. 'That seems apt.'

Marli unlocked the door and opened it wide, eager to be entering the house in the proper way for the first time. Didi and Dad chattered away, trying to guess what each room might have been used for originally.

'You can tell by the white marble mantelpiece that this was the drawing room,' Dad explained. 'The feminine rooms had pale colours, while the masculine rooms — the library, billiard and smoking rooms — had the black marble mantels.'

Marli was nearly bursting with impatience as they toured each room.

'Shall we go up?' Dad suggested, standing at the bottom of the grand cedar staircase.

'No,' Marli insisted, motioning down the hall. 'There are more rooms to see on this floor yet.'

'The ballroom must be here somewhere,' said Didi. 'My mother said that Dame Nellie Melba sang a concert here in 1915.'

Marli hurried to the rear of the house and flung open the ballroom door.

'What on earth?' asked Dad, staring around in amazement. 'How did you do this?'

The ballroom had been transformed. Not only had every surface been polished so that the crystal chandelier sparkled and the parquet floor gleamed, but Luca and

Marli had set up a party. They had rummaged through the garage for ornamental bric-a-brac and borrowed bits of furniture from Luca's family. Old chairs and milk crates with cushions had been set up in various groupings. A long table was set with candles in jam jars and bunches of fragrant roses arranged in old tins. The antique gramophone stood on a tea chest, its brass horn polished until it gleamed. A stack of old records had been placed alongside.

Eight sets of French doors were wide open to let the fresh air and sunshine flood in.

'So this is what the mysterious surprise was,' Didi chuckled.

'That's not all.' Marli smiled so wide that her cheeks ached. She led them out onto the western terrace, bathed in late afternoon sun.

While the garden at the front still looked overgrown, the back looked completely different. The lawns were mown, the hedges clipped and the garden beds weeded. It was far from perfect, but it gave an idea of what the gardens must once have been like with pale roses, blue agapanthus and mauve-pink hydrangeas blooming.

'You certainly have been busy,' said Didi. 'What a glorious afternoon to see it.'

'And our guests are arriving,' Marli announced, waving towards the southern wall. Luca led the procession, followed by Nonno and Nonna, Dani, Marc, Lia, Caterina and Siena, all carrying platters, bowls and baskets of food and calling out greetings.

'I hope you don't mind, Dad, but I used the money you gave me to buy party food for tonight,' said Marli. 'And Luca's Nonna helped us do some cooking.'

Dad laughed as he looked around in wonder. 'Young lady, I don't think that even comes close to explaining what you've been up to.'

Marli twisted her bangle. 'Well, you see, there is something else to celebrate. Mum's been offered an awesome job at Melbourne University, so we're moving down here to live.'

'Do you mean it?' begged Dad. 'That's incredible news!'

Dad and Didi both beamed with joy as Marli told them the details. Then she had to explain it all over again to Luca and his family.

All the food was laid out on the table. Marli and Luca had bought prosciutto, mortadella sausage, marinated olives, sun-dried tomatoes, roasted capsicum, creamy brie, fetta and loaves of bread from the Italian delicatessen to make huge antipasto platters. Nonna had made meatballs, her famous *pitticelle di zucchine*, and *arancini* balls made from rice and mozzarella cheese, which were still warm from the pan. Dani had made raspberry *tiramisu* in individual glasses to eat with a spoon, while Marc carried an esky filled with ice-cold drinks.

'What a feast!' Dad said.

Everyone helped themselves to drinks. Marli pulled the top off her orangeade and clinked bottles with Luca.

'*Salute*,' said Luca.

'*Salute*,' replied Marli. 'To new beginnings.' Everyone clinked drinks and chatted. Nonna passed around the platters of *pitticelle di zucchine* and cheesy *arancini* balls.

'You have to try the *pitticelle*, Dad — they're amazing,' Marli urged, helping herself to the fritters.

'And so are Nonna's *arancini* balls,' Luca added.

'Eat up, Luca *caro*,' said Nonna. 'My darling boy was pale and sick and far too thin. But now he looks well again.'

Marli realised Nonna was right. The sunshine and fresh air of Riversleigh gardens had put a rose in Luca's cheeks and a sparkle in his eyes.

Dani nodded. 'And he's so much nicer to be around. He's been like a grumpy bear for weeks!'

Luca hugged his mother. 'Sorry, Mum, but it was very boring being sick for so long. It's been much more fun since Marli arrived.'

Marli opened the peacock hatbox and spread some of the items from it out on the table.

'Luca and I have been researching the Hamilton family,' she explained to the others. 'We've found out the most amazing things.'

She showed Dad the scrapbook with the photographs, articles and mementoes, and told him some of the stories they had discovered.

'Violet was disinherited in 1928 when she insisted on marrying Nikolai as soon as she turned twenty-one,' Marli explained. 'It caused a huge scandal at the time because not only was he poor and Russian, he had been her father's chauffeur. Shock-horror!' Marli struck a dramatic pose, hand on forehead. 'But it all worked out well, though. Violet became a successful photographer while Nikolai Khakovsky changed his name to the more socially accept-able Nicholas Peterson and became one of Melbourne's top lawyers.'

Didi continued the story. 'Albert Hamilton was already devastated because Violet's older sister, Imogen, was doubly disgraced. She was engaged very young to one of her father's business associates, but she broke the engagement a few months later to marry for love. It was a "mixed" marriage, as they called it in those days, to an impoverished Catholic doctor called Tommy O'Byrne, who preferred treating poor slum-dwellers to making money from the rich. Albert refused to attend the wedding and didn't see her again for years.'

'Poor Imogen,' said Marli. 'But I bet she and Tommy were amazingly happy.'

'No-one would raise an eyebrow in this day and age,' said Dani. 'It seems strange to let a family be torn apart by something so trivial.'

Dad squeezed Marli's hand.

Luca pointed at the formal black-and-white photograph of the Riversleigh staff lined up outside the house. 'There's our great-grandfather Giuseppe and his cousin Alf, although when he became a gardener the butler changed Giuseppe's name to Joseph. He said no-one could be expected to pronounce it otherwise.'

Everyone laughed. Lia, Caterina and Siena crowded around to look, giggling and chattering.

Luca showed them one of the other servants in the photograph, a maid in a black dress with a prim white cap and apron. 'And that's Nonno's mother, Sally. She worked as a housemaid here until she married Giuseppe in the late 1920s. They eventually started a hugely successful *trattoria* restaurant in Lonsdale Street.'

Dad pored over the photographs with Dani and Marc. Marli passed around the meatballs.

'So why did Albert Hamilton give the house to the state

government?' Dad asked as he helped himself to more *pitticelle*.

'He lost all his money in a bad investment before Violet was married,' Marli explained. 'Albert tried to auction off Riversleigh and all its contents, but by 1929 Melbourne was in the grip of the Great Depression and no-one would buy it. So he offered the house to the government as a convalescent home for soldiers, in memory of his two sons who died in the First World War.'

Marli took a piece of bruschetta. Luca took over the story.

'Albert lived here for a while, stubbornly refusing to see his daughters,' he said. 'When Violet's son Michael — otherwise known as Didi — was born, she brought him to see his grandfather. Albert was sick, so Violet insisted on taking him home with her and looking after him. Eventually he was reconciled with Violet and Imogen.'

'There's one more surprise, Didi,' said Marli, giving her grandfather a hug. 'I found something hidden in the very back of the scrapbook.'

Marli opened the scrapbook to the back cover. There was a loose black-and-white photograph of a couple on their wedding day. It wasn't the usual stiff formal shot — this photograph was more natural with the couple arm in arm, gazing into each other's eyes with utter adoration. The bride had a large, dark gemstone on her ring finger.

'Violet and Nikolai,' said Didi, his voice heavy with emotion.

On the inside back cover of the scrapbook was a leather pocket for storing extra photos or papers. Marli opened the flap and fished around inside, pulling out something that she hid in her closed fist. She slowly unfurled her fingers to reveal an oval cornflower-blue sapphire ring, surrounded by sixteen diamonds set in rose gold.

'Oooh,' said Dani.

'It's Violet's missing engagement ring,' Marli explained. 'She must have hidden it there.'

Marli passed the sapphire to Didi, who held it up to the light with trembling fingers, the gemstones flashing brilliantly.

'The Khakovsky Sapphire,' said Didi, his voice lowered with reverence. 'The ring that my father, Nikolai, smuggled out of Russia, sewn into the hem of his waist-coat. I thought it was lost forever.'

Didi weighed the ring in his palm for a moment before slipping it onto Marli's finger. 'It's yours now – the ring given to my grandmother, Countess Khakovska, by Tsarina Alexandra as a wedding present. It's priceless.'

Marli felt a sting of tears. 'I'll treasure it always, Didi.'

Dad examined the ring closely. 'Simply stunning, and what a history!'

'Just like Riversleigh, Dad,' Marli said. 'Please promise me you won't bulldoze the house. With all your building contacts, you could do an amazing job restoring it back to its former glory, just like you used to do in Brisbane. We could run it as a guesthouse or a wedding venue . . . It's far too precious to destroy.'

Dad pulled a sheaf of papers out of his inside pocket. 'Actually, there is one more surprise, Marli. You know that Didi and I went to see the lawyers today to sign the paper-work for the handover of Riversleigh back to the Peterson family?'

Marli frowned. 'Yes?'

'Well, the house doesn't actually belong to Didi as we thought,' Dad continued. 'When Albert Hamilton was on his deathbed, he changed his will. The house had been signed away to the government for ninety years, so he couldn't leave it to his daughters.'

Marli's heart sunk with disappointment. 'Oh no. Who did Albert leave it to?'

Didi beamed at Marli. 'To you.'

'*Me?*' Marli shrieked. 'That's impossible!'

Dad laughed. 'Yes, well, technically he left it to Violet's eldest female descendant. Who is one delightful young lady called Amalia Violet Peterson.'

Marli was speechless.

'Wow! You're an heiress,' cried Luca. 'So I guess you'd better start behaving in a more ladylike fashion. No more climbing trees and breaking into abandoned houses for you.'

Marli put her hands on her hips and raised an eyebrow. 'Why ever not?' she demanded. 'I don't want to be ladylike. I'd much rather be a brave and an intrepid adventuress, just like Violet.'

She looked at her father beseechingly. 'Please don't knock my house down, Dad. I love it.'

Dad raised his hands in surrender and laughed. 'I wouldn't dare do that, myshka.' He gave Marli a hug. 'It will be hard work, but we can make it beautiful again, together.'

Fast Facts about 1920s Melbourne and Russia

- More than one million Russians fled Russia between 1917 and 1920, mostly via Turkey.
- Nikolai's hometown of St Petersburg has had several name changes over the years. In 1914 the name was changed to Petrograd, then in 1924 to Leningrad, then back to St Petersburg in 1991.
- Melbourne — often called 'Marvellous Melbourne' — was the capital of the Commonwealth of Australia from 1901 until 1927, when Canberra was built.
- The years after the First World War and before the Great Depression were ones of enormous change.

- Nearly sixty-two thousand Australian soldiers were killed during the war. Of these, about sixteen thousand were from Victoria (the youngest of whom was James Charles Martin of Hawthorn, who was only fourteen years and nine months old when he died at Gallipoli). In Australia, two thousand eight hundred sets of brothers died in the First World War. A further ten thousand Australians died of the Spanish influenza, including approximately four thousand Victorians.
- In the 1920s, Australia was still primarily a population of British descent, and migrants from non-British backgrounds were often treated with suspicion.
- The Australian Government placed an embargo on Russian immigration to Australia during the Russian Revolution and Civil War from 1917 to 1922. However, the prohibition was lifted once the White Army had been defeated by the Bolsheviks. Most of these White émigrés came to Australia via Siberia and Manchuria after the Red Army seized control of Vladivostok in 1922.
- On 31 August 1922, a Russian national, Alexander Zuzenko, was deported from Australia after being arrested in Melbourne as a Bolshevik spy. Zuzenko had travelled to Australia on a false Norwegian passport, via New Zealand, hoping to escape detection. Zuzenko believed that Australia in 1922 was ripe for a communist revolution. While in Australia, he helped establish the Communist Party in Melbourne and spoke at numerous gatherings, encouraging Melburnian workers to rebel against capitalism by burning down buildings, cutting telephone wires and shooting perceived enemies.

- There were many articles in the newspapers in late 1922, discussing the threat of Russian Bolshevik spies in Melbourne, including interviews with Madame Varvara Kossovskaia, a Russian prima donna and a former soldier in the White Army, who said her life had been threatened by a secret society of Russian Bolsheviks in Melbourne.
- Italians are the second-largest ethnic group in Melbourne after Anglo-Celtic Australians, with nearly half the Australians of Italian descent living in Melbourne. Italian migration to Australia increased markedly in the early 1920s, primarily with peasants from the northern regions escaping poverty and those opposed to the rise of fascism in Italy.
- In 1922, the average male worked forty-six hours per week, and the average wage for factory workers was about four pounds per week (or two pounds per week for women). However, servants worked much longer hours, up to fifteen hours per day, from 5.00 or 6.00 am until 10.00 pm, for much less pay.
- During the early 1920s, Australia was one of the few countries where most women could vote. Women in South Australia received the right to vote in 1895, with Australian women having the right to vote and stand for election in all states from 1902, although Indigenous Australians did not receive this right until 1962. All women could not vote in the USA until 1920 and the UK until 1928. Many European, African and Asian countries did not give women the vote until much later – France (1944), Italy (1945) and Switzerland (1971).

- Edith Cowan, in 1921, was the first woman elected to an Australian parliament in Western Australia.
- The national currency from 1910 until 1966 was based on pounds, shillings and pence. There were twelve pennies to a shilling, and twenty shillings to a pound.

Acknowledgements

There is something totally fascinating about walled gardens and abandoned houses. One of my favourite books as a child was *The Secret Garden*, written by Frances Hodgson Burnett in 1910. Some of the ideas for *The Lost Sapphire* were inspired by this book, particularly family secrets and discord, and the idea of a girl and a boy, who initially don't get on, building a friendship and being healed by bringing a lost garden back to life. The cheeky robin, who helped show the way into the garden, inspired my fairy wren.

The first idea of writing a book about an abandoned house was suggested to me by Leeza Wishart and her daughter Ella. The Wishart family, who love my books, raised money for me to visit their home town of Tenterfield in northern New South Wales, to visit a number of local schools and run writing workshops. While I was there, Leeza organised for me to be invited to visit Tenterfield

Station homestead, the original homestead for the area established in the 1840s, which had been abandoned for many years and was slowly being restored. This old house was filled with history and stories — it was where Banjo Paterson met and later married one of the daughters of the station family, Alice Emily Walker, and the homestead is rumoured to be haunted by the ghosts of old tragedies.

I loved writing this book, particularly the vibrant history of the 1920s. Some of the books I used to research etiquette, entertaining and homes in this era included *The House in Good Taste* by Elsie de Wolfe, and *Etiquette* by Emily Post, written in 1922. For an insight into the experience of refugees fleeing the Russian Revolution, I studied several memoirs, including *Russians in Exile* by Valerian Obolensky, *Lost Splendour* by Felix Youssoupoff and *The Russian Countess: Escaping Revolutionary Russia* by Edith Sollohub.

Life in Melbourne during the 1920s was brought to life by newspaper articles, film clips and memoirs of wealthy debutantes, factory workers and servants. The Hamilton Glove factory was inspired by the Simpson's Glove Factory, which was located on Victoria Street, Richmond, and its collection of artefacts held by Museum Victoria. Riversleigh was inspired by several old Melbourne mansions I visited, including Como House, Labassa, Balmerino and Rippon Lea.

My father's family was originally from Melbourne, and I spent many long summer holidays playing and swimming on the banks of the Yarra River. More recently, I have explored this beautiful city on multiple trips, visiting old mansions and gardens; wandering the streets, laneways and markets; and eating food from many different cultural backgrounds, including Vietnamese, Chinese, Italian, Greek, French and Russian. It is one of my favourite cities in the world!

A big thank you to my wonderful Random House marketing team, Dot Tonkin and Zoe Bechara, together with my illustrator, Serena Geddes, who have spent many hours showing me around Melbourne on book tours.

As always, enormous thanks go to my brilliant publishing team — publisher Zoe Walton, editor Brandon VanOver and agent Pippa Masson — who always have plenty of brilliant ideas, advice, suggestions and support. I have been working with them now for ten amazing years.

Much love and gratitude to my first readers and research assistants, Rob and Emily Murrell.

About the author

At about the age of eight, Belinda Murrell began writing stirring tales of adventure, mystery and magic in hand-illustrated exercise books. As an adult, she combined two of her great loves — writing and travelling the world — and worked as a travel journalist, technical writer and public relations consultant. Now, inspired by her own three children, Belinda is a bestselling, internationally published children's author. Her previous titles include four picture books, her fantasy adventure series, The Sun Sword Trilogy, and her seven time-slip adventures, *The Locket of Dreams*, *The Ruby Talisman*, *The Ivory Rose*, *The Forgotten Pearl*, *The River Charm*, *The Sequin Star* and *The Lost Sapphire*.

For younger readers (aged 6 to 9), Belinda has the Lulu Bell series about friends, family, animals and adventures growing up in a vet hospital.

Belinda lives in Manly in a gorgeous old house overlooking the sea with her husband, Rob, her three beautiful children and her dog, Rosie. She is an Author Ambassador for Room to Read and Books in Homes.

Find out more about Belinda at her website:
www.belindamurrell.com.au

THE LOCKET OF DREAMS

When Sophie falls asleep wearing a locket that belonged to her grandmother's great-grandmother, she magically travels back to 1858 to learn the truth about the mysterious Charlotte Mackenzie.

Charlotte and her sister, Nell, live a wonderful life on a misty Scottish island. Then disaster strikes and it seems the girls will lose everything they love. Why were the sisters sent to live with strangers? Did their uncle steal their inheritance? And what happened to the priceless sapphire — the Star of Serendib?

Sophie shares in the girls' adventures as they outwit greedy relatives, escape murderous bushrangers, and fight storm and fire. But how will her travels in time affect Sophie's own life?

Shortlisted for the 2011 KOALA awards
OUT NOW!

THE IVORY ROSE

Jemma has just landed her first job, babysitting Sammy. It's in Rosethorne, one of the famous Witches' Houses near where she lives. Sammy says the house is haunted by a sad little girl, but Jemma doesn't know what to believe.

One day when the two girls are playing hide-and-seek, Jemma discovers a rose charm made of ivory. As she touches the charm she sees a terrifying flashback. Is it the moment the ghost was murdered? Jemma runs for her life, falling down the stairs and tumbling into unconsciousness.

She wakes up in 1895, unable to get home. Jemma becomes an apprentice maidservant at Rosethorne — but all is not well in the grand house. Young heiress Georgiana is constantly sick. Jemma begins to suspect Georgiana is being poisoned, but who would poison her, and why? Jemma must find the proof in order to rescue her friend — before time runs out.

**A CBCA Notable Book
OUT NOW!**

THE FORGOTTEN PEARL

When Chloe visits her grandmother, she learns how close the Second World War came to destroying her family. Could the experiences of another time help Chloe to face her own problems?

In 1941, Poppy lives in Darwin, a peaceful paradise far from the war. But when Japan attacks Pearl Harbor, then Australia, everything Poppy holds dear is threatened — her family, her neighbours, her friends and her beloved pets. Her brother Edward is taken prisoner-of-war. Her home town becomes a war zone, as the Japanese raid over and over again.

Terrified for their lives, Poppy and her mother flee to Sydney, only to find that the danger follows them there. Poppy must face her war with courage and determination. Will her world ever be the same again?

A 2013 KOALA awards Honour Book
OUT NOW!

THE RIVER CHARM

When artistic Millie visits a long-lost aunt, she learns the true story of her family's tragic past. Could the mysterious ghost girl Millie has painted be her own ancestor?

In 1839, Charlotte Atkinson lives at Oldbury, a gracious estate in the Australian bush, with her Mamma and her sisters and brother. But after the death of Charlotte's father, things start to go terribly wrong. There are murderous convicts and marauding bushrangers. Worst of all, Charlotte's new stepfather is cruel and unpredictable.

Frightened for their lives, the family flees on horseback to a stockman's hut in the wilderness. Charlotte's mother and the children must fight to save their property, their independence and their very right to be a family. Will they ever return together to their beautiful home?

OUT NOW!

THE SEQUIN STAR

After her grandmother falls ill, Claire finds a sequin star among her treasures. Why does Claire's wealthy grandmother own such a cheap piece? The mystery deepens when the brooch hurtles Claire back in time to 1932.

Claire finds herself stranded in the camp of Sterling Brothers Circus. She is allowed to stay — if she works hard. The Great Depression has made life difficult for everyone, but Claire makes friends with circus performers Rosina and Jem, and a boy called Kit who comes night after night to watch Rosina perform.

When Kit is kidnapped, it's up to Claire, Rosina and Jem to save him. But Claire is starting to wonder who Kit and Rosina really are. One is escaping poverty and the other is escaping wealth — can the two find happiness together?

OUT NOW!